## Praise for *The Guilty Can't Say Goodbye*

"A gripping story which weaves a multitude of flavors and perspectives! Mariam has creatively captured the subtleties of life in my home city of Lisbon, Portugal, in a story that is inventive and suspenseful, while also heartwarming and culturally masterful."

**Lisa Lynn Ericson**
Poet, artist, and author of *Simplicidade Vibrante: Pensamentos Poéticos de um Fado Feliz*

"Mariam has nailed the expat conundrum. The twists, turns and buried secrets build tension as the well-paced prose delves into the intricacies of a nomadic life to produce a lush, sometimes sinister, debut novel."

**Apple Gidley**
Author of *Have You Eaten Rice Today?*, *Crucian Fusion*, *Transfer*, *Fireburn*, and *Expat Life Slice by Slice*

"This is a novel filled with intrigue and surprise, and haunted by themes of identity, memory, and the past. Mariam Navaid Ottimofiore beautifully evokes place and the experience of displacement. As three women try to reinvent themselves in a new country that is also an old country, it becomes clear that the past will follow wherever you go. *The Guilty Can't Say Goodbye* is an enjoyable and immersive read."

**Michael Langan**
Author of *Shadow is a Color (as Light is)*

"In her cleverly crafted novel, Mariam Ottimofiore untangles the long-held secrets of three international women, illustrating with insightful accuracy the adjustments they and their young families must make relocating to Portugal. Whether you're already living in or considering moving to Portugal, *The Guilty Can't Say Goodbye* is a page-turning read, and a window into expat family life."

**Louise Ross**
Author of *Women Who Walk*
and *The Winding Road to Portugal*

"What a pleasure this book was! How wonderful it was to discover three different destinies of expatriate women, united under the clear skies of Portugal. Beyond the epic thread of three life stories which will keep you guessing till the last page, there is a multicultural fragrance of life that radiates with every word. You close your eyes and see the jacaranda in bloom, smell the aroma of coffee or the strong scent of freshly cooked food. It's an enchanting mix that makes you want to discover more; this is a lovely invitation to go experience the world."

**Alexandra Paucescu**
Author of *Just a Diplomatic Spouse*
and *Boni Goes Around the World*

"Mariam Navaid Ottimofiore's *The Guilty Can't Say Goodbye* follows three women from diverse cultures whose lives and secrets intersect in Portugal. Through a pacey and enjoyable plot, Ottimofiore shines a light on the characters' struggle to hold together all facets of who they've become, as they search for true belonging in a life of constant change—an enlightening read for expats and TCKs worldwide."

**Nigar Alam**
Author of *Under the Tamarind Tree*

"Ottimofiore takes the reader through a complex tale of smoke and mirrors that plays out across the world. Global nomads and armchair travelers alike will find themselves in this story, as certain themes—of longing and belonging—are universal. An intriguing novel with multiple cultural layers."

**Kristin Louise Duncombe**
Author of *Trailing* and
*Five Flights Up*

"Rich, multi-layered and gripping, this is a novel to be cherished and savored. Mariam Ottimofiore is adept at creating engaging, diverse characters, and this novel only cements her reputation as one of the most talented writers alive today. "

**Awais Khan**
Author of *Someone Like Her*,
*No Honour*, and *In the Company of Strangers*

"*The Guilty Can't Say Goodbye* is a testament to the author's deep expat experiences and genuine curiosity about diverse cultures. As a global nomad myself, I found this novel to authentically capture the challenges and intricacies of expat life. Mariam N. Ottimofiore has written a thoughtful, gripping story that builds to a dramatic and satisfying ending. A rapid-paced novel, steeped in the adventure and realities of expat life, that addresses how we all pine for belonging and the destructive nature of keeping secrets. *The Guilty Can't Say Goodbye* teaches that it's only when we stop stifling our shame that we can truly embrace the opportunity for a joyful, authentic, multicultural life."

**Lainey Cameron**
Award-winning author of *The Exit Strategy*
and host of 'The Best of Women's Fiction Podcast'

"*The Guilty Can't Say Goodbye* is a fascinating insight into expat life for three women who become friends yet are all hiding something about their past. The story is driven by the mystery of hidden secrets, and the suspense kept me turning the pages. Friendships, family and food in a beautiful setting made this a lovely, warm read. I really enjoyed it!"

**Aliya Ali-Afzal**
Author of *The Big Day* and *Would I Lie To You?*

Also by Mariam Navaid Ottimofiore:

*This Messy Mobile Life: How a MOLA Can Help Globally Mobile Families Create a Life By Design*
(Springtime Books, 2019)

# The Guilty Can't Say Goodbye

*a novel*

Three stories. Three women.
Three broken lives.

**Mariam Navaid Ottimofiore**

*For those who are brave enough to move—*
*because home is a story that comes with you,*
*not a place you leave behind.*

"The best way of keeping a secret is to pretend there isn't one."
—Margaret Atwood, *The Blind Assassin*

# PROLOGUE

*Karachi, Pakistan*
August 1996

*There was no time to waste. His gaze fell on the pomegranate and turmeric Persian carpet in the living room, the one he had frequently admired for its rich floral pattern, lavish texture of wool and cotton, and the elaborate design of peacocks and paisleys. It made him imagine the Garden of Eden. How could a thing of such beauty now hold an unspeakable truth?*

*I don't want to be a part of this, he prayed silently. Please don't ask me to do this.*

*But she came forward and whispered, "Drive out to the Indus Delta. Don't come back for a few days. Make sure no one sees you." She held out a bulky envelope in her trembling hands. A peace offering.*

*He looked at the envelope. Within it were enough rupees to stock up on flour, wheat, and rice to feed his family of seven for a year. But instead of taking it right away, he combed his fingers through his venerable, dark beard. His moth-brown eyes could not look directly at her, so instead, he looked up to the heavens and prayed, his palms outstretched in front of him. "Ya Allah, please forgive me." He unclasped his hands, took the envelope from her, and left without a word.*

*The crescent moon shone like a silvery claw in the dark sky. Driving out into the ebony night, his mind wracked with guilt, he knew what he was doing was wrong. He was a simple and hardworking man. He prayed towards Mecca five times a day on his faded green prayer mat. He earned an honest living. But he was also the sole provider for his family. That money would help send his five sons to a public school in the city. He prayed that God would direct his fury at him and not his family.*

*He drove out far into the interior of Sindh, the vigor of youth propelling him to leave the metropolis behind in only a few hours, until he reached the mouth of the Indus River. Here in the surrounding alluvial plains, the great Indus Civilization once flourished, its vast settlements stretching for thousands of miles across Pakistan into Afghanistan and India.*

*The silent and spectral mangrove forest was an impenetrable tangle of roots that made the aquatic green trees appear to be standing on stilts above the brackish water. It was here, in a remote creek, surrounded by the densely knotted desolation of the muddy mangroves, that he carried out the task with which he had been entrusted. Then he watched the light of dawn rise over the silent river delta behind him, swallowing his sin whole.*

# PART ONE

# 1

# FATIMA
*Cascais, Portugal*
August 2022

Fatima Khan was only eleven years old when she knew she had to move away from her hometown of Karachi. Twenty-six years later, she carefully checked her rear-view mirror, adjusted the seat to her petite five-foot-two frame, and steadied herself for driving on the 'wrong' side of the road. All those years living abroad, and driving on the right still felt unnatural. Like drinking water straight from the tap; that had been a hard one to get used to. She needed to get into the zone and concentrate. Thankfully, her UAE driving license had been converted into a Portuguese one without too much fuss, but she hadn't anticipated the feeling of loss that washed over her when she handed in one of the last ties to her expat life in Dubai. A tiny piece of her story exchanged for a new start in a new country.

"Hey, *beta*, excited about today?" She turned around to peer at her ten-year-old daughter in her brand-new red and blue uniform sitting in the back seat of their new Nissan Qashqai. Although '*beta*' literally meant 'son' in her native

Urdu, it was used interchangeably to address both sons and daughters as 'child,' and for Fatima it was fitting to call Maya *beta*. She was her daughter and her son rolled into one. Her only child.

"I think you're more excited about orientation than I am, Mama. I hate being the new girl in school—again."

"I'm sure you won't be the only one, Maya. There'll be plenty of new students starting this term. And besides, that's why Papa and I chose an international school. They'll be kids from all over the world, just like you're used to."

There was no response—just a grunt as Maya tucked a strand of her dark hair behind her ear, propped her chin against a clenched fist, and peered out of the window, watching Cascais whizz by. The alluring seaside town on the Atlantic, a twenty-minute drive from Lisbon, was their new home. Once a summer escape for Portuguese nobility, Cascais—pronounced 'Cush-Caish' by those in the know— had blossomed into a busy cosmopolitan town full of locals and expats proudly calling it their home.

Fatima maneuvered her car through the narrow winding streets of Cascais, past brightly colored houses adorned with blue and white azulejo tiles like something from a medieval village and then past a funky art mural in the shape of a wave on the side of a pharmacy. She turned up the radio, but neither she nor Maya could follow the rapid, stress-timed Portuguese. It sounded more like slurred, nasal, mumbled Slavic than a melodic Romance language to their South Asian ears.

"I miss listening to Dubai 92 on the way to school, Mama."

"I know, sweetie. Me too."

They would need a new morning routine for their new expat life, something else for Fatima to add to her long to-do list, which currently read in her mind like this:

*Fatima's To-Do List for Week 3 in Portugal*

1. *Start driving in Cascais.*
2. *Sign up for Portuguese lessons.*
3. *Settle in Maya at her new school.*
4. *Figure out where to buy Za'atar.*
5. **Find a new radio station to listen to in the mornings.**

Adele's latest hit started to play on the radio—a welcome touch of familiarity in an otherwise completely foreign place—and Fatima felt the knots in her shoulder loosen. She looked out at the traffic ahead and thought about her time in Dubai. It hadn't been far enough from Karachi for her liking, and she fervently hoped Cascais would be. Secretly, she was happy to be living in Europe again, even looking forward to starting her Portuguese lessons.

Crossing the border between countries was always a messy and unpredictable process, but crossing the border from one language to another was her forte. She was always surprised at people who expected it to be easy to learn a new language. Learning languages was hard work, and it was precisely this challenge—mastering something difficult—that she enjoyed. Fatima grew up bilingually with Urdu and English, spoke good German and decent Danish, had a basic command of Arabic, and was curious to see how much

Portuguese she could pick up while living in Portugal. The other day, she'd heard the familiar lilt of Danish on the streets of Cascais and slowed down to listen for a while, to savor it. It had warmed her from the inside, like a plate of *daal chawal.*

The names of so many places and streets in Cascais and Lisbon—Alcoitão, Alcabideche, Alfragide—started with the Arabic prefix 'Al' ('the'). It was a stark reminder of Portugal's past, the 500 years of Muslim rule when the Moors built castles and fortresses and planted orchards of oranges, pomegranates, and grapefruit in the Algarve, once called Al Gharb—'The West.' And it was the Moors who had introduced thousands upon thousands of Arabic words into the Portuguese language. While shopping at Ikea in Alfragide last weekend—Ikea, the obligatory first stop for any expat in a new country—Fatima had smiled to herself when she'd realized the Portuguese word for a cushion, *Almofada*, was derived from Arabic. Fatima used her *Sprachgefühl* like code to grasp new languages and find similarities in new words, even in the most unfamiliar of places.

"We're here," she said as the school came into view. It had clearly been given a fresh coat of paint over the summer. White walls shone in the sun, and the arches, windows, and balconies were painted a cheery yellow. Her almond-shaped brown eyes grew big with excitement, and she shook her caramel-colored long hair out of her ponytail. Maybe she should have made more of an effort, dressed up more, or done something about the chipped turquoise nail polish around the edges of her fingernails, a result of prying open too many packing boxes with her bare hands, but she looked casual and chic in her dark navy jeans, crisp white-collar shirt, and her favorite Ralph Lauren wedges; there was no way she could manage heels on the slippery cobbles of the Portuguese *calçada*. She wished Stefan was with them, but it was the first day of his new job in Lisbon. If she could get Maya to be a little more excited about starting at her new school, and perhaps make one mom friend herself, Fatima would consider it a great start to their new lives in Portugal.

*Fatima's To-Do List for Week 3 in Portugal*

1. *Start driving in Cascais.*
2. *Sign up for Portuguese lessons.*
3. *Settle in Maya at her new school.*
4. *Figure out where to buy Za'atar.*
5. *Find a new radio station to listen to in the mornings.*
6. *Make one mom friend at school.*

Driving in Cascais was manageable, but parking was proving to be a challenge, and her palms were sweating as she slowed down to attempt a parallel park on the steep, narrow road outside the school. As she nudged up towards the curb, a car zoomed out of a side street. There was a sound of screeching tires, and Maya shrieked as it slammed into the rear of Fatima's car with a loud metallic crash.

"What the …! Maya, you okay?" Fatima felt panic, disorientation, and then nothing. There was a moment of silence. Everything was still. As if to allow the world to catch up with what had happened. She could smell burnt chemicals coming from the airbag propellant, and her chest grew so tight it became hard to breathe. She closed her eyes, too scared to look up, too scared of what she'd see if she opened them.

A car door slammed. A tall woman—six foot maybe— came over to survey the damage: pale skin, celery-green eyes, short strawberry-blonde hair that bounced with every move, and an American flag pinned to the lapel of a matching blue pantsuit. She touched the fender of her Range Rover and searched for the passengers in the car she'd just hit.

Fatima and Maya stepped out, Fatima hesitating a little as if she was surprised her legs could carry her weight.

"I'm so sorry!" said the woman. "I clearly wasn't looking. Ya'll okay? I hope you're not hurt? I'm Kate. God, I'm so sorry. What a way to start the first day of school."

Fatima took a moment to hug Maya and then, in spite of herself, smiled at Kate. There was something about her un-assuming Texan drawl that brought her back to the moment, put her at ease.

"No, I … I think we're fine. I'm Fatima and this is Maya. My backlight's broken, and there's a bit of a dent from the impact, I mean, collision."

"Thank God. Listen, this was totally my fault. I'll pay for all damages. I'm obviously not used to driving anymore. I didn't need to drive in Singapore, and clearly I've forgotten how. We've just moved here, and those roundabouts, they're so confusing; I swear I never know when it's my right of way." She took a breath and pointed to a boy sitting inside the Range Rover. "My son, Eric. It's his first day as a fourth grader. What grade is Maya?"

Eric took off his headphones over his blond hair, stuck his head out of the car, and waved.

"Also fourth grade," said Fatima, suddenly realizing she had no idea what the protocol was in Portugal after a car accident. Should she call the police? Notify her insurance? Where were the car registration papers from the car leasing company? God, what if the police didn't speak any English? She'd only been living in Portugal for three weeks, and her Portuguese was still basic—*Olá*, *Bom Dia*, and *Obrigada* was about it. She doubted that hello, good morning, and thank you would get her that far. In Dubai, accidents were so common that she'd had the Road Transport Authority number saved as an emergency contact, but here she had no idea what to do. She thought it best to call Stefan and explain what had happened, but when he didn't pick up, she sent him a quick text and tried Google.

As she was typing, a blue Peugeot pulled over with two kids in the back, and the driver poked out her head.

"Hey, I saw what happened. Are you guys alright?"

The concerned witness was a beautiful black woman with boyish dark hair, a thick British accent, a bright neon shirt, and a mess of bangles clattering down her forearm. Even though she was sitting in a car, Fatima could tell she was tall.

"Thanks, we're not hurt, thankfully," said Fatima, grasping her phone and looking down distractedly at the scar on her left arm. She liked to tell people it was a childhood injury after she fell from a tree. She ran her fingers along the scar but then stopped herself. Now was not the time to focus on old wounds; she had to stay focused on her fresh start. *Stop it, Fatima.*

"Totally my fault," said Kate. "I drove into Fatima's car. Just grateful no one was hurt. What a great first impression

I'm making with parents on our first day." She gave a nervous laugh and unbuttoned her blazer. "I'm Kate, by the way."

"Definitely an eventful start to orientation day. I'm Abena. Nice to meet you, Kate and Fatima. We're new arrivals. From Ghana originally, just moved over from the UK. I'll go park the car and join you. Oh, these are my two: Kakra and Panyin. They're in fourth grade."

"Looks like Maya, Eric, Kakra, and Panyin will be together," said Fatima, looking over to Kate, who was already on the phone explaining to someone what had happened.

Fatima's phone pinged. "My husband says we need to report the accident," she said to the others. "I'll call 112 for the Portuguese police."

"No need to involve the police," said Kate. "I've called the office to let them know. Forgot to mention, I work for the US Embassy." She grinned. "Small accidents are covered under my diplomatic immunity."

Fatima bit her lip, and her stomach contracted into a tight ball. She felt certain she needed to report the accident to the police and the car leasing company. But in truth, it was a minor accident, and Kate was offering to pay to get her backlight fixed. With Kate's diplomatic immunity, it was probably the best course of action and with the least amount of stress for everyone concerned. If there was one thing Fatima had learned in her first few weeks here, it was that Portuguese bureaucracy required a great deal of patience. Besides, there was something about Kate she immediately liked. Perhaps it was her unassuming nature. Or her honesty in admitting she was a bit lost on the roads over here, the kind of vulnerability only the most seasoned expat women feel confident enough to show to complete strangers. And anyway, Fatima was eager to make new friends and not get off on the wrong foot. *God knows, I could use some new friends over here.*

"Sure," she said. "Let's sort out the details after orientation. Anyway, we don't want to be late. Shall we go in?"

Kate nodded, clearly relieved, and Abena came over to join them with Kakra and Panyin in tow, both in their smart new uniforms and sporting neatly tied braids.

And so it was that on the first day of school, Fatima and Maya walked in with Kate and Eric on one side and Abena, Kakra, and Panyin on the other. In years to come, Fatima would say *that* was almost certainly the moment the story began: the day three new arrivals collided into one another when no one was looking.

THE FIRST DAY at an international school was always a medley of first impressions. New principal, new teachers, new rules, new campus, new parents, and new students. This gave Fatima an endless amount of anxiety; meeting new people and making friends didn't come naturally to an introvert. She was terrified of walking into a room full of people she didn't know; it was something that never got easier, no matter how many times she moved. But she'd learned to mask her feelings, put on a brave face, and get on with it. She usually set herself at least one achievable new goal, like getting added to the class WhatsApp group or making one other mom friend from Maya's class. More things to add to the to-do list.

*Fatima's To-Do List for Week 3 in Portugal*

1. Start driving in Cascais.
2. Sign up for Portuguese lessons.
3. Settle in Maya at her new school.
4. Figure out where to buy Za'atar.
5. Find a new radio station to listen to in the mornings.
6. Make one mom friend at school.
7. Get added to the class WhatsApp group.

But today, she was still shaken up from the accident and found it hard to focus and listen to what was being said. Her mind was fuzzy, and the sound of Kate's car crashing into hers was still playing on repeat in her head. There was no sound in the world like a car crash.

She looked across the fourth-grade homeroom, where families were walking in to meet their kids' teachers. Hers was the only brown face around. Where were all the other South Asians in Portugal? The Indians, the Pakistanis, the Bangladeshi, the Sri Lankans, the Nepali? Where was the *desi* diaspora, who shared her South Asian heritage? She'd noticed a few desis on the streets of Lisbon and felt their inquisitive stares in return. Maybe Cascais was too small. Maybe international schooling was a price point not available to many. Part of her was relieved at the absence of desi folk at the new school, but then she was dismayed at her own sense of relief. Fatima never felt she was the best representation of her own culture and often struggled to make friends with other Pakistanis. Perhaps Portugal would truly be the place where she could escape her cultural identity without feeling guilty about it.

A woman in a yellow sundress came over to introduce herself. "Hi there. I'm Henrietta, the fourth-grade homeroom teacher," she said to Fatima in a heavy South African accent. She smiled at Maya. "And who's this?"

"I'm Maya. Maya with a 'y,' " whispered Maya.

"Welcome, Maya. You're going to love it here, I'm sure! Where are you from, or where did you move from?"

"Dubai!" said Maya quickly.

"Amazing. I had a lovely holiday in Dubai once. I'm sure you're missing your old school and your friends back home, but hey, you'll get to make new friends here in Cascais. Would you like to start off with a fun exercise adding your name to our class world map?"

Maya turned to get some stationery and Fatima smiled gratefully at Henrietta. "Thank you so much for the warm welcome. It's been a tricky transition for us; we're hoping Maya will settle in soon."

"Ah yes, transitions at her age can be hard. Don't worry. We've got a great orientation week planned where students will get to know each other and explore bits of Portugal."

They both watched as Maya walked over to the world map and put her initials on the United Arab Emirates. Henrietta smiled encouragingly and moved on to talk to the next parent. Fatima went over to Maya and squeezed her hard, then saw Kate and Abena deep in discussion walking towards her.

"I love this school already," Abena was saying. "The girls are so lucky. It's our first time at an international school, and everyone's so friendly—not exactly like that back in Brighton."

Kate smiled. "Ah yes, the British stiff upper lip. Must have been a huge change coming from Accra?"

At the mention of Accra, Abena welled up. "I *do* miss Accra, especially the laidback vibe. Living abroad has been a huge adjustment for me. Ben, my husband, is Ghanaian too but raised in the UK. He says I couldn't get used to Brighton, even with its by-the-sea vibe. Still, I'm excited about our new lives here and looking forward to all things Portuguese. I'm so glad we took the leap."

"Me too," said Fatima. "How about you, Kate? Missing Singapore?"

"Hell no. Certainly don't miss the heat or humidity. Singapore was great, but as I said to my husband Michael earlier, I reckon I suffered from island fever towards the end. I was happy to leave. This move couldn't have come at a better time. And you, Fatima, how hot would it be in Dubai right now?"

"I don't even want to think about it. 46 degrees in August—that's the Arabian Desert for you. Feels like someone's following you around with a hair dryer. One of the first things Stefan and I checked about Portugal when his job opportunity came up was the weather."

More parents and children streamed in and one by one the kids were taken to icebreaker sessions in their new classrooms, leaving the parents to wander over to the school auditorium for coffee and cake—Portuguese style.

FATIMA TOOK A bite of her creamy *pastel de nata* and looked across at the others. "Well, this is nice."

"Mmmm, yes," said Abena. She took a sip of her *bica*, the

Portuguese equivalent of an espresso shot, and the three of them sat in awkward silence while they polished off their quick breakfast on the go.

"Well," said Kate, reaching for a napkin, "what do you ladies think of getting together regularly for coffee and *pastéis de nata* as we all settle into our new lives here?"

"Great idea," said Fatima and Abena together.

"I'm happy to have met you two this morning," Fatima added quickly. "What a stroke of luck that Kate jammed her car into mine."

Kate laughed. "Ah yes, after living in Mexico, China, and Singapore, I guess I've finally found a foolproof modus operandi to make new friends in a new country." She gave herself an exaggerated pat on the back.

Abena looked at Kate in awe. "So many countries. Is this for your diplomatic career?"

"Sure is. We move around every three years on assignments. People think my Foreign Service career is a cushy number but in reality the pressure's intense. To be honest, I don't often get to attend these school events; my schedule's too demanding. As the stay-at-home dad, Michael usually brings Eric to school. He's the official parent for all things school-related." She put down her coffee and grimaced. "But I really want things to be different here. New country, new rules, right? Aside from hitting your backlight, Fatima, I'm so glad I insisted on coming today. The first school orientation I've attended in years."

"No harm done. I'm sure it'll get fixed in no time. Actually, can I have your number so we can sort it out later?"

Kate took out her cell phone and Fatima noticed it ringing on silent and flashing with "Michael calling." Kate rejected the call, flipped to her contacts list, and searched for her new number.

Strange she was so quick to reject the call, thought Fatima, but who was she to judge? She and Stefan had certainly had their moments—and distinct roles. She was disappointed he hadn't picked up when she'd called him after the accident, and his WhatsApp message had been annoyingly short, without so much as a "Geez, honey, I'm so glad you and Maya are okay." He was probably stressed out on his first day of work, but still, a bit of concern for his wife and daughter wouldn't have gone amiss.

A woman with short brown hair and impossibly high heels tottered over to the three ladies with a list in her hand.

"Excuse me, but are you Ms. Nyator?"

"Yes, that's me," said Abena, wrinkling her forehead in surprise.

"Great, happy I found you. I'm Joan, the admissions administrator here. I wanted to see if you had a moment to follow me to my office and fill out a health care form for Kakra and Panyin—it's missing from their files. I've printed out two copies for you."

Abena froze and Fatima watched the blood drain from her face.

"Sure, no problem," mumbled Abena, getting up to follow the admissions administrator and giving the others an *I'm sorry, please excuse me* look.

"Hey," said Fatima, catching Kate's eye, "would it be okay if I put your name down as Maya's emergency contact at school? It has to be someone other than my husband, and we don't know anyone else here yet."

"Of course, I'd be delighted. Would you be mine?"

"Sure. It's a deal."

They shook hands and exchanged the new phone numbers neither had memorized. Expat living had taught both of them the importance of making friends and building a support system in the absence of family, neighbors, and friends, though it hadn't necessarily made them good judges of character. But that didn't matter right there and then. All Fatima cared about was the happiness she felt at making such a promising start to a new life. And she felt something she hadn't felt in a very long time: she felt safe.

## Nine months later

*She was running. She mumbled a half-hearted apology after colliding with a fellow parent on the football field. She ran, past the colorful stalls, past countless people, all of them looking surprised. She ran as fast as she could. Panic boiled up inside her and made her forget all about her surroundings. She ran, and she didn't stop to think. All she wanted was to get out, to get as far away from this place as possible. She ran blindly. She couldn't believe that after all these years the past had finally caught up with her. She was afraid. She ran, and nobody tried to stop her. She was running from that little voice in her head, the one telling her to stay where she was, that everything would turn out alright.*

# 2

## KATE
### *Lisbon, Portugal*
### August 2022

Kate pushed open the glass door of her Lisbon office and was relieved to find it empty. She needed time to think. And figure out what she was going to do. She fired up her laptop and started a Google search:

"Where to get a car light fixed in Cascais"

She had thrown around the term 'diplomatic immunity' to Fatima as a cover after she'd pretended to call her office about the car accident, but the truth was, most people didn't understand how diplomatic immunity worked. It didn't mean she had immunity from her actions abroad, just that she wasn't subject to local laws. Annoyingly, this was one part of life in the Foreign Service that all the movies and books got wrong. In reality, if a Foreign Service Officer like her messed up abroad, they could get pulled back to the US to deal with the consequences there.

The embassy obviously wasn't going to pay for fixing Fatima's car. Fine; she didn't need them to. It's not like she needed another reason to draw attention to herself at work when she was still dealing with the fallout from Singapore. The curtailment of her Singapore posting had raised many eyebrows and questions in the Foreign Service, even though she had argued her case convincingly and been granted it on compassionate grounds. But the less she thought about that, the better.

Her phone rang. Michael again. *Shit.*

"Hey, honey," said Michael. "Just checking in. How'd the school orientation morning go?"

"It was fine. Eric seemed happy; he made a few new friends. We met a family who have moved from Dubai and another from the UK. All their kids are starting fourth grade with Eric. His teachers seemed nice too. I think he'll be happy there." There was no need to mention the car accident; he didn't need to know.

She wasn't sure when she'd started keeping secrets from Michael. Perhaps after what had happened in Singapore she'd felt the need to keep some secrets of her own.

After some small talk, where Michael went over the menu for the dinner he would be cooking later, Kate hung up. He was a good cook. Thanks to his Italian heritage—he'd grown up as a third-generation Italian American—Kate knew she'd always come home from work to an amazing spread.

Kate hailed from Sugar Land, small-town suburbia on the outskirts of Houston. She'd grown up hearing Spanish around her thanks to the large Hispanic population in Southern Texas, and after studying Spanish in high school and accepting a diplomatic posting to Mexico City years later, she was now pretty much fluent. But speaking Spanish in Portugal was a big no-no; the Portuguese hated any comparison with their bigger neighbor. Still, as she trawled car repair websites in Cascais, her Spanish know-how helped her decipher some of the Portuguese words. She selected a place and was about to call the number when there was a knock at the door.

"Oh, you're back," said Helen, her secretary. "Folks were asking about you. How was orientation morning? Please tell me you said no to joining the class WhatsApp group and the PTA? You seriously don't have the time, trust me." Helen knew the limitations of Kate's schedule better than she did. She fixed her wiry glasses and smoothened the crease out of her black skirt. She was at least a decade older than Kate, but with her hair dyed a mahogany brown, it was sometimes difficult to tell. Resourceful and experienced, she was like Siri, but with a personality.

"I'm happy to report I haven't joined any school cult yet," said Kate. "Although I did have a little problem with jamming my car into a pole inside the school parking lot. Actually, Helen, would you contact this car repair shop and make an appointment?"

"Sure."

"It's just a minor dent," added Kate nonchalantly, her heart beating just a little faster than usual.

"No problem, leave it to me. This ninja in a skirt is ready to help." She made a taekwondo move and formed fists like she was ready to fight. Kate laughed and breathed a sigh of relief. She would figure this out somehow.

After Helen left, Kate put off checking her daily schedule of meetings and found herself looking down at the tattoo on the inner wrist of her left hand: Mandarin calligraphy, two syllables etched side by side in black ink representing truth and honesty—the two most important things in her life but also the most troublesome. The office felt suffocating. She needed fresh air. Maybe the car accident had rattled her nerves more than she cared to admit. It had certainly made her think back to that awful day in Texas. However hard she tried to erase the memory, it remained there, stubbornly, like the cellulite in her thighs.

She left the concrete facade and marble finishings of the American Embassy, stepped out of the front gate onto Avenida das Forças Armadas, and took a deep breath. Not for the first time, she was struck by the contrast between the harsh lines of the reinforced concrete and the leafiness of the embassy grounds.

In August the air in Lisbon was thick with the smell of grilled sardines. She took a walk to the nearest Padaria Portuguesa bakery, a ten-minute stroll from the embassy, and ordered a *galão* in Portuguese, still finding it hard to believe that 1.35 euros got you one of the smoothest and creamiest coffees in Lisbon. Who needed Starbucks?

She knew that the Portuguese could always pick out the fresh-off-the-boat Americans in a crowd—the ones who always wanted ice and lemon with their Coke, regular Coke not Diet Coke, please, as if the distinction should be obvious to everyone, the ones who were too busy to sit down and enjoy a coffee the way the Portuguese did, always in a rush, always wanting their coffee "to go." Guilty as charged, at least today.

She sipped her coffee and walked slowly back to her office, thinking about her past and how far away she was from home. She'd come from a privileged background. Her

Texan parents had always voted red. They didn't even own a passport, and they certainly didn't get Kate or understand her fancy life abroad. The chasm had been created years earlier, starting the day she left Texas at the age of eighteen to study at Mount Holyoke College in Massachusetts, a double major in Economics and Political Science, and it widened when she moved to Washington DC for her Master of Science in Foreign Service from Georgetown University's Edmund A. Walsh School, which was where she met Michael. She'd never looked back.

Once or twice her friends in new countries had asked if her family would come out to visit, but she'd been too embarrassed to admit the truth to anyone. It hurt to say it out loud, but her mother and father had no interest in visiting her anywhere in the world, even though they had the financial means to do so. They didn't see any reason to leave the US, and holidays were taken in Hawaii or Florida, but never in Mexico, China, Singapore, or Portugal, where their only daughter lived and served. Worse still, they didn't consider Kate to be patriotic. Staying in your birth country was the patriotic thing to do, but leaving and representing your country abroad was something close to treason.

She'd tried to make peace with all of this a long time ago, and certainly before embarking on her 15-year diplomatic career that saw her moved from one country to the next with short periods spent in DC in between. Now, as the Political Counselor at the US Embassy and Consulate in Lisbon, she was obligated to attend social engagements sponsored by the embassy and local organizations. Last night's tortuous dinner hosted by the American Club of Lisbon had been a case in point. She and Michael had been greeted by a guy with a strong Southern accent, sounding a lot like her Uncle Steve.

"Hi, my name's Scott," he'd said, locking eyes with Michael. "One of the guests tells me you're the new Political Counselor. As a long-term resident of Lisbon, I just wanted to say welcome to Portugal."

Unsurprisingly, this rubbed Kate up the wrong way. It was her pet peeve: assuming traditional gender roles in the Foreign Service. *For God's sake, is this 2022 or 1952?*

Michael cleared his throat and shifted his weight from one foot to the other. "Ah, that would be my wife, Kate," and he gestured to Kate with a melodramatic sweep of both hands.

"Thank you so much for the warm welcome, Scott," said Kate after an exaggerated laugh. She reached out to shake his hand.

Scott was already turning a beetroot red. "God, I'm so sorry. I just assumed … well, isn't it great our women are holding top-notch jobs. Home *and* abroad."

"Thankfully, things are gradually changing," said Kate, determined to make her feelings on the topic clear. "More and more women have careers that take them abroad, Scott. Now it's the husband's turn to be the everything-else partner." She smiled at Michael.

"The everything-else partner?" asked Scott.

"Well, tell you what," said Michael, "I refuse to call myself a 'trailing spouse.' No one's trailing the other. I'm the everything-else partner who on the surface has little to no official role, but underneath the surface has the bulk of the responsibility, especially when it comes to settling the family into their new country. So hi, that's me."

"Sounds to me like you have the tougher job," said Scott with a wink.

"I probably do," said Michael, and he started to list his job description on his fingers. "Be a professional at packing, moving, and dealing with shipping companies. Conduct extensive research on which neighborhood to live in, which school to send your kids to, and the reasonable price to pay for an avocado at the local market. Do the laundry, pack the school lunches, attend the parent-teacher meetings, volunteer for the school bake sale, drop your kid off at birthday parties, take language classes, meet new people to create a support system in a new country, fumble your way through a new grocery store with a foreign currency in your hands, and learn your new city inside out." He stopped counting when he ran out of fingers, his point made.

"In essence," said Kate, squeezing Michael's hand, "you're the reason I can do the job I was sent abroad to do."

"I guess you're both lucky," said Scott. "Seems you've adjusted to your roles well. My wife—she's not here tonight—struggled when we left Kentucky to move here for my retirement. It's taken her years to embrace her new identity and start to enjoy life in Portugal."

"It's always an adjustment for both partners, isn't it?" said Kate, and with Michael and Scott nodding in agreement, the three of them had headed off to grab some drinks.

By the time she'd got home from the dinner, grabbed some sleep, attended this morning's school orientation, and headed back to the office, Kate already had newcomer fatigue from so many new connections and first impressions. She checked her watch. She was late for her morning briefing, which she'd already pushed back a few hours. She would soon be advising the senior staff at the embassy on bilateral and transatlantic relations. She felt the familiar nerves but gulped down her anxiety, took a sip of coffee, grabbed her notebook and laptop, and strode confidently into the conference room.

## *Cascais, Portugal*
## August 2022

It was close to six p.m. when Kate got home that evening. She enjoyed working in Lisbon, but coming home to Cascais at the end of the day felt good. Somehow it felt appropriate to keep the two parts of her life separate. All the people who had warned her that the long commute in rush hour could take up to fifty minutes had clearly never driven in Houston, where such a distance would be characterized as a 'breeze.'

She closed the aquamarine front door behind her and looked up at the high-ceiling entryway of their new home, a villa in the hillside coastal resort of Monte Estoril on the Cascais coast. There was a mishmash of furniture, most of it acquired through the housing and furniture pool organized by the Foreign Service, the rest still in unpacked boxes from their shipping container, which had recently arrived from the US. Their realtor had explained that a sea-view property in this part of town would typically cost thirty percent more than the average in Portugal. After all, this was a "sought-after location." Monte Estoril was old money, a historic and aristocratic district. Most of the homes in the neighborhood had been built as summer residences for the Portuguese nobility in the early twentieth century, with terracotta-tiled roofs and often three or four floors built on a steep slope. At first, Kate and Michael had fretted about the steep incline; reversing out of the garage was going to be a challenge. But the unobstructed view of the Atlantic made up for some minor inconveniences, as did the south-facing balcony, the beautifully manicured garden with a lemon tree and an orange tree, and the small swimming pool on the ground floor.

Sunlight was filtering in through the oval-shaped windows as Kate went through to the lounge, the smell of roasted garlic wafting through the air.

"Hey, honey, I'm home."

"Hey, welcome back, honey," said Michael as he swept in from the kitchen, wiping his hands on the kitchen towel slung over his shoulder, his blond hair tucked under a Yankees baseball cap. Denim shorts completed the look.

Eric, who had been picked up from school by his father, was lying on the sofa with his iPad. He got up and gave his mother a kiss. "Mom, I had the *best* first day at my new school."

"So happy to hear that, sweetie. I have to say, I had a really good impression of your teachers this morning too." She smiled at him, relieved that at least her son was off to a good start.

It had been hard talking to Eric lately; he'd been moody ever since they'd left Singapore prematurely, six months before completing the three-year assignment. They'd spent those six months living in limbo in DC, where Kate had waited for her re-assignment and had continued to lobby fiercely for the soon-to-be-vacant posting in Lisbon. Being pulled out of the familiarity of Singapore and placed in DC for a while hadn't been easy on any of them, but Eric in particular had been distant and quiet throughout. Kate wondered how much of the fighting he had overheard. Kids his age were pretty clued in to their parents' fighting, and there had been some ugly fighting this summer—arguments, shouting, slammed doors, and tears. Eric was a perceptive boy, and as an only child, he was especially attuned to the moods of his parents.

He had been begging them for a pet, especially a dog, but Kate had resisted for a long time because of their globally mobile lifestyle. Besides, pet relocation was a nightmare and not something supported by her work. But now they were living in Cascais with its ample outdoor spaces and beaches and Eric was excited about starting a new life here, maybe having a dog to look after and take on regular walks would help him adjust and feel more at home. She would need to broach the subject with Michael again.

"Dinner's almost ready," said Michael. "I had a great time shopping at the Cascais *Mercado*. It's this huge open-air market—fresh fruit, vegetables, and an incredible variety of seafood."

Kate followed him into the kitchen and watched as the risotto on the stove crackled when he poured in the boiling stock and gave everything a gentle stir.

The house was still in a half-unpacked state and quite frankly a mess, so Kate was amused to see Michael chopping sage and parsley with his favorite Chinese knife. It was less a knife and more a gigantic silver square machete, something she'd gifted to him in Beijing, sourced from a local kitchenware store in their old Chaoyang neighborhood. Over the years it had become his favorite knife, and he refused to cook with anything else. It was the one thing that simply couldn't get lost on their international relocations, not without Michael losing his cool. They'd always instructed the movers to pack the knife in the treasured "first to open" box along with other essentials, a little expat trick they'd learned after so many international moves.

"Smells great in here," said Kate, feeling the familiar surge of love at watching him cook for the family. God knows she was useless in the kitchen; you could count on her to burn toast. She was grateful that Michael was a culinary rebel forging his way through various international cuisines one recipe at a time. His last name, Russo, had given her a hint of his Italian heritage, but it was much later—when he invited her to his dorm in Georgetown for dinner one evening— that she'd fallen in love. She'd shown up with a bottle of Chardonnay, but he'd prepared a fully-fledged Italian dinner of *bruschetta, risotto alla Milanese,* and *osso buco.* The *tiramisu* dessert had sealed the deal.

"So, tell me, how was your day?" asked Michael. "You mentioned meeting some other moms at school this morning?"

"Yeah. Fatima's from Pakistan, married to a German. They've moved over from Dubai. Their daughter Maya is in Eric's class. And we met Abena, from Ghana, but she's been living in the UK with her husband, who's British and Ghana-ian. They recently moved over with their twin girls, Kakra and Panyin. In the same class as the others. They all seem nice. To be honest, it was good to meet people other than the American crowd at work, the ones who keep complaining they can't find decent bagels in Portugal." She rolled her eyes.

"I'd *love* to meet some new parents," said Michael.

Kate knew all too well that he was feeling left out. Resentful, even. This was usually his realm of responsibility.

"Oh, you know who I heard from today?" he said, still stirring the risotto. "I got an email from Maryanne. Fancy that. I'm not sure if she's allowed to contact us, but she did anyway. She was asking about you and Eric. Said she misses us all."

Kate had turned to grab some plates to set the table for dinner, but she stopped in her tracks, stung by his betrayal. How dare he bring up Maryanne like that—so casually—in the middle of a conversation about their new lives. The new lives they had been forced to create after Michael's actions made it impossible to stay in Singapore. Her resentment bubbled up just as the risotto came to a boil. Before her tears could escape, she grabbed a paper towel and ran out of the kitchen.

# 3

# ABENA
## *Cascais, Portugal*
## August 2022

Abena looked over the blank school form and fiddled with the gold charm bracelet on her right hand. It had her three favorite *Adinkra* symbols dangling from it, symbols that held traditional wisdom from her Ghanaian culture, and in times of uncertainty, she drew strength from them. *Sankofa*, in the shape of a bird, signified learning from the past to build for the future; *Aya*, in the shape of a fern, was for endurance and perseverance; and *Odo Nyera Fie Kwan*, in the shape of a shield with scrolls, was a reminder that love didn't lose its way home: those led by love always ended up in the right place.

Her name, Abena, meaning 'born on Tuesday' and pronounced A-bay-na, was inscribed inside the bracelet, and she considered Tuesday to be her lucky day. In West Africa, and particularly in Ghana, it was common to name a child based on the day of the week they were born, or sometimes on their place in the family, making it apparent who was older or younger. It was the first thing you were asked about a new-born—'What day was the child born?'—and it was information Abena had memorized for each of her girls so she would always be able to give a quick answer if anyone asked. Like any mother should.

But now as she pored over the health form, it became clear she would need help to fill it out. The questions on allergies and dietary restrictions she could complete right away, but the detailed questions on family history were more difficult to answer on the spot. She would need to call Ben for advice.

Since she didn't want the school nurse to understand what she was saying, she spoke in Twi, grateful to have a 'secret' language they could communicate in.

"Ben? Hi, it's me. Listen, I'm sitting at the nurse's office at school … Yes, that's right … No, no, all is okay with the girls. I need to fill out some extra health forms, but I don't know what to put for the girls' family history … Okay, we can discuss it later."

She hung up and smiled at Marta, the school nurse. "So, I just called my husband and I think it's best if we take the forms home and check against their previous medical records since my husband has a complicated family history. Then we'll fill everything in and get back to you soonest. Would that be okay?"

"Of course. End of the week would be fine. I'll make sure to update their medical records on our system afterwards."

Abena breathed a sigh of relief. It was only once she was out in the school corridor that she realized the underarms of her neon shirt were soaked in sweat. She desperately needed some fresh air, a chance to clear her head. She had been told that one of the best ways to get to know the beaches of the Estoril–Cascais coastline was to take a walk along its seafront and appreciate its crystal-clear water and fine sand. It was a three-kilometer stroll from Praia do Conde da Azarujinha in São João do Estoril, passing through Poça, Tamariz, Conceição, and ending at Praia da Rainha in Cascais, and was one of the perks of her new life as a digital nomad in Portugal.

Armed with her laptop, she walked along the *paredão* in search of a café to sit and work in. She settled on an inviting outdoor café perched on the curve of a bend, which offered a bird's-eye view of the glistening Atlantic and the people who walked by: the morning joggers, the regular exercisers, the moms pushing their babies in their strollers, the dog walkers, the beachgoers in their swimsuits, the surfers in their wet suits, and the cyclists not necessarily sticking to the bicycle lane. The tide was often high, even in summer, and Abena had already learned how to spot the tourists from the locals: they would walk close to the edge and jump back in surprise when a giant wave crashed onto the boardwalk and drenched them.

"*Olá, bom dia! Tudo bem?*" asked a young waiter as he approached her table.

Abena was far from confident when it came to speaking Portuguese and was instantly flustered. Worried she'd make a mistake, she took out her phone and opened up Google Translate.

| ENGLISH | PORTUGUESE |
|---|---|
| Do you speak English? | Fala inglês? |

She looked up at the young man, smiled her brightest smile, and asked tentatively, "*Fala inglês?*"

He nodded. "*Sim, um pouco.*"

"Okay, I'd just like to order a coffee, please," she said, slowing things down so she was understood.

"With milk?" he asked without skipping a beat.

"Yes, thank you," she replied with relief.

"Anything else?"

"No, that's all."

She sighed. It was so embarrassing when you asked a Portuguese speaker if they spoke English and they replied with a humble "just a little" but then proceeded to speak fluent English. She knew she'd have to get better at speaking Portuguese. She'd grown up bilingually, speaking Twi at home and English at school, a legacy from Ghana's colonial history under British rule, but had never learned a foreign language as an adult, and it certainly wasn't as easy as it looked on all those YouTube videos she'd seen prior to moving to Portugal. She needed a good Portuguese tutor and then she'd really try to learn.

With her ebony skin, many locals assumed her to be of Angolan or Mozambican descent and were surprised when she couldn't speak Portuguese. Lisbon and Cascais were both multi-ethnic and had a sizable African diaspora, in large part due to Portugal's history of colonization, and it was usually the inherited British accent that made her stand out in a crowd, not the color of her skin. She'd attended an English-speaking school in Accra, but it was only after a decade of living in England that she had started to sound British. Like most bilinguals, she realized she could 'turn on' her British accent upon will, and tune it down too, especially when she was back in Accra. In Ghana, it was common for the educated elite to code-switch while talking—they'd start off telling a joke in English but switch to Twi, Ewe, or Ga by the time they'd got to the punch line. For Abena, this switching back and forth between languages often meant a switch in personalities too. In Twi, she sounded more open, carefree, and relaxed. In English, she sounded more formal, more reserved, more polite. She wondered how she was going to sound in Portuguese.

Her coffee arrived, and she took out her laptop to tackle the day's emails. She couldn't usually work in busy outdoor cafés, finding it hard to concentrate with all the chatter around her, but since moving to Portugal, it had been all too easy to tune out the Portuguese hubbub around her because she didn't understand a word. It was an interesting development; her lack of Portuguese had pros as well as cons.

Abena had a great eye for fashion and colorful *Kente* fabrics and had an impressive knowledge of textiles, baskets, and handwoven goods. She had used that knowledge, picked up informally on the streets of Accra, to good use: she was now the creative brain behind 'Akan,' their basket-weaving business named after the largest ethnic group in Ghana. Akan sold all kinds of household goods, mostly to the European market, with Ben taking care of the business, financial, marketing, and customer side of things. Both of them were staunch advocates for 'Made in Africa' and passionate about bringing West African aesthetics, home décor, and fashion to the rest of the world. Through her work, Abena would travel regularly to Ghana to meet her team, source new workers, buy the latest textiles, and stay in touch with the home market.

She had thought visits back home to Ghana would envelop her in a sense of warmth and familiarity, but instead, each trip confronted her with a sense of displacement and loss. No one had prepared her for this, the uncomfortable reality that her new life would cost her something very precious: her old life. It was a loss she hadn't properly mourned, and she wasn't sure how to anymore. The comments from relatives, the looks from friends, the never-ending requests for financial help, drained and depleted her. It was an unsettling paradox; belonging in one place meant unbelonging in another. But one person she always loved meeting on her visits back home was her only sister, older and wiser Akosua. The siblings had always been close. Which is why it hurt all the more that visits with Akosua were no longer possible.

Abena's coffee date showed up at the café: shaved head, beard, dark-rimmed glasses, florescent yellow running shoes, and an ear-to-ear smile. He walked over and pulled out a chair to sit next to her. "Getting started without me, eh?"

"If I waited for you, I wouldn't start anything, honey."

Ben was notoriously late, but she loved the confident energy he brought to any setting. It was his confidence that had attracted her to begin with. He had moved with his Ghanaian parents to the UK at the age of twelve and was a perfect blend of British and Ghanaian cultures: assertive yet friendly, confident yet humble, friendly but firm. He was a great organizer, though not very punctual. He was at ease eating *foie gras* in a fancy setting or eating with his hands when Abena cooked West African *fufu* at home. Together they made a great husband and wife team and great business partners.

"So, isn't it nice to sit out here?" said Ben, looking over

at the sea. He mimicked drinking a cup of coffee when a waiter came to take his order. "No Auntie Janet ringing up from Birmingham to ask for the secret ingredient in your *jollof* rice recipe and then showing up unannounced to see how you cook it." He laughed, throwing his head back.

Abena shuddered. "God, I hated her surprise visits." It was true, and she didn't miss all those nosy Ghanaian relatives back in the UK either. Whether it was Birmingham or Brighton, Ben's extended family was always poking their nose into their business. They had expressed their amazement when Ben had chosen to marry Abena rather than a Ghanaian girl who had been raised in the UK like him. But Ben had traveled to Accra and fallen in love with Abena when he'd spotted her at the Villaggio rooftop pool and bar. The rest, as they say, was history. The criticism and comments from his family were never-ending: the fake concern about how Abena would adjust to life in Brighton, the constant questions about baby plans, the pretending not to be able to eat her home-cooked food because it was too spicy. Several micro-aggressions later and after a decade of living together in the UK, Abena and Ben were grateful for the distance Portugal provided them.

The decision to move to Portugal had not been an easy one, though. With no one but themselves to drive the process, they worked side by side to turn their dreams into reality. As soon as they discovered Portugal was one of the few countries offering a visa scheme for entrepreneurs, they immediately applied, and instead of hiring professional immigration lawyers and relocation consultants, they did it all themselves.

Ben applied on his UK passport, not thinking for a second

there would be a problem. For Abena, it would have been an ordeal applying on her Ghanaian passport, with a never-ending number of hoops to jump through. So she too applied on her UK passport, having obtained dual citizenship after living in the UK for a decade. You only understood passport privilege once you'd experienced both sides of it, making the unfairness all too apparent and an uncomfortable reality.

Being buried in paperwork and bureaucracy while trying to keep on top of their business had been a tough juggling act. They'd constantly quarreled and nagged each other, but they'd also loved spending time together on their special project, and it had brought them closer than ever. They knew they would be relocating their life, but now they realized they were relocating their marriage too. They sold off everything they owned and arrived in Portugal with only eight suitcases: two per family member. It had felt liberating. They'd chosen a semi-furnished apartment in Cascais, near Casa da Guia—a nineteenth-century palace—and were proud of how far they'd come.

"So, what exactly happened at school this morning?" asked Ben, looking earnest. "You sounded worried when you called. Sorry I'm late. I got here as fast as I could."

"I was totally caught off guard. The nurse was asking me to fill in these detailed health forms for the girls. I just panicked."

"Look, I can get their recent health records from Brighton by calling up our pediatric clinic there. I'm sure they can email us a copy. But the family medical history … I suggest we err on the side of caution and say there's nothing of concern. We don't want them asking even more questions."

"How can you be so calm about this? I can't believe that

on our first day of school, I was put on the spot. I mean, everything I've done so far has been to protect the girls, to give them a proper future." She started sobbing.

Ben squeezed her hand and then enveloped her in a hug, holding her close until her breathing had calmed. "Look, we should have been better prepared for this. We should have realized that moving to a new country would mean we might get asked to provide the girls' medical records. I'm uneasy about the deception too, but you know it's a risk worth taking. We must do everything we can to avoid anyone finding out the truth. Especially Panyin and Kakra."

"Will we be able to build a good life for ourselves here, Ben?"

"Why are you suddenly having doubts?" He pulled his chair closer to hers.

"It's just that … I want to focus on what lies ahead, but I keep getting pulled into the past and what we left behind. And each time it happens, I lose my focus."

"D'you mean *who* we left behind?"

"You know I'd rather not talk about her." She pulled away and leaned back in her chair.

"Fine," he said, "but bottling up your feelings won't help in the long term. Moving abroad doesn't take away or solve our problems. We can change where we live and meet new people and still have the same old problems."

Abena looked over to the horizon. She would happily exchange her old problems for new ones but had a feeling that life abroad didn't work that way. If only it did.

# 4

# FATIMA
## Cascais, Portugal
## September 2022

Fatima looked around her new home. It still didn't feel like *her* space yet, but thanks to many weeks of unpacking, it was coming along nicely. The defining feature of their new home in São João do Estoril was the panoramic view of the Estoril coastline. Waking up to the sea every day was an indescribable feeling. Who needed a pool when you had a private view of the Atlantic from your bedroom, living room, and balcony? It was something she'd never had, her own tiny slice of the Portuguese Riviera, and it was worth all that stress from moving, all those headaches, all the endless bureaucracy.

"Look, Mama. Guess what I found?" said Maya, running into her parents' bedroom holding a box.

"What is it?" said Fatima. "Can you unwrap it carefully?"

"I can't believe you haven't guessed what this is!" said Maya. She tore off the packing paper to reveal a canvas of the Dubai skyline, a farewell present from friends. Fatima ran her hand along the white canvas, along the Jumeirah Beach

Club, the Burj al Arab, the Bur Dubai Mosque, Atlantis the Palm, and the Burj Khalifa. Their memories, and Maya's childhood, were scattered all over the glittering skyline, a poignant reminder of 'home.'

Before they'd moved to Portugal, Fatima had researched how children growing up internationally can have a difficult time processing transitions to a new country. Saying goodbye to her friends in Dubai had been difficult for Maya. Fatima had arranged a "good goodbye" for her daughter: a sleepover with her best friends, a goodbye party with their close neighbors, one last play at their favorite Al-Barsha park, a last meal at Zuma Dubai, and a final camping trip in the Al-Qudra Desert, sleeping under the stars. But Maya had only grown quieter with each 'last.' As for Fatima, she'd kept all the parts of their relocation moving without stopping to say her own goodbyes. She'd kept her own feelings of loss bottled up, as if there was no space for them.

But for every international move, there comes a point when the finality of the decision becomes apparent, when it's clear there is no going back. For them, that moment came once their villa in Arabian Ranches had been packed up and they had boarded the Emirates flight from Dubai to Lisbon. On the plane Fatima had felt something slip into her hand. Her silver necklace, engraved with *inshallah* in Arabic calligraphy, had fallen from around her neck. Inshallah, the word that had dominated their lives in Dubai. Inshallah, 'God willing,' used by locals and expats alike to give a vague answer to when anything would be done: out of your hands and into God's. As the plane took off, Fatima couldn't stop herself from thinking about her necklace breaking, about the symbolic timing, and she broke down and sobbed. It felt silly, a grown woman crying over a necklace, but it was the moment she finally realized what she was leaving behind, the moment all those emotions that had been building up over the past few days and weeks were released. Fatima had always become attached to the places she'd lived in, even the ones she hadn't wanted to move to or hadn't liked in the beginning—like Dubai. Call it her flaw or her superpower, but she was incapable of living in a city without forming a deep attachment to it. Leaving somewhere that had become her home was like grieving the loss of a relationship that had ended prematurely. In this case, it had been a love-hate relationship, but leaving Dubai still felt like she was leaving a part of herself behind. She clutched the broken necklace and mourned this version of herself, something that would cease to exist once she reached Portugal. Why was it that shutting the door on an old life took a painfully long time, but starting a new one could be done so rapidly, lightly even?

Maya had noticed her mother's tears and leaned in for a hug. "*Ma'salama* Dubai," she'd whispered for both their sakes, a quiet farewell to Dubai as the plane circled over the familiar skyline, offering them all one last glimpse of the city.

Fatima and Stefan had both reached out to hug Maya. Half Pakistani and half German, Maya had been born in Copenhagen and lived in Dubai for the past five years, so it was the only place that felt like home. She couldn't remember much about Denmark, and her parents' home countries of Pakistan and Germany were just holiday destinations in her eyes. No matter how many times they visited either Karachi or Berlin, Fatima knew that Maya, fluent in both Urdu and German, felt most stable with the sand beneath her feet in the Arabian Desert. And moving to Portugal had not been part of the plan, until Stefan's Danish company offered him a job and a promotion he couldn't refuse.

"Mama? Did you hear what I said?"

Fatima looked up from the canvas. "Sorry, what were you saying, *beta*?"

"Can I hang this in my new bedroom?"

"Yes, of course."

"Thank you, Mama!"

Maya clutched the canvas and ran out of the room. Fatima smiled and realized she needed to find a way to help Maya stay in touch with her friends in Dubai. Another thing to add to her to-do list:

*Fatima's To-Do List in Portugal*

56. *Set up an email address for Maya so she can email her friends in Dubai.*
57. *Continue with Maya's Arabic lessons?*

Fatima looked back in the box and found one of her old notebooks. She couldn't wait to start writing again and set up her office in their new home. After years of building a corporate career, she'd made a major career switch to full-time writing when they moved to Dubai. As a freelance writer, she'd been published locally in *The Khaleej Times* and internationally in many expat magazines and websites. Now she had a thriving writing business and could write for any client from anywhere. Finally, her life abroad was matched by a portable career.

She put on her house slippers, came down the dark wooden stairs, and stepped into the garden. "Oh, there you are," she said. Stefan was attempting to assemble outdoor furniture on the patio.

He looked up, wiping his brow. There was a dark map of sweat growing down the front of his white T-shirt. He looked younger than thirty-nine, even with the hint of some grays in his straw-like short brown hair, which was matted to his forehead. His eyes, a deep indigo blue, were squinting in concentration.

"Coming along nicely," she said, gesturing to the patio table.

"Almost done. Thought we could sit outside for lunch. It's such a sunny day." Stefan had no hint of a German accent when he spoke, although, as Fatima liked to tease him, sometimes he did mix up his words in English. The other day, she'd given him a grocery list with 'ground cumin' on it. When he'd called her from the supermarket, unable to find "grounded cumin," she'd simply said, "I wonder what the cumin did that was so naughty?" He hadn't got the joke of course, and that had just made Fatima laugh even more.

She secretly loved how sometimes things got lost in translation in their multicultural marriage. It's what kept their spark alive. She now understood that although he wasn't always openly expressive, Stefan showed his love for her in other ways. Like cutting a *Brötchen* in half over breakfast and asking if she wanted the top or bottom half of the bread. When they first met, in a rather corporate setting—a work meeting at their multinational's head-quarters in Copenhagen—they barely noticed each other. It was only the following week, when they bumped into each other standing in the queue at the cafeteria, that Stefan dared Fatima to try some pickled herring, a Danish specialty but rather an acquired taste. When Fatima refused, Stefan put some on his own plate and followed her to her table to discuss the peculiarities of Danish cuisine. It was a conversation that ended with Stefan asking Fatima out to his favorite Danish restaurant for *smørrebrød*, and in spite of herself, Fatima found herself saying yes. Food was her language, and she could tell it was his too.

Falling in love with a German guy while living and working in Denmark had not been part of the plan. Fatima had left Pakistan as a teenager, eager to move as far away as she possibly could at the first chance she got. She had received many offers of admission from colleges and universities in both the US and the UK but had eventually opted for the prestigious London School of Economics. Unlike the majority of the desi diaspora, she didn't enjoy living in London. Too many reminders of home, too easy to get her favorite curry, too easy to hear Urdu or Punjabi on the streets, too many invitations to Ramadan and Eid get-togethers; it was all too close to home. After graduation, she'd applied for finance jobs all over Europe—Brussels, Copenhagen, Amsterdam, and Berlin—and when her double round of interviews with a Danish multinational ended in success, she had very happily moved her modest belongings to Copenhagen.

She looked over at Stefan and his newly-assembled patio table and smiled. She knew she was one of the lucky ones. "It's a gorgeous day today," she said. "What do you feel like eating?"

"Easy," he said without hesitation. "Your *biryani*."

"Not sure I've got all the ingredients for that yet," she

said, thinking aloud, "or where to find star anise. Maybe I'll try my luck at the market." Fatima's recipes tasted different each time she moved countries or when she moved from a gas stove to an electric one; it would take her a few tries to get things right.

"But the car's not back yet," said Stefan.

"Oh yeah, right."

She'd forgotten that Kate had called to arrange for the car to be fixed. That whole business had been rather strange. Kate had personally come to pick up the car from Fatima's place and take it to the repair shop. Fatima appreciated her dedication, but it struck her as odd that a high-flying diplomat career woman would have the time. Still, she'd expressed her gratitude, and they'd made plans to meet up the following week for lunch with Abena. Kate took her lunch break between noon and one o'clock, and she knew a café near her workplace. Fatima was looking forward to it. A lunch date with her new friends. A chance to get to know them better.

FATIMA AMBLED THROUGH grid-like Baixa accompanied by the freshness of the September Tagus breeze. Lisbon's elegant beating heart was alive with the buzz of an early morning, its shops and restaurants as busy as they always were.

In August, Portugal would sleep and holiday. The heat would drive people to take lazy days at the beach. But when autumn strolled around and calm returned after the frenzy of a busy summer, colors changed, stews and soups replaced the salads and ice-creams, and in the historic squares the blooms of the Jacaranda trees gave way to brilliant green foliage. And those colorful skies, and the chestnut smoke that flooded the streets with the smell of the season; after all those years of living in the Arabian Desert, Fatima had missed the changing seasons and the shifts in mood.

She had put extra thought into selecting today's outfit: a white summer cotton dress with ruffled sleeves paired with her trusted Fedora, and red nails to complete a classic look. She was meeting Abena and Kate for lunch later but had decided to spend the whole day in Lisbon. She sauntered from one neighborhood to another and quickly found herself falling in love with the city. She was used to city-dating, switching homes the way other people changed clothes, but it usually took her time to like a place, and at least six months to unpack her heart. But with Lisbon, it was love at first sight, something that had caught even her by surprise. Maybe its history of reinvention and exploration across oceans somehow mirrored her own journey and how far she had come in reconstructing her new identity.

With midday approaching she turned the corner and pulled out her phone to check what street she was on. Fatima's sense of direction was always put to the test in a new city, and the café wasn't where she expected it to be. She had turned one street too early. Realizing her mistake she walked back and took the next left, and sure enough, there it was. Cozy tables were set up under the shade of a fig tree. There was a smell of grilled shrimp, and people were ordering jugs of Sangria. In the middle of the throng, she spotted Kate and Abena waving her over.

"You made it!" said Abena, pulling out a chair for her. Abena was looking as colorful as ever in a lime green shirt and turquoise pants, an African beaded purse hanging on her chair.

"I did, but not before getting a little lost—as I always do," said Fatima, a bit breathless from her walk.

"Just a minute ..." Kate was on a work call. She took an ear pod out of her ear and asked the two of them, "Shall we order a pitcher of Sangria for the table?" She was dressed impeccably in a semi-casual navy suit, her green eyes sparkling with excitement.

Abena nodded yes, but Fatima shook her head. She didn't drink alcohol and hated being put on the spot. In her book, the only question worse than "where are you from?" was "why don't you drink?" It irked Fatima how this little piece of her cultural identity hung around her neck like a noose. She hated being asked and hated explaining herself. She had grown up without alcohol in her Muslim family, and now, of course she could sip sangria if she wanted, but she didn't feel the need for something she'd never missed in life. She was no longer conforming for the sake of conforming; she genuinely didn't want to drink.

"Nah—I'll just get a lemonade," she said, not wanting to explain herself. She saw Kate and Abena exchange a look, but both of them were obviously too polite to say anything.

Fatima ordered the drinks and food in decent Portuguese, something that clearly impressed Abena.

"Where are you learning Portuguese? You sound so confident already. I can barely string two words together."

"Oh, I'm happy to share my tutor's details. Her name's Inês; she's from Lisbon and a really good teacher. I arranged for private lessons to speed things up a bit. She does groups too, if you fancy it, up to three or four at a time."

"Sounds fantastic," said Kate. "I'd love to join and learn with you two. The online lessons my work arranged suck so bad. Honestly, who can learn a new language through a screen? My only issue is time. Today's an exception; I barely have time to eat lunch most days." She glanced down at her phone as it beeped away with incoming emails.

"Well, I can set up a WhatsApp group for us with Inês," said Fatima. "Let's see what she says. We can agree on dates and times that work. Morning or afternoon, Kate?"

"That's tricky. I'll have to really sell this to my boss. As it's for Portuguese lessons, my office might get on board, but I'll need to work around my schedule. Perhaps I can sacrifice my lunch hour for language lessons. I need a high level of functioning Portuguese for the job so they'll probably be thrilled I'm taking this seriously."

"Great, it's settled, I'll just—"

But Fatima was distracted by a slender woman with a mane of thick dark hair who had walked out of the café in a skin-tight white dress, dangling a Prada purse on her left arm. She'd stopped right at their table and was taking off her oversized sunglasses.

"Oh my God. Is it really you, Kate?"

Kate knocked over her glass of sangria and looked down at the shards of broken glass on the pavement.

"Patricia!" she said, gathering herself together. "Wow, what a surprise. Didn't expect to run into you here. What brings you to Portugal?" Judging by Kate's reaction, this wasn't exactly a welcome chance encounter.

"Oh, you know, just a pleasure trip at the moment. But Chris is interviewing for a position here, so you never know, I may join you in ditching the humidity of Singapore for an afternoon of drinking sangria al fresco in Lisbon." She laughed.

It was increasingly clear from the pained look on Kate's face and the way she was squirming in her chair that she wanted nothing to do with Patricia. You could cut the tension with a knife.

Patricia prattled on regardless. "But you seem to be looking well … many of us at SAIS didn't even know you were leaving Singers. No goodbye party, nothing. The way you skipped town had all of us at school wondering if things were okay."

"Everything's just fine," said Kate blankly. "Just my line of work. You know, can't say anything till the last minute, until it's official, so we missed saying a few goodbyes."

"Well, let's stay in touch over Facebook. If we end up moving here, I'll message you to get some advice on schools et cetera."

"Sure."

"Right, well, goodbye. Enjoy your lunch, ladies."

"Bye," said Fatima, relieved to see her go. She tapped Kate's arm. "You alright, Kate?"

"Hmm? Oh yeah. I'm fine. I'm such a klutz for dropping that glass. Hold on. Let me grab a waiter to come clean it."

Kate left the table and Fatima looked over at Abena. "Did you see that? What just happened here?"

Abena shrugged. "No idea. Whatever it was, it's clear Kate doesn't want to talk about it."

Fatima took a sip of her lemonade. She had a hunch. And her hunches were never wrong.

THE BREEZE WAS picking up when Fatima stepped out of the Uber at the end of her street. She fumbled in her purse for the house keys and walked along the street, stopping momentarily to take in the perfume of the balmy evening air. *Such a beautiful place.* She felt happy. That was a fun day out in Lisbon. She was starting to build a life here, make friends. But as much as she liked Kate and her exuberant Southern charm, she couldn't shake off the feeling that something was decidedly off. Her reaction at lunch after being recognized by Patricia was, well, strange. It felt like she wasn't being open. Or honest. Like she was scared to be found out. But why? Maybe she was in a witness protection program or something.

A sudden loss of balance pulled Fatima back to reality, and she steadied herself against a tree trunk. She giggled to herself. As much as the cobblestones and tree roots added to the unique charm of Lisbon and its surroundings, they really made for a toxic cocktail when coupled with daydreaming and high heels. She recovered herself and walked briskly along the tree-lined suburban street she now called home, finally fishing her keys from her purse.

There was a beep from her bag. She took out her phone and opened the WhatsApp message, and with a rattle, her keys dropped to the ground.

And she read the message again and again.

*No, please. Anything but this.*

Clearly, it was far from being over.

# 5

## FATIMA
*Karachi, Pakistan*
August 1996

*I*t had started with the sound of the traditional dhol *beating loudly in her ears—dhum-dhama-dhum-dhum—while the intoxicating smell of fruity jasmine wafted through the air. The oppressive heat meant that the whirring of the creaking ceiling fan created far too much noise and didn't provide enough respite from the humidity. Karachi sat on the Arabian Sea, but in August its unrelenting heat and humidity reached its peak. Load-shedding and electricity cuts were a daily reality. Air-conditioning was a luxury few could afford in this bustling metropolis of a city, but Fatima drew her bedroom curtains to block out all the natural light and then turned on the small air-conditioning unit. In order to keep electricity costs down, her mother only allowed her to turn on the AC at night to sleep, when Fatima would bring her pillow and put it straight in front of the AC and hold it there for a few minutes until it was cool enough to sleep on again. But today, she defied orders and wanted to sit alone in her cool, dark room and avoid everything and everyone.*

*There was a sudden knock on her door and her mother walked in.*

*"Arey, Fatimaaa! What happened? How come you're not even dressed yet? Your ironed shalwar kameez is hanging in the other room. Why is the air-conditioning on? You have to get ready now, or else we'll be late."*

*Fatima continued sitting cross-legged on her bed but looked up at her mother to meet her eyes. Gulzar was the picture of elegance. Glasses perched on her nose, kundan earrings dangled from her ears, an emerald-green chiffon sari draped around her body, and her black hair parted smoothly in the middle. As far as Fatima could remember, her mother was always dressed immaculately. She also took immense care in planning her young daughter's outfits, particularly for special occasions such as Eid or weddings. But today Fatima sat lithely on her bed, barely moving. "Ammi, I really don't feel like going."*

*"What do you mean 'not going?' What will people say if you don't show up to your own cousin's wedding?"*

*"I don't care what people will think. I just feel too ... too tired. Can I please stay at home? Maybe Shazia can stay with me?"*

*"Shazia is our maid, not a babysitter. Besides, she has already gone home. I gave her the rest of the evening off since we will eat our dinner at the wedding. I know you are not fully well, but you have spent the past week moping in your bedroom. All alone. Now it is time to snap out of it. All our relatives are coming. There is a lavish wedding next door in your grandparents' garden. We have to get ready and we have to look good. We cannot give anyone a reason to suspect anything."*

*So, this is how she was going to play it. Gloss over everything Fatima had been through. What they had been through together. Because keeping up appearances was obviously more important.*

*"Fine. But I'm going to sit and not talk to anyone. Please don't expect me to 'participate,' okay?" Reluctantly, Fatima got up to wash her face and get dressed. Ammi had laid out a fuchsia shalwar kameez for her with a jade green dupatta scarf, a perfect fit for her petite eleven-year-old frame. It was customary to wear bright colors to see the bride given away at the* rukhsati. *She slipped into her gold sandals, brushed her hair, sighed at the 24-set of multicolored* choorian *Ammi had stacked for her on the dressing table, and reluctantly put the bangles on. There was an art to doing so without breaking them, making a tight fist before squeezing each one on. Too much pressure and the bangle would break. It was an art Fatima had mastered. She had also learned how to make a strong fist, a skill that had recently saved her life.*

*She opened up her bedroom curtains and saw the red and gold wedding tent with the glittering fairy lights. The excited chatter, the beat of the drum, the smell of the henna-laden candles, and in an instant, Fatima felt still and empty, like a sponge squeezed of all its water.*

## Cascais, Portugal
## October 2022

"Fatima, will you please calm down," said Stefan. He got up to pour her a glass of cold water from the fridge, then sat down and re-read the WhatsApp message on her phone.

Fatima looked at him in horror. Never in the history of being told to calm down had anyone ever calmed down. She took a gulp of water. "How can you expect me to stay calm? She's coming here—to Cascais—to ruin everything we're building. You know how she is. As if she's going to help us settle in. Yeah, right. All she'll do is poke her nose into OUR business and tell us how to live OUR lives!"

"Okay, fine, so how about you just write back and tell her you don't need her help. Maybe she won't bother coming."

"You don't know her the way I do. Ammi will never back down. She'll guilt-trip me into welcoming her here and make sure I cater to her every need. She's probably already told the entire family about her plans, and now if I tell her not to come, the whole thing will blow up in my face and I'll come across as the ungrateful, selfish daughter."

Stefan shook his head. This was one of those times when their cultural differences were in plain sight. Sure, his mother wasn't demanding like Fatima's, but none of his German relatives would even consider just announcing a visit, come and stay, and then dictate the itinerary. And if anyone ever did try and pull a stunt like that, he would just put his foot down firmly and say, "Let me know if you need any help planning a trip to Portugal. Happy to recommend some hotels if you like. It would be great to meet up when you're here."

But with Fatima's Pakistani family, that's not quite how it worked. Plans were never discussed, just made. Itineraries were never suggested, just booked. Hotels were never considered; it was just assumed any or every relative and friend would be hosted at their place. No questions asked. Hospitality was an admirable trait, but taken too far and it just ended up creating resentment.

Fatima paced around the bedroom, thinking out loud. "I don't think I can stop Ammi's visit, but maybe I can convince her to delay it somehow? We need some stalling techniques."

"I know," said Stefan, "just tell her the house is yet to be unpacked and there's no bed for her to sleep on." He dusted off his hands as if he'd just offered up the perfect solution to her problem.

"Are you freaking kidding me? That will give her the perfect reason to fly over right away—to help us unpack, to set up the house. She LIVES for such opportunities. And then the way she'll spin it: *Fatima needed my help in getting her new house set up, so of course I had to drop everything and fly to Portugal right away.*"

"Okay, we'll think of something, but first of all, you really need to calm down." He held her hand, but she pulled away.

"Look, I'm sorry. I just need some time to process this. By myself. Maybe a nice warm shower will help."

Without waiting for a response, Fatima went upstairs and slipped into the bathroom, locking the door behind her. She turned on the shower so that Stefan wouldn't suspect anything, then stood in front of the bathroom mirror while she undressed.

She let her gaze fall on the scar on her left arm. This time she didn't look away. She didn't repress her feelings, she didn't distract herself, she didn't tell herself now was not the time. She ran her fingers over the seven-inch scar as if it were a roadmap to her survival, and as she touched the lacerated, uneven skin, she realized it had changed over the years. What was once a pink discoloration now resembled a gnarly brown caterpillar creeping unapologetically up her left arm. She was ashamed to show it and she would dress in a way that covered it with sleeves. No sleeveless dresses and tops for her. Another price she had to pay. Her guilt was carved onto her as permanently as her scar.

Her throat began to constrict as if she was struggling to swallow a still-beating heart. But the real struggle was with the memories. The painful memories.

Unable to take it anymore, she broke out into violent sobs and slumped to the bathroom floor, curled up like a child, rocking her body back and forth as if to comfort her own inner child. In her mind, she relived the suffering again and again, and she rocked harder and harder, not bothering to wipe away her tears, letting the pain engulf her, swallow her whole. And so it continued until, eventually, her breathing eased, her watery eyes dried, and she became still. She felt triggered, overwhelmed, lost, adrift. She couldn't get her mind to concentrate or focus on anything. She stared into the distance and for the first time noticed that the tile pattern on the bathroom floor was blue, not black.

There was a soft knock at the door.

"Fatima, you okay in there?" Stefan was whispering.

"Almost done," she shouted. She didn't want him to see her like this. No one could.

She turned off the shower, wrapped a towel around her dry head, put on her bathrobe, and took a breath. *You can do this. You've been through much worse.*

Stefan was sitting on the edge of the bed when she came out. He got up to hug her and pulled her in close.

"Listen, I know you don't get along with your mother, and I know she's not the easiest person to be with, but I think we can get through a visit if we stick together. Be a team, you know?" He tucked a strand of her hair behind her ear and cupped her chin in his hand.

Fatima looked at Stefan. Years ago, she had made the decision not to tell him. It hadn't been an easy decision, but it was too late to reverse it now without facing terrible consequences.

The simple truth was, she needed him on her side.

# 6

# FATIMA
*Lisbon, Portugal*
October 2022

"So, ready to begin today's lesson?" asked Inês. She smiled, took a sip of her macchiato, zipped open her cotton blue hoodie, and put on her glasses in anticipation. "My name is Inês. *E-nesh*."

"Thanks, Inês, let's do it," said Fatima, looking over to Abena and Kate.

They were finally having their first Portuguese lesson together at a hidden little café perched on a hill near Park Eduardo VII. Inês was thrilled to be giving them private lessons as a group of three, and with the weather still pleasant enough to sit outside, they had decided each weekly lesson would be held at a different café in Lisbon or Cascais. Inês thought it would be good practice for them to start feeling comfortable ordering food and drinks in Portuguese. She'd also suggested that at the end of each language class, they would put fifteen to twenty minutes aside to discuss cultural norms, history, and local traditions to help enhance their knowledge of Portugal as a whole.

Fatima wondered how old Inês was. She wasn't sure if it

would be impolite to ask. She glanced at her short brown hair, pulled back in a ponytail, and her tiny, slender frame in her navy blue Lycra leggings and a ribbed white tank top. She looked like she'd just come from the gym. She must have been in her late twenties. Born and raised in Lisbon, she'd lived there ever since—a true *Alfacinha*. Married, no kids. She'd told them she couldn't imagine leaving her friends and family in Portugal to move to a different country and start there afresh.

The three students had smiled knowingly at that one. For many people, doing what they regularly did sounded like complete madness. Why would you leave behind everything you've ever known to move to a country where you don't know anyone, don't speak the language and have to learn how things are done? But it was this very process of self-discovery, exploration, and adventure that fueled the start of many expat journeys. What scared one excited another. What one saw as 'leaving' the other saw as 'expanding' in new directions.

They started by delving into topics like how to introduce your family in Portuguese, the words for sister, brother, mother, and so on. It got Fatima thinking about her own mother. She'd managed to stall the impending visit by pointing out all the practical and logistical steps in applying for and obtaining a visa for Portugal, something that would require months of planning. This had bought her some time, at least two months if Portuguese and Pakistani bureaucracy could be relied on; there was always a silver lining to look for in expat life. In the meantime, she was determined to focus her mind on other things, such as learning Portuguese and starting to feel more comfortable with it.

After an hour, two flat whites, and her head full of Portuguese, Fatima felt strangely satisfied. "Thank you for today's lesson, Inês."

"Oh, my pleasure. By the way, I wanted to ask you. There's a place in Portugal called Fátima. Have you heard of it?"

"I have. I saw it mentioned on an online expat group. I was intrigued. Especially as Fatima is one of the most common names in the Muslim world. I've heard the town is a holy site for Catholics?"

"It is. In fact, it's named after the Moorish princess Fátima. She was kidnapped by a knight but then fell in love with her kidnapper and converted to Christianity so she could marry him. Anyway, the place is named after the original Arab name of the princess, not her Christian one."

"I had no idea. I'd just heard that some children had seen an apparition of the Virgin Mary there—leading to the town becoming famous."

"Correct. There's a small chapel: the 'Sanctuary of our Lady of Fátima.' It attracts millions of Catholic pilgrims each year. It's also why devout Catholics in Portugal name their daughter Fátima. You might be interested in seeing it." Inês folded her arms and looked at her expectantly.

Fatima took a second to wrap her cross-cultural mind around this. The fact that one of the holiest Catholic sites in Portugal had a Muslim name was a testament to how closely the world was intertwined, almost without realizing it. While living in Denmark, Fatima knew that her name sounded foreign to the Danes. They would usually misspell it or mispronounce it, placing emphasis on the first syllable 'Fat' and then hurry through the rest. But from the moment she arrived in Portugal, she could tell her name was well-known.

Revered almost. Certainly no one had trouble pronouncing 'Fa' and 'tima' in one fluid sound. Now she knew why. Home is where people can pronounce your name correctly. In some small way, it made her feel that she belonged a little more.

"I'd definitely like to visit Fátima and see it for myself," she said. "Would you guys like to come with me?" Kate and Abena had been listening in and both nodded.

Kate leaned forward in her chair. "Inês, I know our language lesson is over, but can you tell us a little bit about the dictatorship in Portugal. It came up at work today and I realized I know so little about that part of Portugal's history."

"Okay, well, Portugal has a complicated past. It only gained freedom as recently as 1974, when *Estado Novo*, the dictatorship, was overthrown through the Carnation Revolution. That's what we celebrate on April 25th every year. The interesting thing is that an oppressive regime was overthrown through flowers! I have a great book on this topic if you'd like to read more?"

"Great," said Kate. "It would be helpful to understand it in the context of my political work at the embassy."

"Is it true that the dictatorship was heavily invested in retaining Portugal's colonies in Africa such as Angola and Mozambique?" asked Abena. As a proud black woman, this was one part of Portugal's past that she was most interested in.

"Yes. The regime basically saw Angola, Mozambique, and other Portuguese colonial territories as extensions of Portugal itself. It tried to act as a supposed source of civilization and stability to the colonies in Africa and Asia."

Abena was taken aback by this. "Back home in Ghana, I went to El Mina Castle, built by the Portuguese during the time they traded the enslaved. It was a gruesome part of our history. I feel a bit of a traitor moving to Portugal of all places, but I guess if we judged every country by its awful past, nobody would move to Germany, the UK, or Portugal, would they?"

There was an uncomfortable silence as Abena's rhetorical question permeated the air.

"Well," said Inês, "interestingly, there were many Portuguese who had settled in Luanda and Maputo. So when the dictatorship fell and Angola and Mozambique gained independence from Portugal, these people had to 'return' to Portugal. They were known as the *retornados*—the returnees. Doubly ironic as many of them were second or third generation and had never even lived in Portugal. So to call it a 'return' glossed over the culture shock, the judgment, the guilt, and the isolation many of them faced when they tried to integrate into Portuguese society." Inês was clearly enjoying the mini history lesson. She'd told them earlier that when she wasn't teaching Portuguese she was a local tour guide.

The three women could relate perfectly well to the experience of the retornados. Sticking out was a common phenomenon faced by expats when they moved to a new country. And repatriation to your home country meant dealing with the "hidden immigrant" reality. You may look the same as others and sound the same as others, but you don't often think the same as others.

"So," said Fatima, "with such a history of travel, exploration, discoveries, and colonialism, how do modern Portuguese reconcile their history? I mean, are they proud of who they used to be?"

Inês shifted in her seat. "Well, this is a tricky question to answer, and the truth is, it is hard to generalize. But I think one thing is for sure: you will notice that Portugal's history as the first global empire has shaped its language today. Words like *saudade* are born out of this melancholic yearning for that which can never be again. The music of saudade is called *fado*. Have you heard of saudade? It is difficult to translate into English. It means something like a bittersweet longing or yearning for people and places loved and lost. It is happiness tinged with sadness; happiness because you experienced it, but sadness because you can never go back in time."

"I get that," said Fatima. "Saudade resonates deeply with me. It's similar to *hiraeth* in Welsh, which also means a longing for that which can never be. I find it so beautiful to have a word to explain such a complicated feeling."

"Yeah, and I think every expat or anyone who moves abroad can relate to saudade, right?" said Kate.

Abena was looking wistful. "I can't wait to share saudade with Ben. It pretty much captures how I've been feeling in the UK and now in Portugal. It's so much more intense than homesickness. It's about leaving a home that ceases to know your name, that somehow continues on in your absence, while you struggle to move on in its absence. It almost feels like a case of unrequited love, but with a place instead of a person."

"A good way to put it," said Inês. "Well, it's time to wrap up this lesson. I'm off to watch a football match at Benfica Stadium. Perhaps our first lesson has been a good introduction to the three pillars of Portuguese culture: Fátima, fado, and *futebol*. Same time next week?" She packed up her gym bag and stuffed her notebook in it. "Whose turn to choose a café?"

"Mine," said Kate. "I'll find somewhere close to work and then WhatsApp you guys."

Inês nodded. "Thanks Kate. *Beijinhos.* That means 'little kisses.' It's how we say goodbye in Portuguese." And with that, she blew them a kiss and left.

Fatima loved the informality of bidding farewell by saying "little kisses," and it got her thinking about how she said goodbye in other languages: *Khuda Hafiz* in Urdu to say may God protect you, *Auf Wiedersehen* in German to say until we meet again, *vi ses* in Danish to say see you later, and goodbye in English, short for God be with you. She was about to say her first *beijinhos* when she noticed that Kate looked tearful.

"Kate, are you okay?" she asked, placing a hand on her shoulder.

"Yeah … I don't know … I'm not sure why I'm crying. Something about saudade suddenly had me feeling sad. As if I've lost so much, and I can never get it back, you know?"

Kate's sudden vulnerability was out of character, but Fatima liked seeing an unguarded side of her, knowing that when someone takes off their veneer and shows their vulnerability, it's easier to see them for who they are. She squeezed Kate's shoulders in a half hug. "I think we can all relate. Don't be so hard on yourself."

"It's what I'm best at," said Kate, accepting the tissue Abena handed her.

"Well, you've got us here to watch your back," said Abena. She fist-pumped the air a bit too dramatically.

"Thanks, ladies," said Kate, and she grabbed her bag and followed them out.

Fatima wondered exactly what Kate was feeling saudade for. But she understood one thing: one of the hardest times to go through in life is when you've moved from one country to another but you're still transitioning from one version of yourself to another. The latter always takes longer because it requires complete honesty in reassessing not just who you were but who you have become.

# 7

# KATE
*Singapore*
January 2019

*I*f there was one characteristic fragrance of Singapore, it was the combined scent of heat, water, and flowers. As Kate stood in the middle of Chinatown inhaling the fragrance of dried herbs and blocks of sandalwood, she took in the shades of jade and olive temples around her. The chili crab made her stomach growl loud enough for a passerby to hear. All she had eaten that morning was a green tea cake from Taka, as the locals called Takashimaya, one of the massive malls on Orchard Road. She sat down at one of the empty bamboo tables, ordered fresh coconut water, and wiped the sweat from her brow. Her white shirt was already drenched, just minutes after stepping out of her front door. She placed her handbag onto an empty chair and wondered why it was so heavy. But in a few short months of living here, she couldn't imagine leaving her condo without sunscreen, mosquito repellent, an umbrella, and Eric's bathing suit, even though he was in school right now. In true expat mom fashion she was always prepared for everything, from a tropical rainstorm to sunburn and dengue fever.

*She was always hungry in Singapore. The locals never stopped talking about food, thinking about food, and now she was just the same. She would be having a gourmet lunch of spicy black pepper beef in a tamarind sauce with sesame rice and a fried egg on top and find herself wondering what she should have for dinner—that Nasi Goreng from her favorite hawker in Holland Village or a plate of Hainanese-style chicken rice. She must have put on at least five kilos in the past couple of months, maybe not such a surprise when you're living in the culinary capital of Asia.*

*"Oh, there you are," said Kate, finally spotting Michael and waving him over.*

*"Sorry, the interview took longer than expected." He stooped down to kiss her and joined her at the table.*

*"More importantly, how did it go? Please tell me you've found the one."*

*"By far the most promising candidate. Her name's Maryanne Cruz. She's Filipino, 39, two kids back in Manila, been working as a helper in Singapore for six years, and she's worked with two other expat families. She can cook, clean, help throw dinner parties, entertain, and babysit if needed. She sounds fantastic on paper, but the only thing is—"*

*"I knew there'd be a catch. What is it?"*

*"She says she can't sleep in the maid's room." He passed her the resume. "She'd prefer to sleep in one of the empty guest rooms. The maid's room is awful—there's no window and it's right next to the kitchen. I don't feel comfortable asking her to sleep in a windowless box. On the other hand, I don't know how comfortable I feel offering her one of our bedrooms. What do you think?"*

*"I think it's a bit worrying she's making demands before*

*she's even started. But I know what you mean. In all good conscience, we can't put anyone in that maid's room. We've plenty of bedrooms; let's give her the last one down the hall. I'd rather she was happy in her work. Better than any unpleasantness developing later."*

*"You sure?" he said. "What about our privacy?"*

*"Yeah, it'll be an adjustment. But if she's as good as you say she is, I don't mind compromising on where she sleeps. I just don't want any drama." She folded the resume and started fanning herself with it. "The stories I hear from other expats over here ... I don't want any headaches."*

*"Right then, I'll tell her she's got the job and start the paperwork with the Ministry of Manpower."*

*"The Ministry of Manpower, the Ministry of Magic ... sounds like something out of Harry Potter."*

*"You know how strict they are about everything here. All those damn rules. You can get fined for chewing gum on the street and even for eating in the metro. I'm not sure how far your diplomatic immunity will get us over here."*

*She sighed. "I just wish the embassy could help a bit more. Looks like it's up to us who we hire as long as we follow the local procedures, I mean rules. Don't laugh, but I've joined Singapore Expat Wives on Facebook. I know, how 1950s can you get? But anyway, if we have any questions, I can post on there."*

*"Great, it's settled then. Now, can we eat? I'm starving."*

**MARELLA CRUISES**

**Marella Voyager**
Pre-Reserved

## ISLAND HISTORY & RUM TASTING

Port:        Basseterre
Date:        16-Dec-2024
Dep. Time:   12:00
Name:        Llelliott, Alan              Adult
Cabin:       4017
Information: PLEASE MEET AT THE END OF THE PIER 15
             MINUTES BEFORE TOUR DEPARTURE

---

## ISLAND HISTORY & RUM TASTING

Port:   Basseterre
Date:   16-Dec-2024
Name:   Llelliott, Alan              Adult
Cabin:  4017

## Terms & conditions

Please bring your ticket with you as proof of purchase. Just so, you know, you are able to review the booking terms and conditions, which you agreed to at the time of booking at http://www.tui.co.uk/editorial/legal/cruise-shore-excursions-terms-and-conditions.html or please contact your Destination Services team on board should you require any assistance. Your booking terms and conditions outline both your and our rights to change or cancel your excursion booking, in addition you will find full details on prices, tour itineraries, dress code, safety, transport, children any restrictions and general terms.

*Cascais, Portugal*
November 2022

The days were getting chillier and shorter. That was the thing about Lisbon and Cascais in November: warm during the day, but quite a different matter in the evening when the wind from the Atlantic picked up. As Kate jogged back home from Praia do Tamariz and up to Monte Estoril, she wished she'd taken a sweater. Still, the run had given her time to clear her head. After a while, she stopped by a bench, took out her phone, and re-read the email she'd received from Patricia. It was official: Patricia's husband had accepted the new job offer, and they were moving to Portugal over Christmas, in time for the kids to start school in January. She was looking for advice on which schools to check and what neighborhoods to consider.

She knew she couldn't avoid getting back to Patricia, especially after bumping into her two months ago. That had been one hell of a shock. Of all the people to run into. Why was it you always ran into the ones you had the least desire to meet? She and Patricia had never been close, just part of the same mums' group at the international school in Singapore. She would reply later, keeping things friendly. She couldn't risk Patricia showing up and asking more questions about why she'd left Singapore in such a rush. The last thing Kate needed was anyone arousing the suspicion of others.

She made her way up Avenida Sabóia, Monte Estoril's fashionable boulevard, admiring the old buildings with their stucco exteriors and tangerine roofs as she jogged past. She was feeling focused. This time around, she would definitely not hire any help—not after that fiasco with Maryanne, who had broken her trust in such an unbelievable way. Hiring part-time help was common in Portugal too, but she couldn't bring herself to go there. Michael had offered to do the cleaning; guilty conscience, maybe, or his way of making it up to her. Either way, neither of them was willing to go down that rabbit hole again.

Michael was waiting for her on the front porch. He'd just finished watering the bougainvillea at the front of the house, a riot of dazzling pink against the pale white walls.

"Hi, honey," he said as she came up the steps. "How was your run?"

"Good," said Kate. "But running uphill isn't for the fainthearted. I'm so out of shape." She took a sip from her water bottle.

"Tell me about it. I've cleaned all the bathrooms today. Feels like my back's about to give out."

Kate gave him a look, and he got the message and quickly changed tack.

"Eric seems to be settling in well. He mentioned inviting some friends over for a play date. I think it's a great idea."

"Yes, of course," she said, "I'll ask him and set something up. If it's with Maya, then maybe I'll invite Fatima over too. I'm kinda curious to meet her husband and see what you make of her."

"Oh. Why?"

"It's probably nothing. She seems to want to do everything by the book, but her personal life screams otherwise. I suppose it's a big deal for her to marry outside her culture and country. By the way, guess who emailed me from Singapore?"

Michael stopped what he was doing. "Who?"

"Patricia."

"Sydney Patricia or Wisconsin Patricia?"

"Wisconsin Patricia."

"Oooh boy. What the hell did she say?"

"Well get this: they're moving to Lisbon. Chris has accepted a job here and they're moving over with the kids in January. She was asking me for schooling and housing advice."

She decided to leave out the part about running into Patricia last month in Lisbon. She wasn't sure why. Maybe if she told him, he would worry too, and what good would that do? And anyway, what happened in Singapore hadn't exactly brought them closer together. Far from it; it had pulled them further apart.

"Are you in touch with any of the other SAIS moms?" he said.

"Nah, not really. I don't want anyone asking more uncomfortable questions about why we left Singapore. I've told so many lies lately I can barely keep my stories straight."

"I'm sorry, I know it was a really stressful period with you being so worried about your mom back home, and then our leaving Singapore in such a rush—it was all a bit much."

"It almost broke me," she whispered.

It was the first time she'd said it out loud, and Michael walked over and held her hand; a small gesture, but it spoke volumes. He still cared about her. It was still his instinct to protect her.

She wished they could go back to the way they used to be, but she didn't know how; they'd lost so much trust along the way. Expat life had taken such a toll on their marriage. You could bubble wrap your belongings when you moved, but there was no way to bubble wrap a marriage. She wasn't sure where or how to start reconstructing their relationship, though she'd been having a recurring thought about something that could maybe help, and as Michael held onto her hand and they shared a moment of calm, she decided it was worth a shot.

"Michael, I've been meaning to ask. Would you be willing to see a marriage counselor?"

He jerked back as if he'd been slapped across the face. "A marriage counselor? Are you serious? How many times have I told you. Nothing happened between Maryanne and me. I thought you believed me?"

"I thought so too," she said, "but I can't seem to move on. I thought talking about our feelings with a counselor, an objective and neutral third person, might help us get out of this rut. But if you don't want to …"

"I guess I do. I do want to fix us."

"Do you? Are you sure?"

He took her hand back in his. "Yeah, I'm sure."

"Okay, let me do some research, find out who we can see, an English speaker, and figure out what our insurance will cover."

"Darling, you've got enough going on with work. Why don't I find us someone?"

Kate smiled. He was taking this seriously; that was a good

start. For the first time in ages, she felt hopeful. Maybe this could fix them. Maybe it was time to put the Maryanne saga behind them once and for all and forget about Singapore.

# 8

# ABENA
*Accra, Ghana*
August 2012

*A*bena *closed her eyes, but she still couldn't block out the incessant noise from the people, traffic, and livestock. The traffic light turned red and her* tro-tro *came to a screeching halt on a road that was littered with rubbish on each side. Hawkers, beggars, and young kids walked left and right in a coordinated traffic flow all of their own. Women in brightly colored fabrics carried their babies on their backs and balanced towering baskets on their heads—baskets overflowing with nuts, biscuits, cool drinks, plantain chips, and more. Kids who looked no older than ten or eleven were selling wallets, watches, and laundry detergent.*

*"We're here," the tro-tro driver shouted, and there was a mad scramble to get out of the little minivan.*

*"Here" was Accra's famous Makola Market. Noisy and insistent, teeming with people, and with goods sprawling over the sidewalk like an open-air garage sale that had spilled out into the road, it was exactly the way Abena remembered it. Baskets of sea-snails, fresh fish, and huge yams were for sale at one end, richly colored Kente cloth, shoes, and wallets at*

*the other, with just about everything in between. Her life in Brighton seemed a world away.*

*She knew how to keep up with the rhythm of the market. The trick was to become part of the chaos. It was fast-paced, but there was a certain flow as women of all ages whizzed past her with their yams and hairbrushes. She was sweating profusely in corners of her body she didn't know it was possible to sweat in, but she navigated the maze deftly, being careful not to knock a banana off the stack a vendor was transporting or to bump into the tall piles of fabrics four feet high or more. After a few sharp turns, there it was: her sister Akosua's fabric shop, 'Royal Designs.' For as long as Abena could remember, ever since it had been set up by their late father, there had been piles of neatly folded fabrics of all colors from floor to ceiling inside, leaving no inch uncovered. Outside, to entice the shoppers, Akosua would stack the fabrics high, one on top of the other, so it was like walking through a rainbow of African prints. She would sit there on a little red plastic stool and watch the world go by. And even though the market had always been a mad jumble of pushing, hurrying, and shooing, this little corner had always felt like an oasis of calm.*

*Inside the shop, family members would mill about, some-one eating* waakye *early in the morning, someone reading The Daily Graphic, someone mopping the floor, someone getting their hair braided by an auntie, a never-ending flow of activity as they all helped each other out.*

*When she saw Abena, Akosua came out from behind the counter and beamed. "Eiii, Abena, is that you?" Akosua was over six feet tall, with dark ebony skin, and almost ten years older than her sister. Despite the age gap, they shared a close bond.*

*"Sorry I'm late-o. The tro-tro was running behind schedule. More than usual."* Abena put down her purse and ran her fingers through an orange fabric with pink swallows on it.

*"You like that one? It's yours."* Akosua took out a measuring yard and cut out six meters of fabric.

*"Oye, it's nice, but I leave to go back to the UK in two days. Not enough time to get it stitched."*

*"Girl, you've forgotten how things are done here. Every-thing last minute. I can have it stitched for you by tonight. What do you want? A dress? Or a matching peplum blouse and skirt? Something you could wear to church?"*

Abena decided this was not the right moment to tell Akosua she had stopped going to church on Sundays. Ben would rather watch football and go out for a Sunday roast in the local pub.

*"Sure, a blouse and skirt. Thank you. Akosua, how are you managing with work and everything else going on?"* She looked down at Akosua's pregnant belly.

*"Abena, I've given birth four times before. Yes, this fifth one is harder; I'm older this time. But the fights with Daniel, that's what stresses me out. He's still not happy. He doesn't want any more babies to provide for. And I tell him, it's a bit late for that."*

Abena reached over and hugged her beloved older sister. She was worried about her. Akosua and Daniel had never had a strong marriage, but somehow they'd made it work. She didn't like what she was hearing. Daniel had barely been visible throughout her trip, and he no longer helped out at the store.

*"Listen,"* Abena said, *"if there's anything you need, call*

*me, okay? Once I'm back in Brighton, I'll plan another supply trip."*

*"Once you're back in Brighton I hope you won't waste any more time, sis."*

*"Waste time doing what?"*

*"Abena, you know what I mean. I only want the best for you. It seems like you and Ben should start thinking about having a family of your own."*

*Abena pictured all those discarded IVF syringes in the yellow bucket back in their Brighton apartment. She sighed. "Sure, sis, sure." And all of a sudden she couldn't wait to get back on that plane and go home.*

## Cascais, Portugal
## November 2022

So far so good, thought Abena as she came into the kitchen to refill the water pitcher. It had been a while since she'd hosted a brunch, but after talking to Kakra and Panyin, she had finally plucked up the courage to invite Maya and Eric over, along with their parents—on a Saturday so that all three families could meet up and enjoy some time together.

"Babe, you've gotta relax," Ben had told her earlier that morning. She'd been stressing about not having enough food or about the chance of rain, obsessing over every detail. She knew he was right. Abena was a nervous hostess, and this was the first time they'd had friends over to their Cascais apartment. No wonder her nerves were on edge. But inviting friends over was an important step; it would help them feel more at home in Portugal and help her girls feel a little more settled. It was actually Kate who had first suggested the idea of a play date for the kids, but Abena had jumped in and invited everyone over to hers, and that was just fine with Kate and Fatima.

"Mum, we need more napkins," said Kakra, who was helping to set the wicker table on the large balcony that overlooked the community pool, with views to the ocean beyond. Although their apartment had come semi-furnished, it was easy to spot Abena's personal touches: the traditional African hand fans hanging on the walls, the woven Ghanaian baskets displaying everything from magazines to house plants, the rich textiles on the dining table, even the placemats and matching coasters, everything was made in Africa. She had positioned all of these accessories to perfection so they stood out against the neutral walls and had taken great pride in putting her artistic stamp on their new home.

Thanks to its cramped entryway and old-fashioned copper tiles, the fifth-floor apartment appeared small at first glance, but as each room opened up into another, leading to the spacious balcony, it took on a whole new feel. The three bedrooms were enough for the four of them; the girls were still happy to share a room, and the third bedroom had become a home office. A desk facing the Atlantic was quite an incentive to get out of bed in the morning. It's true the bathrooms were a little dull and dated, with their gray tiles and mirrored cabinets, but you couldn't have everything on your wish list. And what the bathrooms lacked, the views more than made up for, and Abena loved to start her mornings on the balcony with a cup of coffee, the soft breeze often bringing her swallows for company.

"Thanks, Kakra. Now we need more glasses for the kids' table."

Kakra seemed happy helping her mum. Both the girls had settled in well, but Abena fretted she was missing something, or that they weren't telling her everything. Adjusting to a new school and a new house in a new country where people spoke a new language wouldn't usually be so effortless. She'd read a book about helping kids prepare for an international move and had expected more problems, more challenges, more discussions. But the girls had taken it completely in their stride. She had decided to ask Fatima and Kate how Maya and Eric were handling things by comparison.

"They're here," Panyin shouted when the doorbell rang, and she ran to the intercom to let them in. After a few minutes there was the sound of footsteps and excited voices as Fatima, Stefan, Maya, Kate, Michael, and Eric came out of the elevator and walked in together. In between hugs and hellos, Fatima handed Abena a bouquet of flowers. Kate had brought chocolates and a bottle of Alentejo wine.

"You guys shouldn't have, but thank you," said Abena, welcoming them into the apartment.

"Wow, your place is so … colorful," said Fatima, taking a long look around the living room, her eyes resting on a coffee table book about Ghanaian textiles. "Just like you."

"Thanks. Come on outside."

Abena led everyone to the balcony. Purple lavender pots and yellow lanterns gave it a whimsical feel, and as they all settled into their tables in the warm November sunshine, drinks were poured and conversations flowed.

Abena glanced over at Stefan and Michael, fascinated to be finally meeting the husbands of her new friends. Stefan

was exactly what she'd expected from Fatima's description—
rather serious-looking but actually very warm and friendly.
He'd started chatting with Ben immediately, sharing anec-
dotes about London and his university days in the UK.
Michael, on the other hand, had surprised her. He wasn't the
loud, gushing, over-friendly, over-sharing American she had
expected—or stereotyped—him to be. He was careful and
measured, waiting for others to make the first move or
initiate the conversation. He had, however, complimented
Abena on her poached eggs. "You have to time them right,"
he'd told her, and she had smiled. It took one foodie to spot
another.

Soon they were all chatting about Ghanaian food,
something Michael hadn't tried, and Abena's *jollof* rice
became the main topic of conversation. She'd been nervous
about serving it to non-Africans, wondering if they would
cope with the kick from the chilis and spices, but Ben had
encouraged her to. It was a typical West African dish made
everywhere from Nigeria to Guinea-Bissau, with its long-
grain rice, tomatoes, onions, spices, vegetables, and meat in
a single pot. But Abena's version had a Ghanaian twist: beef
seasoned with ginger, onions, and garlic, sautéed alongside a
scotch bonnet pepper, which turned dark during cooking to
give it a deep, smoky flavor, all presented with a cabbage
salad and *shito* sauce on the side for anyone who wanted it
extra spicy.

"This is delicious, Abena," said Kate, who had just
swallowed a large spoonful of the rice with a dollop of shito
sauce, her eyes watering and her cheeks flushing as the slow
burn at the back of her throat intensified. "Who taught you
to cook this?"

"Oh, thank you. Actually, it was my s—"

"It's a closely guarded family recipe," said Ben, jumping up to stand next to Abena. "It's been passed around for generations, so we've lost track. We dare not share it and risk incurring the wrath of our ancestors." He put his arm around Abena's shoulders and gave her a squeeze.

Fatima laughed. "Gatekeeping recipes is a guilty pleasure in Pakistani society too. I'm totally against it. I don't think there should be any secrets in the kitchen."

"Agreed. This is like a *biryani*, but different," said Michael after his first mouthful.

"A lot of people say that," said Abena. "I think biryani and jollof have different flavors and textures. I'd say biryani is more fragrant, with all those spices, and has a softer texture, and it's cooked in layers. But jollof is stirred, so the ingredients are evenly distributed." She was relieved the conversation had moved on from the source of the family recipe.

"All this talk is making me think we should host the next party at ours," said Stefan. "Wait till you try Fatima's biryani." He smiled at his wife. "Her mom's recipe. Never fails."

After brunch, Kakra and Panyin took Eric and Maya into their room to build some Lego. The adults lingered in the sun, saying yes to more coffee and another *pastel de nata*, and the conversation drifted to their kids.

"So how are Eric and Maya settling in?" asked Abena. "Has it been a smooth transition?" She took a gulp of her coffee, finally able to relax now that the brunch had gone so well. "I feel so guilty sometimes for taking the twins away from the UK and our family there, and I worry so much about how they're adapting. It's such a big change."

"Eric's used to moving countries," said Kate. "Mind you,

he was considerably younger when we left Mexico and China. He does miss Singapore a lot, and we encourage him to stay in touch with his friends there. The almost eight months we spent back in the US in between the Singapore and Lisbon postings were a bit tricky. I think he felt in limbo. I've been encouraging him to make friends here, which he's slowly starting to do, but you know, it does take time."

"I agree," said Fatima. "An international move can be exciting for kids, but when there are loads of moves, when it becomes a lifestyle, your kids need extra support, and so do you. I could see it this time with Maya. She was only young when we left Copenhagen to move to Dubai, but these days her emotions are way more complex. We discussed things more openly this time; that helped. And I read a book about raising Third Culture Kids—TCKs. It talked about building a RAFT when you move. It's an acronym for Reconciliation, Affirmation, Farewells, and Think destination."

"Wish I'd known this stuff before we moved the girls here," said Abena.

"Why?" said Ben. "Would it have changed our decision?"

Abena looked uncomfortable. "Maybe. Maybe not."

"I found out about the book by joining FIGT," said Fatima. "Another acronym. Families in Global Transition. Great organization. They support globally mobile families."

"Sounds great," said Abena. "Maybe share their website link on our chat group later?"

"I think I'm already a member of FIGT," said Kate. "It's a good reminder to look up their resources. We get some support through diplomatic circles, but I do wish there was more awareness, more support for the trailing spouses."

"I refuse to call myself a trailing spouse," said Michael.

"Just call me the 'Chaos Coordinator.' "

Stefan laughed. "Definitely an apt description for anyone who moves abroad with kids."

As the chatter continued around her, Abena went over to lean on the balcony railing and take in the view, and she stood there, bathed in sunlight, holding the universe together. The life she had dreamed of for so long was finally within reach. And she would make sure nothing and no one got in her way.

Once their guests had left, she joined Ben, who was clearing up in the kitchen, and the masks came off.

"Well, that went well?" she said, handing him some empty glasses, her sarcasm hanging in the air.

"It was a close call, Abena. I *had* to step in, and you know it." He started stacking the dishwasher.

"You're the one who kept telling me to relax. So I did. But apparently I relaxed too much. You shouldn't have interrupted me like that, belittled me in front of everyone. How do you think that made me feel?"

"I was trying to save you," he shouted. "From saying too much!"

Abena's shoulders slumped. "It's a bit too late to save me from myself," she whispered, "don't you think?"

She turned away from him and went back to the balcony.

# 9

## FATIMA
### *Lisbon, Portugal*
### December 2022

Lisbon's fashionable Avenida da Liberdade was all set for the festive season, with its twinkling Christmas lights in the shape of wreaths, angels, and snowflakes, and at number 102, house of designer jeweler Maria João Bahia, the entire building had been wrapped in an enormous green ribbon and bow. Fatima smiled at the ingenuity, and her heart soared when they reached the giant *Feliz Natal* sign across the roundabout from Marquês de Pombal Square. The Wonderland Lisboa market had been set up directly behind the roundabout, with gingerbread houses, a Ferris wheel, stalls selling handmade arts and crafts, an ice ramp, a giant Christmas tree, and food stalls selling hot chocolate churros made on the spot and lightly spiced *bolo-rei*—king cake.

"Let's grab some *castanhas*," said Fatima, squeezing Stefan's hand.

He looked over to the little stand selling roasted chestnuts and inhaled the rich, smoky aroma. Stefan's command of Portuguese wasn't up there with hers, so she helped him order and they meandered over to Park Eduardo VII to sit and enjoy the chestnuts. Just the two of them for a change. Maya was over at Kate's house watching a holiday movie with Eric, Kakra, and Panyin.

"You okay, honey?" she said. "You seem a bit quiet."

"*Scheisse!*" Stefan had burnt the tips of his fingers trying to peel a hot chestnut. "Yeah, I guess. All this 'it's the most wonderful time of the year' stuff. It's the most difficult time of the year if you're an expat living abroad and your family's guilt-tripping you for not coming home for Christmas."

"Listen, maybe we should take a short trip to see your mother in Berlin."

"I don't know. It *would* mean a lot to her. Even Maya's been asking when she'll see her *Oma* next. I guess a few days in Germany over Christmas would be manageable."

"We could finally take Maya to a German Christmas market. She has school holidays till the third of January, so we'd have plenty of time."

"Well, that would be nice. Okay, I'll look for flights once we're back. Just a short visit to meet up with close family members—four to five days max. Each time I go back, it's difficult."

Fatima knew what he was saying. Going back home was something they looked forward to and dreaded at the same time. It was an uncomfortable feeling realizing you'd out-grown a place. It was something that just happened over time; the more you learned about your new country and the more you adapted to it, the more out of sorts you felt in your passport country. And the people who were still living there weren't particularly interested in hearing about your life abroad.

Each time they went back to Germany for a visit, Stefan's mother, brother, and family would ask him, "But when are you moving back home?" Fatima knew he was tired of telling them that home was something he carried with him, inside of him, that home was wherever he, Fatima, and Maya were. His family had never moved from Berlin, so it was difficult for them to relate to a globally mobile lifestyle. And Stefan could barely relate to his brother's life in that tiny town near Wolfsburg, where life followed a predictable pattern: marry the girl next door, work at Volkswagen, and spend your weekends supporting your local football team. Stefan craved acceptance from his family about his life choices, but he knew it was difficult to accept something you didn't understand, something you'd never experienced yourself.

"Can we agree that if we do go," he said, "you and I won't fight? Every time we're there, the family dynamics are such that we … stop seeing eye to eye."

"Well if your mother or brother suggest one more time that I should speak to you in German instead of English, I'll explode. And I'll tell them, no, how about we speak in Urdu? Seriously, it bothers the hell out of me that they presume your language is somehow more important than mine."

"I'm sorry, I've tried to explain to them. My mother's biggest fear was always that she wouldn't be able to communicate with Maya in German, which thankfully we've put to rest."

"It's the same for Ammi. She loves the fact that Maya can understand and speak Urdu, even though you have to sometimes insist she doesn't respond in English. Ensuring Maya learned Urdu was the one non-negotiable part of my parenting. Urdu is what I carry with me, no matter where I go.

I can move away from home and marry someone outside of my culture, but I can never stop speaking my mother tongue. And speaking of my mother, I should probably call her once we're back."

Not wanting to ruin her festive mood by thinking about her mother, Fatima suggested walking all the way to Rossio and Praça do Comércio to see the giant Christmas tree and lights before they headed back.

"But we just came from there, Fatima." Stefan laughed at her awful sense of direction. "It's one of the things I love about you."

It didn't matter to Fatima where they walked. Maybe it was the chestnuts or the Christmas lights, but as they flitted from one magical square to another, she felt warm and fuzzy inside.

HER GOOD MOOD didn't last. When they got home, Stefan looked for flights to Germany, and she called Ammi as she'd promised.

"Finally you found the time to call me back," said a petulant Ammi.

"Ammi, I told you I'd call you once I was home."

"It hurts that you give such little importance to talking to me when all I do is wait eagerly for your phone calls."

If there was an Oscar for best emotional blackmail, Ammi would be a leading candidate, but Fatima decided to change the subject and indulge her mother. "How's your knee?"

"What can I say, *beta*? I'm getting old. There are days when I can barely go down the stairs. So I ask Shazia to bring my dinner upstairs. I don't know how much longer I can go on like this. I want to come see you before I'm not fit to travel at all."

"Ammi, I'm worried about you. How will you travel with your bad knee? And you know, the streets are hilly and steep in Portugal, with cobblestones everywhere, so you have to be very careful."

"Are you saying you don't want me to come?"

"No, of course not." Fatima cleared her throat. "I want you to be extra careful when you do come."

"Okay, good, because actually, I wanted to tell you that I want to come visit you for an extended period of time. The house here needs some painting work to be done, and it is best it happens when I am out of the way. Muhammad will take care of the repair work and supervise what needs to be done. I was thinking how nice it would be to stay with you for maybe four to five months, to spend time with Maya too. Probably she has forgotten me by now since she hasn't seen me in so long."

"Ammi, she saw you plenty in Dubai and has not forgotten you at all."

"If you say so."

"I do say so. Listen, I will have to look into the paperwork, okay? I might need to sponsor you as a family visit of an EU citizen. Let me check and see what I find out."

"You always make it sound so impossible. Shagufta next door has spent six months with her son in Toronto. Six months! And you act like me coming to Portugal to see my only daughter for a few months will be such a big deal."

"Ammi, calm down. I never said don't come. All I said was, let's look at how long a visa the Portuguese Embassy grants you."

"Well make it happen. I can help you with the house, with the cooking, you know."

"Ammi, I don't need your help in the kitchen. I will find out what paperwork is required to sponsor you for an extended family visit."

"Good, because you owe me this. After all I've done for you."

And there it was again. Guilt from a parent never added up to love. Fatima sighed. "I haven't forgotten anything. But I still need to discuss it with Stefan. He'll wonder why you're coming for such a long time."

"You still haven't told him, have you? Of course not. I can only imagine his reaction when he finds out the truth about you."

Fatima felt herself tense up. She was too tired to fight this battle again, and she wouldn't rise to the bait. She would keep her cool, accept that the visit was going to happen, and simply make the best of it. It was the only way to proceed without losing her mind.

"Stefan doesn't know," she said, "and I'd like to keep it that way."

"I've always helped you keep your secrets. This is why you need me there."

"Fine, Ammi. I'll find out what's required and be in touch soon."

"By soon, I hope you really mean soon this time."

"*Khuda Hafiz*, Ammi, goodbye."

She put the phone down and stared blankly ahead. Her

mother always made her feel like this. Ammi's visit would hinder her settling into her new life in Portugal, not help it. She looked down at the scar on her left arm and ran her hands over the raised skin. This time, she vowed, it would be different.

# 10

## ABENA
*Cascais, Portugal*
December 2022

A bena looked over at Ben, who was sitting opposite her sipping a mojito in the dimly lit restaurant. Finally, she thought, our first date night. It had been quite an exercise in courage and logistics to make it happen. Abena had been nervous about leaving the twins with a new babysitter, especially in a new country and with the language barrier too. It was the reality of expat life. You couldn't just call your mom, your sister, or your neighbor to babysit. In Brighton she would have called Ben's sixteen-year-old niece; she loved looking after the girls. But in Portugal, they barely knew anyone. She'd thought of asking Fatima but knew from a message on their WhatsApp group that Fatima was sick and would be missing this week's Portuguese lesson. In the end, they'd hired a professional babysitter through a nanny agency and crossed their fingers.

Abena was forcing herself to relax. It was quite the setting. The sun burnt a bright orange over the Cascais Marina and the yachts rocked gently in their moorings. This was the high-end part of Cascais, with prices to match. *25 euros for a bowl of linguine with shrimp. Ouch*. No one had warned her about the rising cost of living in Portugal, and dining in expat-heavy, tourist-dominated areas was particularly expensive.

"So, I'm glad we're finally doing this," said Ben. "It's been such a busy few months adjusting to life here. We need some alone time before this hectic year comes to an end." He leaned across the table and took her hand in his.

"I know," she said. "And I'm glad we didn't cancel tonight. I just hope the kids are okay."

"They're not babies anymore, Abena. Of course they'll be okay. I'm sure Teresa will have an easy time babysitting them. She'll let us know if there's anything."

"Have you checked if you've had any messages from her?"

"No messages. And now I'm putting my phone away, and so should you."

"Okay, okay, I get the hint." She looked through the menu. "How about sharing some *Amêijoas à Bulhão Pato*— clams in a garlic and white wine sauce."

"Sure, let's be adventurous and try local food," he said, and once the waiter had taken their order, he moved his chair closer to the table and looked over at Abena. "There's something I've been meaning to discuss with you."

"Oh?"

"A business opportunity has come up. I've been contacted by this big-shot entrepreneur. Nana Afua. He came across our business and is proposing a joint company venture. He's got a full-scale export business supplying Ghanaian homeware goods to some of the big-name brands in Accra, and he's looking to expand into the European market. I can see an opportunity for collaboration, but there's one thing …"

"What is it?"

"He's invited me to fly to Accra next month to discuss it in person." He scanned her eyes for a reaction, looking as if he already knew what the answer would be.

"You can't go, Ben. It's too risky."

"Even if only I go?"

"I don't think it's a good idea. And you know why. Why don't you invite him here instead?"

"It would be more productive to have the meeting in Ghana and visit the local suppliers firsthand. That's what he wants to show me. And as you know, this is something I've always wanted to do: connect to my roots and explore business opportunities that connect my culture to my creativity. Of course, I wanted to discuss it with you first and see what you thought."

"The business opportunity sounds promising, but you going back to Ghana right now, it makes me nervous. What if you get caught? What in the world would I do, sitting here in Portugal?"

The waiter arrived with their food. When he was gone, Abena reached over the table. It was her turn to take his hand in hers.

"Look, I know none of this is easy. But we made our choice. We made our decision. And now we have to live with it." She looked down at her charm bracelet.

"Why do you still wear that thing?"

"You know who gave this to me." Her voice cracked. "It's all I have left."

Ben sighed. "I'm sorry. I wish we could move on. I know it's easier said than done, but we've talked about this. You know that for years I struggled with where I belonged. A black Ghanaian boy in Britain. I always felt I had to negotiate my sense of belonging—in Britain, in Ghana, or within black communities in London, Birmingham, and Brighton. It's like I fit in everywhere but belong nowhere."

"It's not been easy for you," Abena acknowledged.

"It created a sort of hybrid identity. As far as I can remember, I've always wanted a space where I could be myself. And going back to Ghana and working closely with other entrepreneurs and businesses in Ghana has always been a part of that plan. It feels like the dream is slipping away, Abena. It's a tough loss to accept." He looked weary, his arms crossed in resignation.

She didn't know what to say next and struggled to look him in the eye. Maybe it was her fault for snatching his dream away from him, but they'd both been willing partners and were equally to blame for their predicament. And now, it seemed, they had reached an impasse, where neither knew how to move forward without backing down.

Ben saw the look on her face and admitted defeat. "I'll make up some excuse about not being able to travel right now and see if we can have the discussion online or set up a meeting here."

"Thank you. I can't take any more stress right now, and you going back to the motherland would make me so incredibly anxious. I'm sorry."

The rest of the dinner date passed mostly in silence.

Abena knew there were two types of guilt. The one that lay buried deep inside of you and the one that constantly came to the surface to nag you into indecision. As she swayed back and forth between both, she couldn't figure out which one was worse.

# 11

## KATE
*Lisbon, Portugal*
December 2022

Kate and Michael sat in the airy reception area at the office of their new psychotherapist. Kate already loved the location. Almada sat on the southern margin of the Tagus River, on the opposite side of the river from the city. It had some of the best views of Lisbon, and it felt good to be sitting here at a distance looking into the city from the outside. In some ways Kate had always been an outsider, drawing a strange sense of comfort and control from being on the outside looking in. But the best part was, it was highly unlikely she would run into anyone she knew on this side of the river. It was anonymous and perfect.

Dr. Teixeira had been recommended to Michael through various expat groups on Facebook. Kate had doubted whether a Portuguese therapist would understand the dynamic of their expat marriage, with all the stresses and cross-cultural factors that affect globally mobile lifestyles, but Dr. Teixeira was a Canadian of Portuguese descent and fully bilingual in English and Portuguese, offering therapy sessions in both languages. Kate had checked her credentials online. She seemed a promising fit, and her clinic accepted their insurance.

An assistant led them into a starkly white side room. White walls, white furry carpet, white leather two-seater couch opposite a white armchair, and a gleaming white desk with the barest number of accessories.

A woman in a white pencil skirt, white tank top, and cream blazer walked into the office, her shoulder-length charcoal hair and dark eyes providing the perfect contrast. "Hello. You must be my two o'clock," she said. "I'm Dr. Melissa Teixeira. It's nice to meet you both." She smiled and extended a hand.

"It's lovely to meet you too. I'm Kate."

"And I'm Michael."

"Please, have a seat." She opened a folder and reviewed the information they'd already filled out online. "So, it says here that both of you are interested in regular sessions for couples therapy. Is that right?"

"Yes," they said. Michael reached over and squeezed Kate's hands.

"Great. Is this your first time attending a therapy session?"

"First time for both of us," replied Kate, inching towards the edge of her seat.

"Okay, let's start by getting to know you both a bit better. How long have you been together?"

"Nearly twenty years," said Kate. "We were university sweethearts. We also have a son together, who's ten."

"I see. Wonderful. And what brings you both here today?"

There was a pause.

"In the past few years," said Michael, "we've been moving to different countries due to Kate's diplomatic career as an FSO—Foreign Service Officer. As you can probably guess, we're both from the US, but we've spent most of our marriage living in Mexico, China, Singapore, and now here in Portugal. Unfortunately, the non Foreign Service spouse—that's me—has to rely on the FSO for everything, and the embassy won't allow us to manage hardly any of the processes ourselves since we're not employees of the government. As with any international marriage, problems have crept up along the way."

"What kind of problems specifically?"

"Well, as the accompanying spouse, I suppose I've struggled with feelings of resentment sometimes. Towards my wife. The lack of a job, of a stable, regular income, the complete dependence on her and her career to dictate our lives, being a stay-at-home dad to our son Eric, and always having to create a new life for all of us, from scratch, in each new country we move to, and all the while questioning my own purpose in this … life, I guess it's taken a toll on our marriage." He shrugged.

"And do you feel the same way, Kate?"

"Well, I agree that the underlying problems are definitely there. It's like no one taught us how to relocate our marriage."

"Has there been any infidelity from either side—physical or emotional?"

It was a question that had both Kate and Michael squirming in their corners of the white leather couch.

"Not exactly," said Michael.

Melissa looked from Kate to Michael and then back to Kate again. "Not exactly? What does that mean?"

"It means," said Kate, now perching right on the edge of her seat, "I suspected him of infidelity in Singapore. But he's always denied it."

"That's because nothing happened," Michael insisted, pressing his hands together like he was praying. "I would never cheat on Kate. I was wrongly accused of infidelity by our helper ... err, our maid, in Singapore."

"And what was her name?"

"Maryanne," he said.

"Did she live with you in Singapore?"

"Yes, she was a live-in maid. It's the norm in Singapore."

"Did she have her own living quarters?"

"No, not exactly. There was a small windowless room that was meant to house the maid, but we both felt uncomfortable putting her in there, so we gave Maryanne one of our spare bedrooms."

"And this was an arrangement you both felt comfortable with?"

Michael nodded.

"Yes, but only initially," said Kate.

"Why only initially?"

"After several months, it felt like we'd lost all our privacy. Maryanne was always there. And with me working long hours at the embassy, Michael and Maryanne spent a lot of time together."

"Did it make you feel nervous?"

"Yes."

"So, what did you do about it?"

"Nothing at first. Because I trusted Michael. But

eventually I told Maryanne she could only continue working for us if she moved over to the maid's room, the one at the back of the kitchen."

"And how did she take it?"

"She was angry and upset. It had been one of her conditions for taking the job, but I felt my own comfort and sanity were being compromised."

"How so?"

"I was afraid that in my absence, Michael was relying on Maryanne more and more to keep the household running." She looked down at the rug, surprised she had admitted that out loud.

"And how did you feel, Michael?"

"I … uh … I agree with what Kate said. In her absence, I came to rely heavily on Maryanne, and we became quite close."

"Close? How so?"

"With Kate working long hours at work, including a lot of travel within the Asia Pacific region, Maryanne and I would eat dinner together most nights. We would discuss all the household chores, plan the groceries and menus for the week, coordinate Eric's schedule and after-school activities, plan birthdays and dinner parties together … I suppose we grew quite close as a result."

"Did you confide in Maryanne?"

Michael could feel Kate's eyes boring into him, but he steadied himself and said, "Yes, I often did. I often expressed my frustration about Kate's job. I also expressed loneliness and other emotions I probably shouldn't have."

"So, although you say no physical affair took place, am I right in saying certain emotional boundaries were crossed?

That Maryanne became more your confidante than your employed help?"

"Yes, I believe that's an accurate reflection of what happened." He brought his hands to his face to cover his mouth, then looked over at Melissa. "In the process, I'm ashamed to admit, I also revealed certain private information to Maryanne about our family."

"I see. So what happened when you asked her to move out of the guest bedroom and into the maid's room?"

"She was furious. One day when Kate came back from work, Maryanne started yelling at her that she had not been treated well by us—"

"And then she accused Michael of cheating on me," said Kate. "With her!"

"What?"

"Maryanne told me that Michael preferred her over me."

"And how did that make you feel?"

"Bewildered. Lost. Confused. Angry. Betrayed."

Melissa paused. "So, it was a case of 'he-said, she-said.' Maryanne claimed she had an affair with Michael, and Michael, you claimed certain boundaries were crossed, but you were never unfaithful to Kate."

Michael squirmed. "Yes, that pretty much captures it. Since then, I've been trying to get Kate to see that Maryanne was manipulating my weakness to cause trouble in our marriage, out of spite. No, not out of spite; perhaps she saw an opportunity and went for it. I don't know. But Kate has never believed me, not completely."

"How can I ever trust you again?" said Kate, finding it increasingly difficult to keep her temper.

"Okay," said Melissa. "This has been an important first

step, telling me what happened. Now let me ask you both this: how committed are you to working this out? From what you have described, we have work to do in lots of areas of your marriage. But are you both prepared to give it a shot?"

"That's why we're here. At least it's why I'm here," said Kate, crossing her arms over her waist.

"Me too. I'm fully committed to working through our marriage problems, to regain Kate's trust," said Michael, who was also folding his arms.

"Okay. Wonderful. Before our next appointment, I need you both to do some homework." She grabbed some handouts and gave them to Michael and Kate. "Your first assignment is to do an exercise we call 10 10, where you write for ten minutes about what attracted you to each other in the first place. Make a list of those qualities and bring it with you to the next session. You'll read your partner's list, we'll discuss it for ten minutes, and then we'll swap. That clear?"

"Sure," said Kate, standing up to leave.

"Thank you, Dr. Teixeira," said Michael.

"Melissa. Please, call me Melissa."

They walked in silence towards the car, which was parked a few blocks away. Kate was relieved to be outside; it was good to feel the ocean air on her face.

Michael took her hand. "Wow. That was tough, honey. But we made some good progress in there, don't you think?"

"You call that progress? We barely scratched the surface. What about the *full* story?" She wrestled her hand free of Michael's.

"Look, it was only our first session. We can reveal more as we start to feel more comfortable with her."

"Are you crazy? You want to tell her the full truth about

why we left Singapore? About why we HAD to leave Singapore? About how we actually got the embassy to curtail our assignment?"

"Don't you think we need to be completely honest with her?"

"Sure, if we want to destroy the career that I've worked so hard to build."

There was nothing more to be said. It would be a long drive over the bridge back to Lisbon.

# 12

## ABENA
*Cascais, Portugal*
December 2022

Abena pushed open the doors of the hospital, willing herself to stay calm, not to panic. Panicking never helped anyone. Thank God she had quickly messaged Kate and Fatima and asked them what to do. Both of them had recommended driving the twins straight to the public hospital and going to the Emergency Pediatric Unit so they'd be seen right away. While Ben figured out the parking, Abena rushed in with Kakra and Panyin and went over to the reception, but the receptionist just pointed at a ticket machine and said, "*Primeiro precisa de ir até à máquina para tirar uma senha!*"

The ticket machine was entirely in Portuguese, but a woman behind Abena came to her rescue, clicked twice, took the ticket, and gave it to her. Number A85. Abena looked up at the screen; they would be next.

After what felt like an eternity, there was a 'ding dong,' and A85 blinked above one of the counters. She grabbed the girls, who were both limping, and headed straight over.

"*Olá, boa tarde. Como posso ajudar?*" said the female official, not bothering to look up.

"Um … *fala inglês?*" asked Abena.

It was a good attempt but the official was having none of it and hollered something to another official sitting next to her. There were nods and looks from some of the people sitting in the reception area.

Kakra tugged on Abena's shirt. "Mum, I think she's complaining about foreigners who move to Portugal and don't learn Portuguese."

Abena blushed and tried to explain in English to the unsmiling official. "I'm so sorry. I *am* learning Portuguese, but it takes time."

The official sighed. "What do you need?"

"My daughters, they were playing and had an accident—they both slipped on the cobblestones. Either they have twisted their ankles or maybe sprained them. I think we need X-rays, to make sure nothing is broken."

"What is your NIF number? And I need the *Número de Utente* for your daughters."

When Abena started scrolling through her phone for the twins' Utente numbers, the official let out another sigh—more of a groan this time—and the crowd in the waiting room turned around to see what the commotion was about.

After a frantic search, Abena found the numbers and read them out to the official in English, who finally said something helpful. "Please, wait here. First the doctor will see your daughters for an assessment."

Abena sat down, her heart racing. It was stressful enough rushing your children to the emergency unit of a hospital in your home country, but to do it in a country where you're not familiar with the medical system or culture and to be shamed for not speaking the local language, well, it was an extra stressor, and in moments of stress, Abena's mind would regress, and what little Portuguese she did know would go out of the window.

She took out her phone and opened up Google Translate in case she needed help telling the doctor what had happened.

After a few minutes of waiting, they were led along the hall to the doctor's office, and a rather serious-looking man with wispy brown hair and black-rimmed glasses introduced himself in Portuguese.

"*Fala inglês?*" said Abena. It was worth a try.

"Yes, I do speak English," he said. "How long have you been living here? Do you understand a little Portuguese?"

"About five months. I *am* learning the language, but it takes time. I know some Portuguese, some small talk." I'm here for medical advice, not language lessons, she thought. "But this is a medical emergency. I want to be sure I can follow and understand everything. So I prefer English, please, if possible."

"Okay, so tell me, what happened?"

"My daughters had a fall on the side of the pavement. They bumped into each other and fell down. They might have sprained their ankles—I'm hoping there's no fracture."

After a quick examination of Kakra's left foot and Panyin's right foot, it was good news. "I think nothing is broken," he said. "But we'll need X-rays to be sure. Please, follow me."

He led the three of them along the corridor to another room, asked them to wait outside the open door, chatted to the lab technician, and then waved them in.

The technician said something in Portuguese, and Kakra, who was first, understood he was asking her to take off her shoes, lie down on the table, and turn onto her right side for an X-ray of her left foot. After a few minutes and some different angles, it was Panyin's turn, and Abena watched on, suitably impressed that both of them could understand so much Portuguese. The kids had clearly been picking up the language at school—and much faster than she was.

By the time Ben had found somewhere to park, Abena and the girls were back in the main reception area waiting for the X-ray results. Abena filled him in, and half an hour later they were called back into the doctor's office.

"See here? A tiny hairline fracture on the left side of the foot for Kakra. Panyin has been lucky: no fracture, only a sprain." The doctor gave Panyin a compression sock. "You need to ice both feet, and wear this." For Kakra it was a compression stocking. "Keep your foot elevated as much as possible and take painkillers every six to eight hours as necessary."

"How long will it take for the fracture to heal?" Abena asked the doctor.

"Two to three weeks. Maybe four. I'll see her after four weeks to assess. It's best not to put too much pressure on your foot, Kakra."

Kakra smiled at the doctor. "Luckily, we have winter holidays for the next three weeks."

He smiled back. "Good. Please rest up. And on your way out, make an appointment at reception for a date four weeks from now. I'll see you in the new year."

Once back in the car, Abena started to relax. Navigating a medical emergency in Portuguese had been a trial, but at least they hadn't needed to pay for anything. What the public health care system lacked in empathy, it made up for in efficiency and cost.

But this had been a real wake-up call for Abena. She vowed to take her Portuguese lessons more seriously. She needed Portugal to be her home, a place where she belonged and felt capable of handling any task. It was going to take a long time to get there.

## *Cascais, Portugal*
## December 2022

It was their last Portuguese lesson before the Christmas holidays. This time they had asked Inês to meet them in Cascais, by the Cascais Mercado. It was a public holiday for the 'Feast of the Immaculate Conception' and everywhere was busy. They'd opted for one of the seafood restaurants; it was a chilly winter day, and the promise of a hot *galão* coffee had enticed them inside.

"So, what have you all been up to?" asked Inês once everyone was seated and coffees had been ordered.

"Well, I think I can finally start spotting the difference between Brazilian Portuguese and European Portuguese," said Fatima, looking pleased with herself. "Take '*Boa noite*.' In Portugal people pronounce the 't' but in Brazilian Portuguese the 't' sounds more like a 'ch' sound. I hear '*boa noiche*' instead."

"Right," said Inês. "You'll hear both variations; there are many Brazilians living in Portugal."

Kate laughed. "Well, I'm glad you're making progress in Portuguese because I sure ain't! The other day I was in a bakery and I ordered *quero um pau*, and the assistant looked at me like I was mad. I repeated *um pau* several times and it was only when I pointed to the bread that I finally got what I wanted."

Inês giggled. "Yes, unfortunately this is a common mistake people make when learning Portuguese. *Um pau* means 'a penis.' Bread is *um pão*. No wonder you got some funny looks, Kate."

Kate shook her head in embarrassment. "Oh boy. Guess it all makes sense now."

"Well," said Abena, "I recently had this experience in the public health care system that left me a bit rattled. I had to rush both my daughters to the emergency unit for a suspected fracture and was constantly shamed and criticized by the receptionist and clinicians for not speaking Portuguese. The little that I do know went clean out of my head. It was just so … stressful managing the language barrier on top of the medical emergency. Inês, I *so* need your help. Can you teach us all some key phrases—what to say and what to expect at a hospital or doctor's clinic?"

"First of all, I'm really sorry you experienced that, and I hope your daughters are okay. Sometimes the public hospitals are a bit less accommodating of foreigners and expats who don't speak Portuguese. The private hospitals are a bit more used to it and may even give you the option to have your consult in English. This is an important topic, and we can dedicate our entire lesson today to understanding what to do in case of an emergency, where to go, what to say, and go through a few helpful phrases. Keep in mind that for serious medical emergencies, you might still need help in English, and that's okay. Learning the local language is important, and it is good to practice in grocery stores, in restaurants, anywhere you can, but when you are being treated for a medical emergency in a hospital, you need to understand exactly what's going on; so don't feel bad if you don't respond in fluent Portuguese. As long as you can speak a bit, it will go a long way."

"To be honest," said Kate, "I've been to the emergency section at one of the private hospitals in Lisbon for a bad tooth, and I did everything in English, and no one said anything. In fact, the doctors and nurses were super helpful and friendly, and the quality of care was amazing. I mean, no comparison to the US. But like you said, Inês, that was my experience in the private sector, and language-shaming someone when they're in the middle of an emergency isn't cool."

Fatima nodded. "Abena, do you think—and I hesitate to bring this up—the color of your skin and the fact you're a black woman played on an unconscious bias when they heard you couldn't speak Portuguese? No offense, Kate, but when you go in as a white Caucasian woman with your blond hair and green eyes, it might be different for you. I only ask because with my brown skin and when they hear I'm from Pakistan, I think it happens to me too. For example, one nurse asked me at my recent gynecologist appointment, 'You're here alone? No husband?' It's more usual for Pakistani women to be accompanied by their husband. And you know the first thing the husbands say? 'I don't want a male doctor to examine my wife.' So I think sometimes it's an unconscious bias that's expressed out loud, or it's what you read between the lines."

"I think maybe you're right," said Abena, wrapping her aquamarine scarf a little tighter around her neck.

Kate wasn't impressed. "I can't believe that nurse said that to you, Fatima."

"Well, it's fascinating to hear all of your experiences with public and private health care systems in Portugal," said Inês. "As a Pakistani, American, and Ghanaian, each of you has lived in different countries, so of course your experiences and perceptions of life in Portugal will vary too. Try not to take it personally. If it makes you feel any better, most Portuguese complain about the Centro de Saúde. They're horrible to their fellow Portuguese over there too."

It was something that elicited some rueful smiles from across the table.

"Right, let's start our lesson: how to navigate hospitals and conduct doctor's visits in Portuguese," said Inês. "I'll show you what to say and expect for a regular doctor's appointment, and then we'll cover an emergency situation. These days, most of us make an appointment on the hospital apps, so let's start with what to say when you show up to your appointment."

Abena was feeling a little better. At least she was learning what to do next time, and with Inês's help, she was sure her experience with the health care system in Portugal would improve. She was determined to do right by Kakra and Panyin and for them to see their mom as a positive role model abroad.

# 13

# FATIMA
*Karachi, Pakistan*
September 1996

*F*atima came home from school in their white Suzuki, *pushing the hair out of her face and looking forward to a quiet afternoon doing her homework in her bedroom. She was always picked up by their driver, Muhammad, and she'd sit in the back of the car, silently watching the world whizz by. Very rarely, Ammi would come to pick her up, usually if she was out running errands or socializing with family. Once home from school, Fatima always followed the same set routine: she changed out of her blue and white uniform, washed up, and went into the kitchen to eat. That day, the cook had made* aloo ki tahiri *with yogurt and cucumber raita on the side. She looked around the kitchen. Sometimes Ammi would join her for lunch, but today it looked like Ammi had been entertaining. Whenever she had guests, Ammi would wheel out a trolley full of sweet and savory delicacies accompanied by chai. Judging by the leftovers, today there had been a platter of chicken tikka samosas, a tiered tray with egg and cucumber sandwiches, and a plate of dainty pastries and lemon tarts.*

*Ammi called out from the living room. "Fatima, are you hungry? Have your lunch first and then if you like you can have a lemon tart for dessert. By the way, do you know who was over today?"*

*"Let me guess," said Fatima, joining Ammi in the living room. "Shagufta aunty from next door."*

*"Yes, she was here, poking her nose into our business as usual."*

*"What do you mean, Ammi?"*

*"She heard the rumors, so she wanted to come and try to wheedle out information from me." Ammi looked up from the purple sari she was mending and gave Fatima a knowing look.*

*"So what did you say?"*

*"What could I say? I had to come up with a cover story—fast."*

*"So basically, you covered up one lie by telling another lie?"*

*"Fatima, people are asking more and more questions."*

*"Which is why we need to tell the truth about what happened. People will understand."*

*"No, Fatima! What we need to do is to come up with better, more convincing lies to silence them once and for all."*

*Fatima looked at her mother with unease. All these lies to hide the truth were making her feel worse than ever. As if she was to blame. As if she had something to hide.*

*Ammi saw the look she was giving her and put her sewing needle down. "Beta, you're still too young. It's my job to protect you. And look how badly I've done. You don't understand the ways of the world. Let me handle it."*

*"But people might understand."*

*"People will never understand! Especially not in this patriarchal society. Not in this conservative family. You need to trust me. I am doing this for you. Trust me, it is for the best."*

*Fatima sighed but then nodded. It was an awful burden to bear at eleven years old, but she was grateful that Ammi was taking care of things. Now she had no choice but to trust her.*

## Sintra, Portugal
## December 2022

Standing on the edge of a continent blew Fatima's mind. This was where Europe ended. It was as though she had run as far as she could but had reached the end of the world and couldn't run any further. There was an entire continent behind her, and in front of her and beyond that jagged shoreline, the vast expanse of the Atlantic Ocean beckoned tantalizingly. It was raw, ferocious, unapologetic, and otherworldly, and on this chilly December day, it was eerily quiet. The tourists would come up here in droves in the summer, but in winter few would venture out to battle the elements. Today it was just a couple of locals out with their dogs and her. The wind picked up from the north, lashing her hair with force, over and over, and she felt a powerful tension between the sea and the land. A battle for dominance. She was hit by a sudden rush of adrenalin. Cabo da Roca, the westernmost point of Europe, a place people once believed to be the edge of the world, was as frightening as it was amazing.

She had driven here after dropping Maya at school. It was the last day before the much-anticipated winter holidays, and they were flying out to Germany that night. She needed some alone time to clear her head, and this seemed to be the perfect place. Cabo da Roca was isolated: a lighthouse, a monument, a gift shop, a coffee shop, but not much else. She'd been meaning to come here for a while but hadn't had a chance. She stood high up on the cliff and noticed the dark clouds gathering above her. She felt a sudden and dark sense of foreboding. It didn't feel comfortable there. It was time to leave. She hurried her way back to the car, which was parked by a remote, untamed field, and looked back up at the sky. It was hard to explain, even to herself, but somehow this place had forced her to confront her fears head-on.

FOR ONCE, PORTUGUESE bureaucracy had let Fatima down by being incredibly efficient. Her mother's paperwork had been processed; Ammi's sponsorship visa was ready. Back home after her clifftop walk, Fatima called Ammi to tell her the good news.

She picked up on the first ring as usual. "*Haan*, hello?"

"*Salam*, Ammi. I have good news to share."

"What is it, Fatima? Are you … you're not … it can't be …?"

Fatima laughed at her mother's typical *desi* reaction to the mention of good news. "No, Ammi, I'm not pregnant. Your sponsorship paperwork has been accepted and your visa is ready. You can come to Portugal now for up to six months to visit and stay with us."

"Such welcome news. Allah has answered my prayers."

"We're looking forward to seeing you. I'll send you the details soon and email you the confirmation letter."

"Thank you, *beta*. I had better start planning my trip."

"I can help you once we're back from Germany."

"Thank you, beta. Okay, you go and finish your packing."

"I'll message you once we're in Berlin."

"Okay. Bye, Fatima."

"Bye, Ammi."

Fatima hung up and looked at the half-packed suitcases with a giddy sense of excitement. Germany would be a fun family time. Maya was excited about visiting the Christmas markets in Berlin she'd heard so much about.

Fatima was fishing out her suede boots, which she'd bought in Copenhagen and would be perfect for the German trip, when her phone rang again.

"Ammi?"

"Sorry, beta, I forgot to ask you one more thing: what is Maya's current size? I thought I could get some nice Pakistani clothes stitched for her and bring them with me, but I need her shoulder, chest, and waist measurements to give to our tailor."

"Thats a nice idea. I'm sure Maya will be happy. I'll take her measurements and send them to you."

"Okay, thank you, beta. Sorry for disturbing you."

"Bye, Ammi."

Fatima smiled in spite of herself. Her mother had impeccable taste and would no doubt pick out some beautiful clothes for her granddaughter. Perhaps she could even wear them for her school's International Day celebrations that were coming up at the end of the school year. She rummaged through her closet and found the suede boots. Her phone rang again.

"Ammi, what did you forget now?"

Silence.

"Ammi? Ammi, can you hear me?" She looked at her phone to check the caller's number, but there was no caller ID. She heard a breath at the other end, a deep, faint breath, then another, and then nothing. Her stomach churned. Suddenly flustered, she hung up.

Stefan walked into the bedroom and found her standing in the middle of the room. "Hey, what's the matter? You look like you've seen a ghost."

"It's nothing." She forced a smile. "Just a wrong number. And look, here are those boots I was looking for."

Later that evening the three of them took a cab to the airport, and as Fatima stared into the darkness, she was no longer sure what the new year would bring.

# PART TWO

"You can change your location,
Meet new people,
And still have the same old problems.

To truly change your life,
You need to look inward,
Get to know and love yourself,
And heal the trauma and dense conditioning in your mind.

This is how you get to the root.
Internal changes
Have a significant external impact."
—Yung Pueblo, *Clarity and Connection*

# 14

## FATIMA
*Cascais, Portugal*
January 2023

The pungent smell of soft, yellow turmeric infused with the earthy blend of garam masala was both disorientating and comforting. Fatima had just got home after the school drop-off and morning grocery run. She went into the kitchen and saw the fragrant cardamom ready to be crushed. But the mashing didn't crush the seeds; it only cracked the husks. Cardamom was strong. It endured. Then they were expertly sautéed in vegetable oil along with a fierce blast of fresh ginger and garlic, and she could hear the smoky mustard seeds crackling alongside the sweet cinnamon sticks, the rip of the fragrant bay leaves, and then everything was stirred in the pan with the spicy red chilies.

It smelled like home.

The woman standing at the stove orchestrating this feast wore a long blue kameez and a baggy shalwar at the bottom. No rings, no watch, no bracelets, but there was an air of sophistication in her stirring of the pot, the smooth, precise movements. Her short black hair, dyed every month, was pulled back into a neat ponytail, and her face belied her age. She picked up the pestle and ground some fresh coriander against the stone. The scent that wafted up matched Fatima's mood—spicy and aggressive.

"Ammi, why are you cooking so early in the morning? It's nine a.m." Fatima took out the bread and eggs from her shopping bag, but there was no place to put them. She surveyed the state of her kitchen. On her usually immaculate countertop there were three chopping boards, one with boneless chicken, one with chopped herbs, and one with freshly washed okra that was sitting in a strainer over a bowl. Jars of spices, most with their caps open, were strewn haphazardly, and little teaspoons were littered in between. Fatima's favorite blue and white Royal Copenhagen porcelain bowl, from their time in Denmark, was stained with turmeric mixed with milk—*holy crap, will that stain ever come out?*—and it took all her resolve not to clear the whole lot up there and then.

"It's never too early to be in the kitchen, *beta*. What a nice kitchen you have here. I love the big windows overlooking your front garden and street. But I have to say, it's not very easy to find things in your kitchen, Fatima." Ammi wiped her hands on a tea towel and turned around to face her daughter, hands on hips, ready for a fight.

"What do you mean?" asked Fatima, feeling thirsty and reaching for a glass. "Where have all the glasses from this cupboard gone?"

"Don't you think the glasses and cups should be in the cupboard near the fridge so you can easily get a glass of water?"

"No, Ammi, the glasses should be in *this* cupboard near the sink because here, in Portugal, we drink the tap water. In fact, that's what I fill up the bottles with and put inside the fridge so we have some cold water." She was trying not to sound annoyed, hoping she'd be able to stave off another confrontation, but that wasn't looking likely.

"*Arey, beta*, while you were dropping Maya at school, I already switched things around—to make it easier for you to access things in your kitchen. It might take you some time to get used to, but I am sure you will agree it is better organized this way." She went back to standing at the stove and lowered the heat, not waiting for or expecting a response.

Fatima started to say something but stopped herself. Ammi heard the split-second hesitation and walked up to her and put her arm around her daughter.

"I took care of it. Like I always do. And tomorrow I will organize your spice drawer too. No wonder you don't cook Pakistani food very often. But do not worry, I am here to cook for you right now."

And there was the problem. Fatima always gave in, always deferred to her mother's iron will, because there was no point in arguing with her, with the kind of woman who had the audacity to change the setup in her daughter's kitchen without asking. Ammi had always been this way: arrogant and conceited to think her way was the only way. Which was why Fatima had always ensured her mother's visits to Dubai had been short. Four days, five maximum, measured, controlled, and with a clear end date. But that had been easier to manage with Dubai only a two-hour flight from Karachi. Now here they were after all this time, together in Portugal for an extended period of time. There were no end dates, just an open-ended ticket and a countless number of weeks stretching ahead. Why, she asked herself, had she agreed to this?

She could feel herself growing more agitated by the minute. She was biting her nails. Her mother's presence was already bringing out the worst in her. And she still hadn't gotten over that phone call, not that she dare mention anything about it to her mother, but it was hard to shake off the paranoia. Some days she even questioned herself: did it really happen, or had she imagined it all in her head? No, it happened. And now she was obsessing, checking her phone for missed calls or any other unusual messages. None so far. It was probably a weird one-off incident that meant nothing, but that feeling in the pit of her stomach refused to go away.

## *Cascais, Portugal*
## January 2023

If ever she needed a breath of fresh air to clear her head, it was now. She had to get out of the house—quickly. Before it was too late, before she said something she wouldn't be able to take back and would regret afterwards.

Today's Portuguese lesson gave her the perfect excuse to step out alone. She was scheduled to meet Inês, Kate, and Abena at a newly opened café—indoors again since January weather in Cascais was rarely at its best. She was the first to arrive and ordered a flat white, her barometer of how good the coffee was in any café.

She sipped the frothy milk with its latte art, and it instantly soothed her nerves.

"Hey Fatima, you're early," said Inês, followed in by Kate and Abena a few steps behind.

"I know. Got here early for a change." Fatima smiled and got up to hug her friends.

"So, how's it going?" Kate asked Fatima once the exchanges of "happy new year" and coffee orders were out of the way. "Is your mom finally here?"

"Yeah, she is. It's going okay," said Fatima, sounding distinctly neutral.

"Lucky you. Family visits are always fun when you're abroad," said Kate.

"Oh God, Ben's aunties and cousins in the UK have already hinted they want to come visit us," said Abena. Her look of horror made her feelings on the topic perfectly clear.

"Are your parents enjoying Portugal, Fatima?" asked Inês. "Is it their first time here?"

"Yeah. It's my mom who's visiting. Dad died when I was six. Sudden heart attack. So I was raised mostly by my mom and her brother, my uncle." She cleared her throat. "But yeah, my mom's really enjoying Portugal so far and wants to see different parts of the country. Good thing she's here for an extended visit, so plenty of time to show her around."

"Lovely," said Inês. "Sounds like you and your mom are close. As you might have observed, Portuguese society is also very family-oriented. Many people live in the same area as their parents. And it is very common for grandparents to help rear the grandchildren by watching them a few times a week or picking them up from school."

"The thing that surprised me the most when we moved here," said Kate, "even more than the stunning Atlantic coast and the tile patterns on buildings, was Portugal's deference to parents and families. It's so unlike the US. I mean, you only have to look at Lisbon's airport and see people being ushered into the fast-track family queue to know how much emphasis they place on kids and families."

"So true," said Abena. "One of the things I struggled with in the UK, especially as a new mom, was how kids are meant to be seen but not heard—the opposite of Ghana. But I think Portugal's more relaxed. I know it's helped me to relax here as a parent."

"Well," said Inês, "that's a perfect topic for today's lesson: families. Let's dive straight in. One of the most important Portuguese traditions is *Domingos em Família*: Sundays with the Family. Usually on Sundays everyone gets together at their grandparents' house or with whoever decides to host the Sunday family lunch. On the table you'll find a whole lot of traditional Portuguese dishes, from the famous roasted meat dish, *assado*, to *bacalhau*—cod—followed by dessert. In Portugal, it doesn't matter if you have the means or not, the tables are always as full as possible. It's how the Portuguese recharge their batteries before heading into a new week at work. Sunday is the most important day of the week for the Portuguese and their family."

Inês's impassioned talk about the importance of family in Portugal left Fatima feeling uncomfortable. From a young age she had learned *not* to express her feelings or emotions. Especially not an emotion as ugly as guilt. Guilt wasn't a rational thing. It would crush you whether you deserved it or not. For Fatima, guilt was like an unwelcome guest in her life;

there was no way to move with it or to leave it behind. She wasn't sure Inês, Kate, or Abena would understand the complicated feelings her mother's arrival had provoked in her. No one ever did. They would only look at her as ungrateful. So, as she always did, Fatima took refuge in keeping her thoughts to herself. Maybe she'd have a stroll through town after the lesson. Anything to avoid going home to *her*.

# 15

# KATE
*Singapore*
January 2020

*E*ven the air-conditioning in the MRT couldn't stop Kate *from sweating on that sweltering afternoon. Singaporeans would tell you their country officially had two seasons: hot and wet and hot and dry. As far as Kate was concerned there was only one season—very hot and very humid. Every morning, the international weather report on the BBC showed Singapore's weather forecast as 29 or 30 degrees Celsius, with a chance of rain. Life on the equator was monotonous, and Kate was pretty sure that being a weather forecaster in Singapore must have been the most boring job in the world.*

*Normally she would escape the worst of the sticky afternoon heat, but today she'd decided to take the afternoon off from work and go home early because she wasn't feeling well—turns out blackmail can make you physically sick. The fact that she had to share her home with her blackmailer was a particular twist of irony that not even she could have predicted. But as Michael kept reminding her, it was "just a little bit of blackmail."*

*Just a little bit of blackmail that threatened to turn their lives upside down. Just a little bit of blackmail that could get Kate fired from her job at the embassy. Just a little bit of blackmail that could probably get them both deported from 'the red dot,' as locals affectionately called Singapore because of how it appeared on a world map.*

*She walked home from the MRT station, noticing some green butterflies drawn on the pavement on Mount Sinai Road, passed a row of small townhouses and turned right into the site of the tightly packed white apartment blocks. Her favorite Indian security guard was there to greet her when she walked in through the pedestrian entrance. She waved back, weaved her way past the Olympic-sized swimming pools and a smaller splash pool for the kids, all empty in the afternoon heat, past the flower beds of white spider lilies, past the small gym, and into the entrance of her block, where she called the elevator. A quick check of her reflection in the elevator as it rose to the twelfth floor confirmed that she looked as haggard as she felt.*

*When she stepped into the gleaming white kitchen of their brand-new condo, there she was, Maryanne, mopping the kitchen floor energetically. Kate took a good look at her. Long black hair, straight as silk, tied in a knot above her head. Her lanky frame made her look more like a teenager than a forty-year-old mother of two, and her usual uniform of a white shirt and black shorts helped with the youthful look. One of the buttons on her shirt was missing.*

*Maryanne stopped mopping and turned around. "Ma'am Kate. You back home so early, lah?"*

"Yes, I'm not feeling too well," said Kate, tiptoeing across the wet kitchen floor. She reached for a Panadol from the medicine cabinet, wondering when did you tell your blackmailer that it was actually their blackmail that was making you feel physically sick?

"Sorry Ma'am. My daughter Tala also very sick Ma'am. Today I talk to her, but she cannot talk much, lah."

"What did the test reports say?"

"We don't know Ma'am. My husband too afraid going back to hospitals. Hospitals in Manila no good anyway. But I think cancer is back."

"I'm sorry." Kate couldn't imagine what she would do if Eric had cancer. Probably drop everything to get him the best treatment in the world. But would she be desperate enough to blackmail her employer?

"Ma'am Kate, please help us, lah. Tala only nine years old. I send money from here, but I don't know what else to do …"

"Look, Maryanne, as Michael and I have both told you, we're willing to give you a bit extra to pay for hospital bills and expenses for your daughter's treatment. But we cannot do more than that. Our hands are also tied. The sum you are asking for is simply not possible."

"Please Ma'am. Please help me. I don't know who else to turn to."

"It would be easier to help you if you weren't threatening to expose us to the authorities here."

"Ma'am. I'm sorry. I don't know what else to do. How else to raise the funds I need to pay for her private treatment and tests. I work so hard, looking after your son, in order to give my own children a future."

*"Well if you share what you've learned about us, then I definitely won't be in a position to help you. So please think carefully about your actions and the impact it will have on all of us."*

*"I'm sorry … I found the newspaper clippings in that old box when I was cleaning. I was not sure. Then Michael told me the rest. He has been telling me a lot of things. I didn't want to cause trouble, but I have nowhere else to go. You are my last option Ma'am."*

*"It's a little too late for that, Maryanne." Kate crossed her arms around her chest. She wasn't going to succumb to this pity party for Maryanne. A woman who accused Michael of cheating on Kate. A woman who had learned the awful truth and decided to use it against Kate for her own purposes. A woman whose child was severely sick and suffering. A woman who made the best homemade dim sum. A woman who her own son was so attached to.*

*Kate's heart and mind were in turmoil. It was just a little bit of blackmail, but it could destroy everything she had worked so hard to build her whole life. It was simply too high a price to pay. She gulped down the Panadol with a slug of water and went to lie down.*

## Lisbon, Portugal
### January 2023

Kate breathed a sigh of relief as she stepped into her happy place. It was odd to call your therapist's office your 'happy place,' but sitting in Dr. Teixeira's pristine white office was the only place where she felt relatively relaxed and able to let her guard down. She was committed to doing the work and figuring this out, and she squeezed Michael's hand as they walked in for another session.

"So, how have you both been? How were the holidays?" asked Melissa Teixeira, wearing another signature white outfit, this time complete with white leather boots that came up to her knees. The temperature in Lisbon dipped in winter, enough for the locals to bring out their winter coats and boots. But after craving a more temperate climate during the three years they were in Singapore, Kate described Lisbon's weather in winter as 'pleasant.' She remembered being in a Zara store at Ion Orchard Mall in Singapore trying on an oversized knit sweater in the air-conditioning and dreaming of the day when the weather necessitated wearing one.

"Thank you, Melissa. We've both been good." Kate turned to look at Michael as if to confirm they were indeed in a much happier place.

"We went to Spain over Christmas," said Michael, "and spent the holidays in Barcelona. Some much-needed family time. Eric loved it too."

"I'm glad to hear it. I'm also happy you were both able to complete your homework and send it to me ahead of today's session. I've had a chance to go over each of your responses, and you have both raised some good points. One thing both of you mentioned in your responses is the need for good communication. How is communication at the moment? On a scale of one to ten, how would you assess it?"

"I think I'd give it a five," said Michael.

"I'd give it a two."

There was an awkward pause.

"Why a two, Kate?" asked Melissa.

"Well, it seems we don't share openly with each other anymore. There's always this fear of how things will be perceived. And sometimes staying silent seems like the best option."

"Can you give us an example?"

Michael looked hard at Kate.

"Okay, for example, the other day, I received an email from Patricia, an old friend of mine in Singapore; not really a friend, more of an acquaintance. Her kids used to attend the same school as Eric, so I knew her through school. Anyway, by coincidence, she and her family are in the process of moving to Portugal. Out of the blue, she sent me an email asking if my old helper Maryanne was available as there was a family she knew back in Singapore who were looking to hire some help. She remembered that I always spoke highly of Maryanne. I mean, did I have a choice back then? I definitely didn't want to recommend her to anyone else, but I was at a loss as to what to say to Patricia, so I hinted that Maryanne had already found work and was unavailable. Of course, just my luck, right before moving here Patricia ran into Maryanne at Lucky Plaza and asked her outright if she was available for work. Maryanne said yes, she was in desperate need of a job, and now Patricia knows that I lied to her. But I haven't told Michael any of this because I hate to dredge up the past. It feels like we can never move on. Every mention of Maryanne drags us back to that awful place of mistrust. And yet, not sharing what's been on my mind is also not good because then there's this distance between us. I'm sorry, Michael. I probably should've told you this earlier."

"It's okay," he said. "The important thing is you're telling me now. I also have something to share. I'm sorry I haven't said anything until now, but the truth is, I received another email from Maryanne yesterday. She keeps contacting me. I didn't want to bring it up again and drag us back to that awful place, as you put it, that we are desperately trying to crawl out from." He took Kate's hand in his.

"Thanks, honey," said Kate. "I don't know how to deal with this. Why does she keep contacting us? What does she want from us? We're not even in Singapore anymore."

"If I may." Melissa took off her glasses and looked at both of them. "I think admitting that you both want better communication from each other is a good step. But trying to avoid the topic of Maryanne whenever it comes up is adding too much unnecessary stress. How about, instead, we come up with a way for you to share your feelings and thoughts openly with each other? To talk each other through it. If you do that regularly instead of shutting off, then perhaps you'll find a healthier way forward."

Kate and Michael nodded in agreement.

"Okay. Let's get started. But there are some ground rules I'd like you to follow …"

KATE WAS DEEP In thought as they walked out of therapy together. There was a cool breeze. She looked across the river at the red-tiled roofs of Lisbon in the bright winter sun, then turned to look at Michael. "Are we bad people for not having helped her more?" she said. "Sometimes I feel so goddamn guilty."

"I think we did enough. And you know better than me that the risk was too big, and the consequences could've been dire. I don't know how long we could've sustained the charade. In the end we had to protect ourselves and our family."

"I guess you're right. And I do think the only way to move past this is to start being honest with each other again. I know it won't be easy, but it's worth a shot, right?"

"I want to make this work, Kate. I want us to be us again."

She looked at Michael, into the dark hazel eyes she fell for all those years back in Georgetown, and she knew that somewhere deep down in the bottom of her anxious, constantly guarded soul, they both wanted the same thing.

She was on the verge of giving him a smile when her phone beeped, and Kate the workaholic couldn't stop herself from checking her emails. "You've got to be kidding me," she mumbled. "What impeccable timing."

"What is it?" asked Michael.

"It's Patricia. Wanting to meet up. Wanting to know all about Lisbon, to have all the settling-in advice, to know why the hell we left Singapore all of a sudden."

"Did she actually say that?"

"Of course she didn't," Kate snapped.

Michael jerked back, surprised by her sudden outburst.

"But come on," she continued, "I'm not an idiot. Can you believe it? We actually manage to extract ourselves from a major pickle and leave it all behind, and then hardly a few months later, this happens. Aren't there like 210 plus damn countries in the world? Why did her damn husband have to get transferred to Portugal of all places?"

She took a deep breath, trying to get her raging heartbeat

under control; even she had been startled by her strong reaction. She looked back at Michael, but whatever brief moment there had been between them had evaporated.

Michael turned around and walked slowly back to the car.

Was he angry at her? At the situation? At himself for having brought this upon them in the first place? But had he, really? Or was she the cause of all of this? She didn't know anymore. But she knew one thing: no matter how she felt about Michael, no matter how she felt about everything that had happened, she wouldn't be able to weather the gathering storm on her own. The stakes were simply too high, and if anyone else found out about her secret, she would lose everything—her career, her reputation, her family, and even her freedom.

# 16

## ABENA

*Brighton, UK*
September 2012

*A*bena Nyator *was not pregnant. The single pink line confirmed her fate. Maybe she shouldn't have gotten her hopes up that their third IVF would work. But she had; she'd pinned all her hopes on it, one last time. She'd forced herself to remain positive during the two-week implantation period, not letting any negative thoughts get in the way. She'd even taken a much-needed holiday from work in order to rest her overactive mind and been to an acupuncturist as a boost to her fertility treatment.*

*Of course, like before, she hadn't told a soul. Nor had Ben. Neither could bear the thought of it not working out. The disappointment. They'd known it was their last chance, and since their families had known nothing about their first try, or the second, it would have made no sense to tell them about the third and final try. So here they were, three strikes and out, with nobody to share their pain.*

*She sat at home at her white wooden desk and logged on to her computer. Her stomach was cramping again. She hated the bloating feeling that engulfed her, the nagging pain in the small of her back, and those horrible cramps, a constant reminder of her failure. She looked out of the window, only to see the dark storm clouds gather. Brighton was Bohemian, hedonistic, quirky. But on that September morning it was a stranger, watching her heartbreak from a distance, coolly, its pastel-colored streets mocking her as if to say, why can't you be happy here?*

*Unable to concentrate on her emails, she got up from her desk, walked over to the large mirror in her bedroom, and stared at her reflection. She'd put on a lot of weight because of the fertility treatments. It had been a gradual shift, but the additional hormones and water retention made her feel like she had become a bloated version of herself lately, almost like a puffed-up whale. She felt like she barely recognized the person that was staring back at her—exhausted and defeated. How had this thing come to define her?*

*A beep from her phone snapped her out of her thoughts. It was a text message from her sister-in-law, Amoafoa, the one person she wasn't in the mood to hear from or talk to. Amoafoa had recently shared on the family WhatsApp group that she was four months pregnant with their first child, and Abena recalled the sinking feeling in her stomach when she'd read the message. She had burst into tears and sobbed for hours before typing a congratulatory message to her sister-in-law and brother-in-law. When had she become this sad person who couldn't even be happy for others or rejoice in their good fortune? She hated how selfish she had become. Infertility had turned her into a jealous, selfish, self-absorbed woman. It brought out all the worst parts of her. No, the worst part was that Amoafoa and her husband were coming to visit them in Brighton next month, and Abena knew it would look suspicious if they refused to host them, so she had resigned herself to feeling even more worthless in their presence.*

*She called the one person who could always cheer her up, her sister.*

*Akosua picked up on the first ring, even though it was probably still early in Accra. "Abena, my girl! I was just thinking of you as I contemplated stepping out to get some* waakye *for breakfast. Do you remember that place by the roadside in Dzorwulu we used to go to as kids? That uncle is still there."*

*Abena chuckled. "He must be at least a hundred by now." If she closed her eyes, she could almost taste the beans and rice and that boiled egg and salad on the side. Waakye had always been her favorite food, but since moving abroad, it had taken on a new status in her mind. The ultimate comfort food. And in that moment, heartbroken, hungry, and homesick, she wished she was back home.*

*But nothing was that simple. She had not confided in any of her family members about her battle with infertility. In Ghana, women who couldn't produce children were socially ostracized and still carried a certain stigma. In rural parts, some believed that a woman not able to bear a child was cursed or bewitched or had had abortions or led a questionable lifestyle. There was no way Abena wanted to be infertile in Ghana. Despite everything, it was better to be childless in the UK than in Ghana.*

*"Wait a sec, sis," she said to Akosua, "how come you're going by yourself to get waakye? Where's Daniel? You're practically full-term now and about to give birth any day. Shouldn't he be running around for you, looking after the kids, and fixing you breakfast?"*

*"Ay. That's a good question."*

*"You don't know where he is?"*

*"No. He … we fought again yesterday. He really doesn't want to become a father again. I thought he would come around by now. But things between us, they're not good."*

*Oh God. This was even worse than Abena had expected. But her mind was full, and in between her own heartbreak and her sister's pain, she could only think to say, "Akosua, leave it up to God."*

*She hung up.*

*There was a gorgeous rainbow forming over the front garden; the brightest rainbows were often found after the roughest storms. The rain had cleared and left behind an answer as clear as day. She knew exactly what she had to do, and she would have to do it in person. It couldn't wait. She had to get on the next flight to Accra.*

# Cascais, Portugal
## January 2023

Abena had so many chores to do, but she was tired. The new year had gotten off to an exhausting start. They had decided to remain in Portugal for the Christmas holidays, but there had been one work emergency after the other. Christmas was their busiest time of the month for business deliveries, and not all had gone to plan. There had been many complaints from customers about delays in order deliveries, and there was a huge backlog to work through. It was January, and she was still working on getting the Christmas orders delivered.

She thought better of catching up on her emails and instead clicked on the twins' school calendar to check when their next holidays were. And wait, what was this? Her kids' school would be celebrating International Day in May, a chance for them to share their different cultures, countries, foods, games, and traditions. She smiled. It would be the perfect way for her kids to share their Ghanaian heritage with their peers. It was still several months away, but that gave her ample time to prepare and ensure their stall would be the best.

Unable to contain her excitement, she gave Kate a call. "Guess what?"

"I hope you're calling with good news, Abena. I'm not having the best of days."

"Very good news. Mark your calendar. The school is celebrating International Day on May fifth. How cool is that?"

Kate laughed. "Okay, Abena. Please breathe. Deep, deep breaths. Eric celebrated many International Days in Singapore. It's a staple event in the calendar of most international schools."

"But this is so exciting! We've never celebrated International Day before. It wasn't a thing in the UK, especially not at the public school the girls were at. I can't wait to be in charge of the Ghana stall. In fact, I'm thinking I'll volunteer to organize the whole event—make different themes and games and ensure each country at the school is represented."

"I can tell you're excited, Abena. Good luck with getting involved with the event planning …"

"But please promise me, Kate, you *have* to be there. You can set up a great American stall."

"I'm sure the other Americans will rally up a table. I'll find out who's leading it and join in. On International Day in Singapore last year, we had snow cones at the American stall. You can imagine what a hit they were, with the humidity over there."

"Amazing. Now you've got me even more excited. I need to call Fatima and tell her too." By now, Abena was virtually clapping her hands in glee.

"Sure, go ahead. I need to get to my meeting. We can discuss this more at the next Portuguese lesson."

True to her word, Abena called Fatima next, but she didn't pick up. She was sure Fatima would be as excited as she was. She could set up a Pakistani stall. Imagine the food! Abena would be there simply for the food.

SHE WAS IN the middle of emailing the school's parents' association to offer her support for International Day when Fatima returned her call.

"Abena, sorry, I was driving earlier. What's up?"

"I've got such exciting news and couldn't wait to share it with you. Our kids will be celebrating International Day at school in May."

"I know, I saw it on the school calendar. That's … great?"

"Could you sound any less excited, Fatima?"

"Well, it's just that, do you ever feel like you're not the best representation of your own culture? I struggle with it sometimes. I'm pretty sure Maya's also tired of celebrating

International Day. Every year in Dubai it was the same story. We'd have endless arguments about what she wanted to dress up as. She hates choosing sides. Sometimes she doesn't feel very Pakistani, or German enough, and struggles to identify with one or the other. Last year we compromised and sent her to school wearing a T-shirt with a big globe on it that said 'I'm from here.' "

Abena laughed. "That's smart. I get why International Day could be complicated for some. I've never really thought about it. Back in Britain we never had a way of expressing our Ghanaian identity at school, so I suppose it's a novel concept for me. I've even signed up to volunteer to help run the whole event."

"You have?"

"Do you think you'll put up a Pakistani stall? Or a German one?"

"I'll talk to Stefan and Maya and see. Maybe we can do both."

"That would be brilliant. Keep me posted, okay?"

"Sure. Bye, Abena."

What a strange world, Abena thought to herself. Some people took solace from their identity but it made others feel incredibly uncomfortable. Some people proudly wore the map of their journey but others simply didn't care.

She was hoping the girls would always be proud of who they were. She had even chosen their names in line with a Ghanaian tradition for naming twins in the Akan language: Panyin (the older) and Kakra (the younger). But was she a hypocrite? She hadn't been truthful with the twins, had she? All because of her shame and overbearing guilt. Should she have been honest with them? Was it too late? Of course, the twins didn't suspect a thing. The family in the UK had been sworn to secrecy, and the family in Ghana had been cut off. Now the only person who could break the silence was Abena herself. Or Ben. And maybe this was the real reason she was so excited about International Day. It was a chance to share their story without admitting the naked truth.

# 17

# KATE
*Sugar Land, Texas*
October 2000

*K*ate had forgotten how boundless the sky seemed in Texas, stretching endlessly over the horizon and enveloping all it could in its embrace. So why couldn't the people here breathe this incredible limitlessness into their soul? Why couldn't they think outside the box and question the predictability of their lives?

She was back in Houston visiting her family for the fall break, and her life in Massachusetts seemed a world away. Texas seemed to get even hotter when the sun went down, but aside from the hell-fire weather, she hated the giant billboards, the clogged freeways full of reckless drivers, the cookie-cutter gated communities, and the faceless suburbs with the same-sounding names. The Texas flag was flying everywhere, towering menacingly over the state. They even mowed the Lone Star onto their lawns for Chrissakes. She hated the giant pickup trucks that everybody drove, oblivious to the soaring gas prices or the slap in the face to more sustainable and eco-friendly energy sources. She hated how a three-car garage in *a suburban house was the norm or the fact that the garages were so full of "stuff" that you couldn't park inside. There was so much stuff. Everywhere. She hated the drive-through culture, the drive-through banks, the drive-through Starbucks, the drive-through pharmacies. As if walking would kill them. But then again, it wasn't a walkable place because you couldn't do anything or get anywhere without a car. Texas was a state-sized lamb chop of misery and Kate had been so thrilled to escape. Now she was back, she remembered all the reasons why she left as soon as she could. Only two things lured her back here—Tex-Mex salsa and family. While the former had not disappointed, the less said about the latter, the better.*

*She came down the stairs from her childhood bedroom into the family living room. She could smell the smoky flavor of the classic Texas BBQ: beef brisket, sausage, and ribs.*

*"What if you have a vegetarian coming over, Mom?" said Kate, wrinkling her nose.*

*"I'll serve them a vegetable plate of a potato salad with raw white onions and pickles." Kate's mother, Alice, was a young 50, her striking gray hair adding a streak of sophistication to the dowdy apron around her neck.*

*"That's not exactly what most people would call a healthy vegetable plate, Mom."*

*"Well it's how we do it in Texas—none of this vegetarian or vegan nonsense like you East Coasters."*

*She went back to prepping the potato salad on the kitchen island and Kate went out to the backyard.*

*Their home in Sugar Land hadn't changed much over the years. Like most of Texas, Sugar Land had been influenced by the Native Americans, the Spanish, the Mexican government, the Mexican immigrants, and the American pioneers. With its rich agriculture and fertile lands, Sugar Land had soon discovered the power of sugarcane production, something that had led to a surge in the town's growth and to its well-maintained homes, parks, and medical facilities. Kate's family took great pride in belonging to the pioneering community in their corner of the US.*

*"Well, there's my gal!" her dad exclaimed, expertly flipping the gigantic steaks on the BBQ. He had aged too, with those gray corners in his hair, and was in his standard casual uniform: checkered blue and white shirt, denim shorts, and a Houston Astros baseball cap. Kate had been used to seeing him in scrubs after working long shifts at the Houston Memorial Hospital downtown, but she'd always preferred his weekend outfit. It made him look more relaxed.*

*"Hi, Dad. Smellin' good out here." She raised the lid of the BBQ to check on the meat. If there was one smell that captured her childhood, it was this: the burnt smell of well-cooked meat on the grill.*

*"Thanks, missy. So, how's it feel to be back? We've invited Ronnie and Janet over from next door. They keep asking about you."*

*"Oh, that's nice."*

*"A lot of us are worried about how you're getting on up there, honey. Do you have a college major picked out yet? I keep thinking if you'd gone to Baylor or UT Austin, I'd have been able to put in a good word for you with the professors."*

*"Dad, I don't need you to put in a good word for me at college. Besides, I'm pleased to tell you I've finally decided. I'm gonna major in International Relations at Mount Holyoke."*

*"And what will you do with a degree in THAT?"*

*"There are other fields, Dad, you know, besides medicine.*

*I don't know … I could join a research think tank, I could become a journalist, I could enlist in the Foreign Service. The options are endless. I'm still in 'merica, you know. There's a whole world beyond Texas."*

*"Wrong, honey. Texas is all the world we need."*

*Kate knew her dad well enough to know this meant the subject was closed. Nothing was resolved, but he had made it clear that as far as he was concerned, she was wasting her life away by moving to Massachusetts, choosing the wrong major, and jeopardizing her career prospects.*

*She spotted the ice box near the patio door and went over to grab a chilled can of Coke. She could hear Ronnie and Janet talking to her mom in the kitchen and hid around the corner with her back to the wall to listen in.*

*"Well, Alice, they printed an article in the Houston Chronicle today, and I thought maybe ya'll hadn't seen it."*

*Kate edged closer so she could peek into the kitchen.*

*Ronnie hesitated then handed over the newspaper to her mother, folded onto a specific page.*

*Her mom froze, then let out a muffled sob. "Sorry, excuse my tears," she said. "This is a tiny sliver of good news in this awful tragedy. It's the right thing to do and it's a good way to honor her memory." She folded up the newspaper and put it on the kitchen island.*

*Janet took her mom's hand. "Of course, Alice, we didn't mean to upset ya'll. We remember Kate's inconsolable grief this past summer. Hopefully, this will bring her some closure."*

*"Thank you, Janet. I hope so too." She picked up the potato salad. "C'mon now, let's go outside and dig in."*

*Kate went around the house, waited till they were all safely outside in the backyard, and snuck into the kitchen. Her fingers were shaking as she reached for the article and smoothed out the creases to read the headline. But her heart was pounding so fast that the words began to swim around in her head. She slammed her eyes shut, took a deep breath, and counted to ten in her mind, as her therapist had taught her. Another panic attack.*

*When she opened her eyes, the room was still.*

*She should have just read it and then put it back. Instead, she ripped the article out of the newspaper, folded it up carefully, and put it in the pocket of her shorts.*

## Cascais, Portugal
### February 2023

If she had to suffer Patricia's company and keep up her defenses, then at least she would sit through the torture in a café she liked. The nightmare had become a reality. Patricia was living in Cascais, her kids were settled in a new school, they'd found a place to live, and Patricia had messaged Kate to suggest a coffee date over the weekend. To catch up "like old times."

Lusophonica was Kate's favorite Cascais café. You had to know where it was or you'd miss it completely, nestled as it was in a hidden little lane close to one of Cascais's most photographed attractions, the blue and white Santa Marta lighthouse. The tiny café doubled as a radio station and served the best flat white in town. The seating was mostly under the massive white umbrellas outside, which fluttered in the wind that came in from Cascais Marina and sometimes blew over if the wind was strong enough. The subtle reminders of Portugal's colonial past were all around; here was a platform to connect the Portuguese diaspora through music, culture, and food.

She'd ordered the usual, a flat white and avocado toast, and had closed her eyes, inhaling the salty sea breeze, when Patricia spotted her outside the café.

"Falling asleep already?" said Patricia, pulling out a chair. "Shall we get you some more coffee?"

"Haha. Well you *are* a bit late. Or perhaps still running on Asian time?" Kate wasn't about to let Patricia get her down.

"You know, old habits die hard. Can I get you some more coffee?"

"Nah, I'm good. You go ahead."

Patricia went in to place her order. Much to Kate's amusement, her friend had already adopted the Portuguese convention of dressing for the season, not the weather. In February, regardless of the actual weather, the standard Portuguese uniform for women included a tailor-fitted blazer, a pair of chunky wedges, and a lightweight scarf. Patricia was sporting all three, Kate none of them. Some people could interpret and then match the vibe of a new city so well, so quickly, so seamlessly. As for Kate, weekends always meant unapologetic athletic wear, a much-needed break from the formal attire of work.

"So, how has the new year started for you?" Patricia was back and nursing a rose-pink cappuccino cup.

"It's been good. Hectic at work, you know, but the usual. I've had a few business trips here and there, so looking forward to the spring break next month when I can take some time off and spend a bit more time with Eric. How about you? Settlin' in okay?"

"Honestly? It's been a harder transition than I expected. I guess I hit the ground running when we moved from Wisconsin to Singapore—everything was in English, and the systems were so efficient. But this time around, not knowing Portuguese has really slowed me down. And the bureaucracy. It's so slow. Feels like I'm still finding my bearings, you know?"

"Sure, I get it. You need a ton of patience for the bureaucracy here. Remember to be kind to yourself in this transition," said Kate, wagging a finger at her.

"How's your Portuguese?" asked Patricia. "Did you take language lessons?"

"Yes. In fact, I'm still taking lessons with a tutor and a couple of friends."

"Oh, speaking of friends, Kate, I wanted to ask you … remember your old helper in Singapore, Maryanne? Seems she pulled quite the runner on the new family she was hired to work for—after asking for an advance of 10,000 Sing Dollars. Have you heard?"

"No. But can't say I'm surprised. I'm not sure I'd recommend Maryanne to be honest."

"Oh? You were always so full of praise for her."

"Yeah, well, that was before she … you know what, never mind."

"Did she break your trust in some way? Or steal from you?"

"No, it was nothing like that. She proved to be a bit nosy while she was cleaning. She found some old newspaper clippings and articles about my family that I keep in a box and read them all. I was furious when I found out."

"Oh my. I see. Sounds like quite a breach of privacy."

"It left a sour taste in my mouth. I wish her well, but yes, I guess it did cost her my trust."

"Totally understand. Say no more. I'm glad I asked. I thought she'd acted out of character, but obviously not."

Kate was relieved that conversation was out of the way. She leaned back in her chair, only now noticing she'd been sitting on the edge of her seat the entire time. Being halfway honest seemed to have done the trick. Patricia, who was naturally predisposed to thinking ill of a helper anyway, had bought her story without needing too many explicit details.

Kate had often been angry with herself for saving that newspaper clipping from the *Houston Chronicle* all those years ago, for holding on to it after all this time and all these moves. What good had come of it? It had only brought harm to Kate and her family. Her secret had been unearthed by an unsuspecting maid hired to help around the house, who'd read the newspaper clippings Kate had saved and had started asking questions. Michael had been too trusting, too drunk, and too ready to blame Kate, and confiding in Maryanne and sharing all the incriminating details had been a massive lapse of judgment. Details that Maryanne had used to blackmail Kate to fund her daughters' cancer treatment. Maryanne believed in divine intervention, but she also made Kate fear for her life, her job, her career in the Foreign Service, and her freedom. Maryanne had made Kate leave Singapore in a rush, with little to no explanations or goodbyes.

Because the guilty can't say goodbye.

# 18

## FATIMA
*Dubai, United Arab Emirates*
November 2021

*F*atima hurried her steps. She was eager to get to the
Arabian Tea House and sit in her happy place to shake
off the stress of the past few days. Parking in the historical
neighborhood of Al Bastakiya had always been a problem, so
she'd taken the Dubai metro to Al Fahidi station and walked
the rest. The Bastakiya Quarter was steeped in history. It was
Fatima's favorite part of Dubai and a welcome break from
the glitz of glass, concrete, and steel that dominated Dubai's
new skyline. Here on the dusty old streets, she could sense the
past, feel it: the narrow, winding lanes, the sand-colored
buildings fashioned from coral, mud, gypsum, and palm
wood, the old Al Fahidi fort, the beautiful Persian mosque,
the wind towers—air conditioners of the past—fitted on the
old houses. For Fatima, the way to truly understand a city
was to walk where immigrants before you had once walked,
to see what they had left behind, to merge your story with
theirs, connected through time and place.

*Here it was. Outside there was a little wooden area with red floor cushions around a teapot to replicate the Arab majlis style of sitting on the floor to drink tea and coffee, while inside, in the middle of a beautiful old courtyard past an old well, were white tables and white linens. The Arabian Tea House was the perfect place to sample a vast array of Arabian teas and coffees and the wonders of authentic Emirati cuisine.*

*She sat down at a small table in the courtyard and without thinking ordered her usual: a piping hot cup of traditional Arabic coffee, a slice of* regag *bread drizzled with honey and stuffed with egg and cheese, and* khabees, *a sweet blend of sautéed flour and molasses. She'd also asked for a glass of fresh mint lemonade. Even though it was November and the temperature had cooled considerably, the midday sun was strong, and she was thirsty after her walk from the metro station.*

*She had come here to do two things. The first was to recover from Ammi's visit this past weekend. The short three- or four-day visits were just about manageable: enough time to see her mother and keep up the pretense of their relationship, but short enough to avoid major conflict.*

*The second was to reflect on something that had been weighing heavily on her mind. Stefan had been offered a new job on promotion within the Danish company he worked for. But it was to be based in Lisbon, so another international move. Were they ready to leave Dubai after five years of living in the Arabian Desert? They had discussed the pros and cons, and as far as Portugal was concerned, there were very few cons. They had visited Lisbon before when they lived in Copenhagen and had been charmed by the steep cobblestone roads, temperate climate, gorgeous beaches—and the custard tarts.*

*But their primary concern was Maya. How would she handle the move, the transition? It was less of an issue moving to a new country when a child was young, but Maya was now ten years old. She was in that awkward pre-teen phase when friends matter more than family, and leaving your friends behind because of your family, well, it was something that required careful research, intention, and planning. Not impossible to do of course, but a lot depended on the child's personality and how they viewed the move: as an adventure or as a burden that would ruin the status quo. Maya had moved before, from Copenhagen to Dubai when she was five, but back then she had viewed it as one big, exciting adventure. One day Maya had walked up to an Arab gentleman at the Mall of the Emirates and tried to lift up his long white robe as they waited in line behind him at a shop. Fatima had been mortified, but luckily, the Arab gentleman hadn't taken offense. He had recognized the curiosity of a child and laughed when Maya asked Fatima loudly, "But Mama, I don't get it. Why do the men here wear a white dress?"*

*They'd made some wonderful memories in Dubai. But Fatima hadn't been completely honest with Stefan about how the potential move to Portugal would suit her just fine. She'd been majorly reluctant to move to the UAE in the first place, given its proximity to Pakistan, and now she was equally keen to get as far away from Dubai as possible. For her own peace of mind.*

*Fatima knew she wasn't being rational. She knew the demons of her past were long buried. Ammi had made sure of that. And she knew the horrors of her childhood would never be able to catch up with her, regardless of her distance from Pakistan. But she couldn't help feeling the way she did. She didn't feel comfortable or safe. And a move to Portugal would take her far away from the one person who stood at the center of it all—her mother. She would never find peace unless she was far away from Ammi.*

*As for Maya, she would have to slowly start growing up, just as she had to grow up at that age. And what Fatima had to do at the age of ten and what Maya would have to do at the age of ten was not comparable.*

## Cascais, Portugal
## February 2023

It was the weekend. Fatima woke up with a jolt, her heart pounding in her chest. She sat up in bed and for a second didn't know where she was. How strange that she was living her dreams and nightmares at the same time. She had supposed that nightmares were a thing of the past, but now they were back with a vengeance, and it was always the same nightmare. There was only one reason for it, only one person to blame—her mother. She couldn't remember the last time she and Ammi had spent so much time together. A month already. *The longest month ever.*

She grabbed a light-pink sweater from her closet and came down the stairs, pausing to look out of the large lounge windows. It was a beautiful spring day in Cascais, and Maya and Stefan were already in the garden.

"You look horrible, *beta*. Did you not sleep? No husband wants to see his wife looking like that first thing in the morning." Ammi was sitting in the kitchen on one of the black countertop stools holding a cup of chai as she gave Fatima the critical once-over.

Fatima scowled at her mother. "Uff, thanks for the lovely compliment first thing in the morning. To be honest, I didn't sleep well. I've had a nightmare, okay?" She switched on the electric kettle to make herself some chai. In spite of their differences, mother and daughter followed the same steps when it came to making a cup of tea: first, the tea bag went in the cup, then hot water was poured from the electric kettle, then a drop of milk; no sugar for either of them. When Fatima had first seen Stefan making a cup of tea, she'd been horrified and called him a "tea destroyer" for adding the milk first.

"So what?" said Ammi. "We all have nightmares. But we get out of bed and fix ourselves up."

"It wasn't just a nightmare, Ammi. It was *the* nightmare."

"You learned to run from what you feel, and this is why you have nightmares. Am I to blame for that too?"

"Well, yes, actually, you are."

"You can't keep blaming me for everything that is wrong in your life, Fatima. If anything, you should thank me. I wish you would learn from your mistakes."

"I made no mistakes!" shouted Fatima, furiously stirring milk into her tea.

"Well maybe you have learned a thing or two. You are raising Maya better than I apparently raised you."

This back-handed compliment was a particular specialty in her mom's arsenal of insults.

"I was a CHILD!" Fatima shouted, and she threw the spoon across the counter, where it fell with a loud clatter. There was silence as Fatima's words lingered in the air. Fatima stared at Ammi, who stared right back.

When Ammi finally spoke, she did so slowly and carefully. "But you knew *exactly* what you were doing. And look what it almost cost us."

Hearing the commotion, Stefan poked his head into the kitchen and saw the look on both of their faces. In an attempt to break the tension, he asked in Urdu if everything was alright, much to Ammi's delight.

Ammi clapped her hands in glee. She loved it when her white *gora* son-in-law spoke Urdu, albeit with a German accent. "Yes, everything is fine, just a mother-daughter chat. Things often get heated between us, you know?"

Fatima was fuming. Her German was so much better than Stefan's feeble Urdu, and it irked her that his five-word Urdu vocabulary was applauded by her mother, while her near-fluent command of German was barely remarked upon by Stefan's family or even by her own family for that matter.

Oblivious to his white male privilege or the inherent hierarchy of languages, Stefan walked over to Fatima and kissed the top of her head. "Hey, listen, I need to get a few tools for the garden. I'll take Maya with me—she's been helping me out this morning."

"Sure," said Fatima quietly, still seething and barely bothering to look up.

Once he was safely out of earshot, Fatima turned to her mother. "Ammi, we really have to be more careful around Stefan and Maya. I think Stefan heard us yelling at each other. He's been worried about me, wondering what's going on. Apparently, I've been acting different lately. The truth is I've been so shaken up ever since that car accident on the first day of school."

Ammi sat up on her stool. "You had a car accident at

school? You never even mentioned it to me. What happened?"

"It wasn't a big deal. It obviously triggered in me ... well, you can imagine."

"Fatima, what are you talking about? What does a car accident have to do with anything?"

"Seriously, Ammi?" Fatima was snarling now. "Don't tell me you forgot? You, who normally doesn't forget a thing?"

"Ohhh. I see what you mean. But you can't live your life like that. You can't be triggered by all sorts of memories or else you'll never move on!"

That was easy for Ammi to say, thought Fatima. Easy for Ammi to blame her for everything. She felt suffocated in her own house and something snapped inside her. She grabbed her keys and wallet, made sure she had her metro card in her purse, quickly donned her black boots, zipped up her leather jacket, tied a scarf around her neck, turned to Ammi, and said, "I forgot, I have an appointment in Lisbon today. Don't wait up for me, okay?" She didn't wait for a reply.

She walked to the train station in São João do Estoril and bought a ticket from Cascais to Lisbon. It wasn't till she stepped out at Cais do Sodré station and took a tram to Alfama that her heartbeat began to return to normal. Alfama, the birthplace of *fado*—the music of destiny, nostalgia, melancholia, love, passion, and of course, saudade. She climbed up through the steep, winding old streets, stopping now and then for a bird's-eye glimpse of the cathedrals, the classic orange roofs, the Tagus River.

She must have taken a wrong turn, finding herself in a deserted lane, paint peeling off graffitied houses and faded laundry hanging from minuscule balconies, but she continued anyway until the street became so narrow that the sidewalk was practically non-existent, tapering into the road until it disappeared completely so she was forced to walk on the road itself.

She thought she heard footsteps behind her, but when she turned to look back, there was nothing, no sign of life, not even someone peeking through a window or a balcony. She thought she heard a cough and immediately swung around, but still nothing, no one, unless they were hiding behind a trash can or something. Now she was imagining things. *Come on, Fatima, why would anyone follow you? Who would follow you? You barely know a soul in Lisbon.*

She recalled the phone call. The heavy breaths. How it had unnerved her. And now this. Something wasn't right. And so she started running, as fast as she could.

# 19

## ABENA
### *Cascais, Portugal*
### March 2023

Abena looked around the school room as parents headed towards the refreshment stand to mingle and chat. She was feeling pleased with herself. The first meeting she had organized as co-chair of the International Day Committee had been a resounding success. Dozens of parent volunteers had turned up after the school drop-off with some great ideas. According to the school admissions office, the school had children from fifty-two nationalities, and Abena had personally reached out to some of the parents, wanting every nationality at the school to be represented at the International Day celebrations. At the meeting, she had asked each nationality group to choose a team lead who would coordinate what to present at their stall in terms of food, culture, games and, if possible, a dance performance. Each nationality had also been asked to choose two cultural icons from their country. Abena had gone over the practical aspects of what each stall would have access to, such as paper plates, cups, drinks, straws, electrical outlets, and access to the school's kitchen and microwaves.

"Great job, Abena. I thought that went really well," said Kate, coffee in hand. "Well worth being a bit late for work this morning." She winked.

"Thanks, Kate. I was so nervous, but I think everyone sounded excited about it all. It's great to see the parents' enthusiasm." Abena's stomach growled; she hadn't eaten a thing all day.

"Great idea to kick off the celebrations with a parade," said Fatima.

"Yes, I was thinking that first the kids will gather on the stage of the auditorium to sing a song about being 'one,' no matter where they come from. The parents can sit and watch. Then the kids will walk out onto the football field with a flag bearer leading each country to cheers from the parents on the bleachers. I need to choose an emcee for the event, someone to introduce each nationality and say hello in their language as they walk past with their flag."

"You've given this a lot of thought," said Fatima, "and I like how you're encouraging kids to represent more than one nationality. That'll be a relief for Maya. She wants to walk behind the German *and* Pakistani flags."

"That makes me so happy. Kakra and Panyin are excited about representing Ghana and the UK. It's a great way to help our kids embrace their multicultural identities."

"It's also great that you're making such an effort to keep your links to Ghana alive," said Fatima. "I sometimes think I haven't done such a good job of keeping Maya's ties to Pakistan as strong as they should be, especially when I look at you and see how proud you are of your heritage. The girls are so lucky to be close to their Ghanaian roots. Do you take them back to Ghana often?"

Abena was caught off guard. She didn't want to lie to Fatima, but telling her the truth wasn't an option. "Yeah, I try to take them back to Accra as often as I can …" There was a tap on her shoulder.

"Can I steal you for a second, Abena?" It was her co-chair, Allison.

"Sure," said Abena, clearly happy to be interrupted. "Ladies, I'll say goodbye for now, but see you next week for our Portuguese lesson." She grabbed her notebook and followed Allison to the football field, and Kate and Fatima headed off towards the school parking lot.

WHEN SHE WAS finally alone, Abena started to cry. Small, quiet sobs at first, but then it became uncontrollable. It was so difficult to admit to anyone else what was going on when she could barely admit it to herself. She felt guilt, so much guilt, for being the biggest fraud—extolling the virtues and importance of the upcoming International Day when she'd never taken Kakra and Panyin back to Ghana, not once, in their whole lives.

But she knew she could never take the twins back to the country they came from. It was too risky. So she tried to compensate in other ways, incorporating Ghanaian culture, fashion, and etiquette into their home and through her work. She had built an entire career around her identity and heritage as a proud Ghanaian woman, exporting its fabrics, materials, baskets, fans, shea butter, and much more around the world.

But was it enough? Her girls would only have secondhand knowledge of their African roots. Would they resent her for it one day? Would they be upset that she'd never taught them Twi? And what about not knowing anyone from her side of the family? Would they wonder why she'd never introduced them to their grandmother or their aunt or their many cousins? Would they want to explore their cultural identity one day and visit Ghana by themselves? How would Abena or Ben stop them? Would they feel safer in a black community, where they didn't always have to think about or be reminded about the color of their skin, where they had direct access to hair, beauty, and skincare products made for them, where they didn't have to worry about facing racism or discrimination because they were black?

Lately, she'd been feeling such a deep, intangible loss. Of course, there were many losses associated with expat life, but no one ever talked about the loss you faced when you moved to a new country and could never go back to the place that brought you up. It was like being placed on a restraining order by someone you loved.

It was why she'd grabbed the opportunity of planning International Day and thrown herself into the preparations and organization of it—a feeble attempt to control the narrative and pretend that nothing mattered more than showing who you were. Nothing, she told herself, should stop you from being who you are. Nothing except the possibility of jail time, maybe, and that's what awaited her if she took the twins back to Ghana. She knew what she had done, and if she was caught, she could lose her girls forever, and that still wasn't a risk she was willing to take.

# 20

# KATE
*Lisbon, Portugal*
March 2023

Kate took a moment to calm herself and looked over at the celebrated plaques on the wall of her office, the framed photographs with dignitaries from around the world, the red, white, and blue flag on her desk. Hers had been a predictable but fulfilling career in the US Foreign Service.

As a senior-level political officer, it was Kate's job to interpret her host country's politics and advise on international issues. So she kept a trained eye on the political climate in Portugal and deciphered events as they related to US interests, negotiations, and policies. She would work behind the scenes to analyze and report on local issues, helping policy makers in Washington DC better understand events and tailor US messages appropriately. She managed a large political section and supervised a number of officers at the US Embassy in Lisbon. This meant she regularly advised the ambassador and drafted policy documents and statements for senior department officials and for the embassy in Lisbon.

She looked back at her laptop and re-read the email. It had come out of the blue. This wasn't how things usually worked in the Foreign Service. The rules, the eligibility, the selection, the career paths; everything was rigid and clearly defined, with little to no space for exceptions or surprises. Jobs were advertised months in advance, and then the Foreign Service Officers would bid on them. Orders needed multiple signoffs.

So why had Ambassador Hill come back from DC and sent Kate a cryptic email to come in for a confidential—and unplanned—meeting that morning? She hated being caught off guard, but that's exactly how she felt. What exactly had happened in DC? Her record was stellar; she had aced the Foreign Service Officer Test before her first overseas assignment to Mexico, and she'd always passed the Suitability Review panels, the oral assessments, and the medical and security clearances. She was sure if anyone looked into her record, it would be squeaky clean. Despite this, her paranoia had reached new heights, and she had to take time to calm herself down before coming out of the office to tell her secretary to cancel her morning meetings.

She made her way to the ambassador's office and knocked on the door.

"Come in, Kate. One moment, please."

Ambassador Dennis Hill sounded more clipped and restrained than usual. He was staring out of his window with his back to Kate. She could see the top of his bald head and the stiff white collar of his shirt. When he turned around, he had that jaded look of jetlag about him—he must have gotten back in the wee hours of the morning from DC.

Back in the day, the Foreign Service had career ambassadors, but these days it was common to have ambassadors

THE GUILTY CAN'T SAY GOODBYE      169

who were political appointees—such as Ambassador Hill, who had been appointed by President Biden for the active role he'd played in the presidential campaign.

He picked up his favorite black and white coffee mug with a map of Florida and the words 'Sunshine State' on it, took a slurp, then stared blankly at Kate.

"So listen, I'll cut straight to the chase. While I was in DC last week, I was informed through the Regional Security Office that a former employee of yours in Singapore had filed a complaint against you. Are you familiar with a Ms. Maryanne …" he put on his glasses and looked down at the printout in front of him to confirm the last name "… Cruz?"

Kate shifted uncomfortably. "Yes," she said, enraged but poker-faced. "She was my hired help in Singapore."

"As you know, the Foreign Service takes these complaints seriously. You know firsthand how rigorous our system is when it comes to performing background checks and security clearances on our FSOs in every city and country they have ever lived in."

"If I may, what exactly am I being accused of? And can I please explain myself?"

"Okay, this employee of yours has alleged that you're not a fair employer, that you're not fit to serve in the Foreign Service. She hasn't provided any proof of misconduct, as far as I can tell. So I'm here to first understand and listen to your side of the story, to assess if there is any truth in these allegations." He leaned forward on his desk and looked at Kate expectantly.

"I see," said Kate. "Well to start, Maryanne was my helper and was employed by us for around a year when she started asking us for money. She had a child back in the

Philippines who was sick, and she needed help to pay for the hospital bills. We tried to help out a bit, but she always wanted more. When we refused, things turned sour, and she started threatening to report us to the authorities for being unfair employers. She has simply reported me out of malice."

"Wait a minute. So did Maryanne have anything to do with the curtailment of your assignment in Singapore? That's a hell of a coincidence, Kate."

"If you look at the records, you will see that the curtailment of my Singapore assignment by six months was actually granted on 'compassionate grounds.' Unfortunately, around the same time as Maryanne started asking us for money, my mother became quite sick in Texas and was diagnosed with stage three breast cancer. As her only daughter, I rushed back to see her through chemo and helped set up adequate medical care for her with my father. But then there was also a danger ... well, the family history suggested that I should be checked out at once. There were multiple medical tests to be done to assess if I carried the various gene mutations—my case was not simple—and to help decide whether I should get a prophylactic mastectomy to significantly lower my risk of developing breast cancer. That's why I left Singapore on compassionate grounds—to attend to my own medical needs in the US. Thankfully, Mom is doing better now, and as soon as I was in the clear, I returned to work and was able to bid on this assignment in Portugal." She smiled at him. "But this is all in my file."

"I'm glad to hear that. As far as I can tell by looking at your file, you have broken no official rules, but I'm sure you understand that we will need to contact this ... Ms. Cruz ... to reach our own conclusions."

*Great. Just great.* The last thing she needed right now was to have this Maryanne saga hanging over her head and have the legitimacy of her premature departure from Singapore questioned. Her guilty conscience gnawed at her. It *had* been a lucky coincidence that Maryanne's blackmail attempts had coincided with her mother's cancer diagnosis. And it was a cruel irony of fate that she had to call something as serious as cancer in the family a 'lucky coincidence.' She'd known right away that, officially speaking, her mother's illness and her own medical tests could be her ticket out of Singapore as far as the Foreign Service was concerned. But she was still furious at Maryanne for reporting her and arousing suspicion at her workplace after all these months. When people went digging, they always found things.

She was in a bit of a daze when she got back to her office and paced around, rubbing her temples, but it only made her headache worse, so she sat down and put her head on the desk.

There was a knock, and Helen, her secretary, poked her head in.

"Hey, you feeling okay?" she asked. She took out her ear pods and stared at Kate. Helen wasn't exactly the maternal type—she was proudly childless by choice—but right now, she was full of concern for Kate.

"I … actually, I'm not feeling too good. My head's spinning. I feel hot."

"Holy moly," said Helen, touching Kate's forehead. "You're burning up. I have some Tylenol in the office. Actually, perhaps you should go home and call it a sick day."

"Perhaps. I can't think straight. My head feels woozy."

"Okay, stay there. I'll call Michael and ask him to come

and get you. Don't worry about anything here. I'll rearrange your schedule."

"I'm so sorry, Helen. I hate adding to your to-do list."

"Don't be silly. At this point, even my to-do list has a to-do list."

WHEN SHE WAS safely in the car, Kate told Michael what had happened.

"Shit. I never thought she'd actually go and report you," he said as they drove off. "I didn't think she had the balls. I'm … I'm sorry."

"That's it? That's all you have to say? That you're *sorry*? How can you be so calm? Do you not understand that she's serious about exposing me? Have you forgotten what's at stake here? If they find out the truth, they'll invalidate my security clearance and my job. They'll send me back to DC to face the US judicial system—it's a federal crime. I'd have to wait and see what happened, with my entire future hanging in the balance. I would lose my job, for sure. I could lose *everything* if there's even a slight doubt about my actions!" She was shouting at him, still holding a hand to her throbbing head.

"But darling, Maryanne has *no* proof. All she has are a few newspaper clippings. Who would believe her?"

"But she doesn't *just* have the newspaper clippings, she has much more than that. You filled in the details for her. You told her explicitly who Carla Mosely was. *You* are the reason I'm in this bind. You are the only person I've ever trusted with this, and you have betrayed me in the most spectacular fashion. You'd better hope and pray that she didn't record your conversation or else I'm doomed!"

Michael went quiet, then went on the defensive. "I've told you a million times, I'm sorry for what I did. It was a moment of weakness. You and I were not in a good place back then. I was tired of supporting you nonstop. I got so drunk that night I didn't know what I was saying until it was too late. I'm sure Maryanne didn't record me." He took a hand off the steering wheel to squeeze her thigh, but she brushed it away.

"It's too late, Michael. Too late. It is what it is. I'm not even sure the marriage counseling is going to salvage things now. What's the point? Maryanne may not have proof, but questions can still be asked, doubts can still be cast, and aspersions can still be made."

And then there was just an angry silence, each of them consumed by their own guilt.

## Lisbon, Portugal
## March 2023

The next day, their Portuguese lesson was being held in a funky café in Estrela, a buzzy neighborhood in the southwest of Lisbon. Usually Kate liked to meander through its streets and discover its hidden gems, but today she was still reeling from the investigation at work and her confrontation with Michael. She'd made a concerted effort to dust herself off and make her way to class, and she was determined to pretend everything was okay so her friends wouldn't suspect a thing. She arrived late at Amelia Café and rushed inside, barely noticing the neon sign, floral displays, and funky décor. They were all waiting for her.

"There you are. Thought you might not be coming today," said Inês.

"Yeah, not like you to be so late," said Fatima.

"Guys, I know, I'm so sorry. Work has been crazy." She beckoned to the waiter to come over and ordered a *galão* and an avocado toast in Portuguese.

Inês applauded. "Well done, Kate. Your Portuguese is sounding better and better."

"Ah, well, I have a good teacher," said Kate, winking at Inês.

"*Então*, well, let's get started on today's lesson on modern Portuguese society. Now that you know quite a bit about Portugal's history, I thought we could try to have a conversation about Portugal as a multicultural society. Where does it draw its sense of identity from?"

Abena sat up. "I'd love to learn more. Identity and how it's formed is quickly becoming my top interest. I guess I've been thinking so much about it with International Day coming up at the kids' school."

"International Day? What's that?" said Fatima.

Kate sniggered.

"Oh, you got me there for a second," said Abena. She grinned at Fatima. "Inês, would you be interested in attending our International Day celebrations? I can share the invite with you later. It's on a weekend."

"Sounds great. If I'm not leading a tour group that day, I'd love to join you. Okay, let's dive into our topic for today."

Inês opened up her notebook. "First, as usual, I have some suggestions for books on this topic that you might find interesting to read." She handed out a list. "They are all Portugal specific but have been translated into English, so they're easy for you to read."

Kate scanned the titles; they would be helpful as part of her work. She raised her hand. "Inês, can I please ask you, how do the Portuguese feel today, I mean do they have a strong European identity or predominantly a local identity?"

Inês took several sips of her *bica* before answering. "That is an interesting question, Kate, and you'd probably get different answers from different people. In my opinion, I think it is correct to say that we Portuguese are trying to reconcile our different sources of identity, to be proud of who we used to be and also who we are today. In Europe, Portugal is the underdog, the poor neighbor. But in Mozambique, Angola, or Brazil, Portugal is still seen as the former colonial power, as the Eden, and the place to move to for a better, safer future. We switch back and forth between our different personas, like a chameleon changing its color depending on the environment."

This was something that resonated with Kate. Sometimes her whole personality changed depending on the language she was speaking, and so did her accent. "I totally get it. I feel like a chameleon most days. I'm sure I've added more spots to my skin since Singapore."

Fatima nodded. "Me too. I change my colors depending on whether I'm living in the East or the West. I guess it's what we do to adapt to each place we move to."

Abena, who'd been deep in thought, looked up and asked, "But is it adaptation? Or are we simply not being true to ourselves? What I mean to say is, are we simply choosing one version of ourselves over the others?"

"I think, just as Inês talked about Portugal's identity having many different layers, so do we," said Kate. "Our global identities have many layers too, based on all the countries we've lived in, all the varied experiences we've had. Sometimes, we show one layer to the outside world and not another—it remains hidden till we feel comfortable enough to share it."

"Yeah, I guess that makes sense," said Abena, not sounding entirely convinced.

Kate looked over at Inês, Fatima, and Abena, each of them lost in their own thoughts. As they got ready to start the revision of their Portuguese grammar, she couldn't help but wonder if her friends were exactly who they seemed to be. Or maybe they were hiding something too?

# 21

## ABENA
*Cascais, Portugal*
April 2023

Abena opened her stainless steel fridge and thought about what snacks she could prepare for the girls and their friends. Every other week, the kids had a short Friday when they finished school at noon, and these days were perfect for playdates. Earlier that day before leaving for school, Kakra had smoothed out the pleats in the navy blue skirt of her uniform and pleaded with her mother, "Please Mum, nothing Ghanaian, nothing too foreign, okay? Don't go serving fried plantain. Our friends will think eating a fried banana is weird. Can we have some normal food like crackers and cheese? Please?" Kakra's request had saddened Abena, and the word 'normal' had rubbed her up the wrong way, but she'd smiled and said nothing. She understood that at the age of ten, her girls wanted to fit in with their new friends.

She cut up some fresh kiwis and strawberries, prepared a small cheese platter with crackers, a slab of brie, beetroot hummus and grapes, and some chocolate chip cookies, and took the tray of snacks to the twins' bedroom, where the kids were busy playing Monopoly. She was about to knock, but the door was ajar and she stopped to listen in.

"Are you guys traveling anywhere for spring break?" asked Eric.

"We've got my Pakistani grandmother over from Karachi for a long visit," said Maya, "so I doubt we'll travel anywhere. We'll probably show her more of Portugal and celebrate Eid here as a family."

"That sounds nice. We never go anywhere," said Panyin.

"Not even a visit back to the UK?" asked Eric.

"Nah. I think our parents are relieved to be living in Portugal, away from all the Ghanaian relatives in the UK," said Kakra. "And so are we."

"Yeah, my parents always make me visit a ton of relatives when we're back in the States over the summer. It's super boring," said Eric.

"We never go back to visit Pakistan either," said Maya. "Usually it's my Pakistani grandmother coming to visit us in Dubai or here. But we do go back to Germany to see my dad's family. They never travel to see us."

"We never go back to Ghana to see our mum's family either," said Kakra, sounding miffed. "In fact, we've never been."

"You've *never* been to Ghana?" said Eric.

"Nope," the twins replied together.

"Why not?" asked Maya.

"I don't know. I don't think my mum gets on with her family in Accra," said Panyin.

"I don't think my mom gets on with her family in Texas either," said Eric. "But she forces us all to visit them. They never visited us in Singapore or China. I doubt they'll come to Portugal."

Maya giggled. "My mama pretends she's on good terms with her family, but whenever my grandmother comes to visit, she gets so stressed out."

Abena stopped listening. It was upsetting to hear the girls talk like that. She had no idea they felt that way. She went back downstairs, left the snacks on the dining table, and curled up on the sofa. When Ben walked in and found her there minutes later, he put down his keys and went straight over.

"Hey, babe. What's going on? You okay? Are the twins' friends here?"

She'd been crying. "Yeah, they're here. I'm fine. It's nothing."

"It doesn't look like nothing." He touched her shoulder.

"I overheard the girls talking with their friends. They mentioned they've never been back to Ghana. I mean, can you blame them for not feeling Ghanaian? It's like they're almost ashamed of their identity. I feel like a terrible mum, like I've failed them completely!"

"Honey, you're not a terrible mum; you had to make a terrible choice. You really need to cut yourself some slack. Kakra and Panyin are well-adjusted, happy children. We've given them a loving home, and that counts for something. And now look at this amazing new adventure we're on together, our new lives in Portugal."

"I guess. I struggle to reconcile how *they* feel with how *I* feel, my identity versus how theirs is developing. I don't want to lose them, Ben."

"You're not going to lose them. Why don't you spend some quality time with them over the spring break? Do things they'll enjoy doing with you. Make some memories together that will bring you closer, things you'll all cherish. I can take care of business if you fancy a few days off?"

Abena smiled lamely. She knew Ben was always there for her and would support her in any way possible. But this was really starting to bother her. She'd have to think carefully, come up with an exciting plan for their spring break. And in the meantime, she'd have to put her feelings aside and think of the kids. "Kakra! Panyin! Please bring your friends to the living room and have some snacks."

A few moments later, the kids gathered around the dining table and helped themselves to the food and drinks she had prepared. Abena hovered over them with only one thought running through her mind. The time had come.

# 22

# KATE
*Cascais, Portugal*
April 2023

K ate pushed open the glass doors of the school, walked in past the uniform shop, and took a seat on the plushy couch in the reception area. It was two p.m. on a Thursday afternoon and normally she would be at her office in Lisbon, but today she had an appointment with Eric's homeroom teacher. It wasn't the regular parent-teacher conference that took place at the end of each semester. Today's meeting was to discuss a particular topic that had drawn the attention of Eric's teacher, who had contacted her via email. Kate's palms were sweating. She felt a little guilty for not telling Michael about the meeting. He would've insisted on being there, but she wanted to hear the objective facts first; she could involve him later if she needed to.

"Ah, thanks for meeting me, Ms. Miller," said Ms. Henrietta, Eric's fourth-grade homeroom teacher, as she led Kate to a little meeting room. "I know you have a busy schedule, so I appreciate you coming in at such short notice."

Her broad smile put Kate immediately at ease as they took their seats.

"Not a problem," said Kate. "I wanted to come and meet you in person and hear exactly what Eric wrote in English class, what it was that raised the alarm."

"Well as you know, we are about to complete our module on poetry. The fourth graders have been reading different types of poetry and experimenting with writing some of their own. Their latest assignment was to write a short poem starting with "I'm from …" Five short stanzas, two lines each. I've got a printout of Eric's poem here. Why don't you read it yourself and then we can discuss it." She handed the poem to Kate, who took out her reading glasses and started reading.

### I'm From
*by Eric Miller Russo*

I'm from a sea of Chinese faces,
Pinching my white cheeks.

I'm from chili crab and kaya toast,
Always thinking about my next meal.

I'm from the pitch-black passport,
Filled with endless stamps.

I'm from the suitcases,
Not always full but tucked in the closet.

I'm from my parents' home,
But I think soon there will be two of these as well.

Kate brushed away the tears forming in the corner of her eyes. *Holy crap.* Eric had obviously picked up on her and Michael fighting and was already preparing for their eventual separation—and two homes.

"If you need a minute to yourself, I totally understand," said Ms. Henrietta, her voice soft and almost apologetic.

"I'm uh … no, it's fine. Thank you for bringing his poem to my attention. I had no idea he felt this way."

"I certainly don't mean to pry into your personal life, Ms. Miller, but I think kids Eric's age can be quite perceptive. He's a talented boy, as you'll agree. The rest of his poem shows immense understanding of straddling different cultures and worlds, so common for Third Culture Kids. Many of his classmates also have diverse backgrounds and express themselves eloquently, but I think Eric in particular has an incredible talent for words. He's not very outspoken in class, but I just thought perhaps if he was facing a difficult time at home, then we could help support him at school."

"My husband and I are currently going through marriage counseling," Kate blurted out, but almost in a whisper, still looking down at Eric's poem.

"I can imagine what a difficult time this must be for you and your family. Please know that we do have school counselors available on campus should you feel the need for Eric to talk to someone."

"Thank you. I appreciate your help and for bringing this to my attention. I'll have a word with my husband tonight. We'll figure out a plan together. Can I keep the poem?"

"Yes of course. Let me know if I can be of any further help."

Once safely back inside her car in the underground school parking lot, Kate let the tears flow. *My poor, poor boy!* She didn't want him to bear such a burden, something that was hers and Michael's to figure out. She decided to drive straight home and talk to Michael before he picked Eric up from school.

KATE HAD COMPOSED herself by the time she walked through the front door.

Michael came out of the kitchen in his apron, spatula in hand. "Hey, what are you doing home so early?"

"We need to talk. It's important. Look at this poem. Eric wrote it in school."

He put down his spatula and she handed him the folded piece of paper.

"Shit," said Michael once he'd read Eric's poem.

"Exactly!"

"How did you get this?"

"Ms. Henrietta called me into school to discuss it," she said, waiting for the fallout.

"Why didn't you tell me earlier?"

"Isn't that part of the problem?" she snapped.

"When it comes to Eric, we have to be a team, Kate. We've discussed this in counseling."

"I know. And I told Ms. Henrietta we were already going through marriage counseling. But I think we need to get really serious about it."

"I agree."

"I mean it, Michael. We have to take our sessions with

Dr. Teixeira seriously. And that means completing all our homework assignments on time."

"I know. I'm sorry. I'll do better, promise. Hey, come here."

They hugged, and for a brief moment she felt safe and the world felt like a better place.

"Do you think we should talk to him together?" said Kate.

"That might be a good idea."

"But what in the world do we tell him?"

Michael pulled away and looked at Kate. "Look, it's not been a smooth transition for him. Leaving Singapore early without warning because of your health scare, then going to a school in DC for six months and then moving here. Let's apologize for all the shouting and the bad atmosphere in the home. And then we can be honest with him and tell him we're seeing a marriage counselor to help us work out our problems."

"But what if it gives him false hope?" This was her number one worry.

"I think it'll give him some reassurance."

"I guess," she said. "I do want him to know we're trying to work this out together."

"We have to help him see that no matter what happens we will always love him, that he is our top priority."

"Agreed," said Kate. "Let's have a family talk tonight after dinner. Shall I go pick him up from school or do you want to?"

"Let's go together," said Michael. "Let's both pick him up for a change."

"Yes," she said. "I'd like that very much."

For once, they were united in purpose.

# 23

## FATIMA
### *Cascais, Portugal*
### April 2023

Fatima woke up with a jolt. Her eyes flew open and she scanned the shadow standing over her bed.

"Mama, I don't feel too well." Maya was still in her lilac pajamas. She was coughing and sounded hoarse.

"Oh *beta*, what happened?" She reached out to touch Maya's forehead.

"I couldn't sleep. My nose is blocked too. I don't think I can go to school today."

"You definitely feel warm. Okay, listen, why don't you get back in bed, and I'll go down and fix you some breakfast and bring some meds, okay?"

Maya smiled weakly and went back to her room, and Fatima forced herself to get out of bed. Stefan was already up. By the sound of the faint clatter coming from the kitchen, he was brewing coffee. It always took Fatima a while to adjust to the sounds of a new house: the three beeps of the dishwasher when it completed a cycle, the shrill timer on the oven, or the scrape of the pantry cupboard being opened.

By the time she'd put on her robe and house slippers and gone downstairs, Ammi and Stefan were sitting on the kitchen bar stools drinking coffee together. Both of them had always been early risers, the first ones up. Fatima knew that Ammi disapproved of her habit of getting up late, but she didn't care anymore. Ever the traditionalist, Ammi expected women to get up and serve coffee and breakfast to their husbands every morning and, God forbid, not the other way around. Ammi had learned not to express her criticism anymore, not verbally anyway, but there it was, written all over her face.

"Oh, you're up," said Stefan. "I was about to bring your coffee up." He went to hug her but she pulled back, hesitant about showing physical affection in front of Ammi.

"Yeah, I'm up. Listen, Maya's up too, but she's not feeling well. She's coming down with a fever and should stay home from school today. I thought I'd make her some breakfast and bring it up."

"Let me help you," said Stefan, already opening the fridge to get the eggs. "I agree; she should stay home today and rest."

"Oh, *bechari* Maya," said Ammi, immediately feeling bad for 'poor' Maya. "I can help you look after her today, in case you need to work?"

"Uh, thanks Ammi. That would be great," said Fatima. "I do have that article to finish up."

"And I can make her some *khitchri* for lunch."

"What's that?" asked Stefan, turning up the heat to scramble the eggs.

"It's what Ammi makes when anyone is sick. It's basically white rice slow-cooked in a pot with yellow lentils."

"Has Fatima never made it for you?" said Ammi, sounding incredulous. "Or for Maya?" She got up from her stool. "You leave it up to me. I'll take care of lunch today."

"Save some leftovers for me," said Stefan. "I'm having lunch at the office today. I'd better get going. I'll say goodbye to Maya." He scooped the eggs onto a plate, left it on the countertop, grabbed his laptop bag, and headed out.

Fatima looked at Ammi, who was now putting two slices of bread in the toaster, taking up where Stefan had left off. Her help always came with a side-serving of guilt, but today was a day when Fatima could really use the extra support so she could focus on meeting her writing deadline. A few minutes later, Ammi carried up a tray of scrambled eggs, toast, and a glass of orange juice for Maya. Perhaps it would be a good opportunity for Maya and Ammi to bond.

THERE WAS AN earthy smell of fresh *khitchri* wafting from the kitchen when Fatima came out of her home office that lunchtime. Even she had to admit that Ammi's khitchri recipe was unbeatable. Her secret was to use two different types of *daal*, yellow lentils and red lentils, and combine them for extra flavor; this made it easier to digest but kept you feeling full for longer. She would always make some cucumber *raita* on the side to refresh the taste buds by grating some cucumbers, mixing with plain yogurt, and adding dried mint and coriander.

Maya and Ammi were eating together at the dining table in the lounge; from the kitchen, Fatima couldn't help but overhear their conversation.

"This is so good, Nani Ammi! I can't believe I never had it before," exclaimed Maya.

"I'm glad you like it, *beta*, anything to make you feel better. This was your grandfather's favorite."

"What was he like? I wish I could have met him."

"Your Nana Abba? He was very fond of food. But only South Asian food. He was born in New Delhi, in India, before the 1947 Independence from British rule. He migrated to Pakistan a few years later with his family, and leaving his home was something he never got over. He was never able to go back to India, you see, as tensions between the two countries deteriorated. He was the perfect gentleman, working hard for his family, and he never said an angry word. He was polite to a fault and tried to see the good in everyone."

"He sounds like an amazing person. Do you miss him?"

"Yes, of course I do. His untimely death came as a huge shock to all who loved him."

"I'm glad I at least get to know you, Nani Ammi," said Maya.

"You are my favorite granddaughter too."

Maya laughed. "I am your *only* granddaughter, Nani Ammi."

"And I wish you didn't have to live so far away. But I am glad we get to spend this time together."

At this point, Fatima came into the lounge and joined them at the dining table with her own bowl of khitchri. "Thanks for making lunch, Ammi, it's so good. Maya, honey, are you feeling any better?"

"Yes, Mama, but I think I'm going to lie down in my room now. Thanks, Nani Ammi, for looking after me." She got up and gave her grandmother a kiss before going up to her room.

With Maya safely out of earshot, Fatima turned to Ammi and smiled. "Well, you two were certainly getting along."

Ammi's affection for Maya was written all over her face. "She really is a good girl. So appreciative and curious about everything. And her Urdu is excellent. I am so glad I can converse in Urdu with her."

"I love that you are spending quality time with her. I guess you're making up for lost time." Fatima took another spoonful of khitchri before looking directly at her mother. "You were never this loving towards me as a child."

"That's not true, Fatima. I did everything for you. How can you say that?"

"I can say that because it's true. I was so lonely when I was Maya's age. I only had my books to keep me company. Well at least you're staying consistent about the lies you're telling about my father."

"How dare you! You know that I did what I had to do to protect our family."

"But did you *really* protect us? I think you made matters much worse by what you did."

"I," Ammi paused for emphasis, her nostrils flaring, "did not do *anything*. And you know it." She got up from the table.

"You know, Ammi, that's our fundamental problem. Sometimes, I don't even know what I despise you more for, the things you did do or the things you didn't do."

"And you? What about you, huh?" said Ammi, going on the offensive.

"What about me?"

"Don't act all innocent. You rebelled the first chance you

got. And in a *big* way! I mean, I've accepted him now, but you know what my first reaction was when you told me you were marrying Stefan." Ammi cocked her head to the left and stared at Fatima as if daring her to suggest otherwise.

"My choice of partner had nothing to do with you!" Fatima shouted back.

"But marrying outside of our culture was your way to escape. Do not try to deny it."

"It was my way to take back control over *my* life. And I don't regret it one bit. After all, I didn't exactly have any positive role models amongst the Pakistani men in our family, did I?"

"And this is my fault too? I forget, with you, everything is my fault. Aren't you proud of your own culture?"

"Of course I am. Why do you think I worked so hard to teach Maya how to speak Urdu? It's the one piece of my heritage I'm *extremely* proud of."

"There is only one piece of your heritage you are proud of?" Ammi snorted.

"Well, keeping up with appearances was always your forte, Ammi, not mine."

"You're always blaming me for keeping up appearances. But what about you? Are you not doing the exact same? Stefan still does not have any clue, does he?"

"I guess you've taught me well. Clearly, I've learned from the best," said Fatima. And then she left the table before she said something she would later regret.

# 24

## ABENA
### *Cascais, Portugal*
### April 2023

"Honey, wake up. Wake up, Abena." Ben was holding a cup of coffee by her bedside.

"Did I oversleep? What time is it? Are we late for school?"

"It's almost nine o'clock. You did oversleep, but don't worry, I dropped the twins off at school. Lucky for you, you have a husband who has it all under control." He smiled.

"I can't believe I didn't wake up."

"I can't believe it either; the twins were really loud getting ready this morning. You were out cold. You had a late night, so we let you sleep in." He bent down and kissed her then opened the shutters in one swift movement, and the morning light flooded in.

"It's been so hectic lately," said Abena, squinting in the sunlight.

"I know this school event is important to you, and I think it's great you're putting in so much effort, but don't let it consume you, okay? Look what happened with the girls last night. I think you pushed them too hard."

She nodded. Ben was right: things were getting a bit too much to handle, and Abena was wearing too many hats. Her work, her kids, her home—all were suffering as the International Day preparations took over her life, her schedule, and every waking moment. The event had snowballed into a massive undertaking, particularly since Abena had gotten her latest idea approved by the school leadership—to invite a few prominent ambassadors from different countries serving in Lisbon to be the chief guests and to inaugurate the parade. Abena had also approached Kate to ask if the American ambassador would be interested in attending, and Kate had made no promises but said she would definitely ask her boss. Then there were all the sub-committees to manage, the volunteer WhatsApp groups, the decoration committees, the food, the security protocol. Oh, the list was endless.

She was still thinking about last night's argument with Kakra and Panyin. It had all started because the discussion on identity at her Portuguese lesson was still replaying in her mind. She'd started thinking about ways in which she could help her daughters feel more Ghanaian, and at dinner last night she had suggested they prepare a traditional Ashanti dance for International Day, and that's what started the rebellion.

"But Mum, none of our friends are dancing," Kakra had said, rolling her eyes at Abena. "It's going to look silly. I don't even know how to do a traditional Ashanti dance."

"I mean, we've never even been to Ghana," Panyin had chimed in. "How are we supposed to suddenly know this dance or perform it correctly?"

"I'd teach it to you both of course."

"Why is it so important to you, Mum? I mean, Dad isn't asking us to do a British pantomime," said Panyin. "Whatever that is. I mean, it's where we both grew up, so if anything, we should be doing more for the UK stall."

"They have a point, honey," said Ben, his raised eyebrows sending a clear signal to Abena. "You can't force this kind of stuff. Let the girls express their identities in a way that feels natural to them."

"But do you remember what happened last week when we were sitting at that café in Cascais? The waiter asked the girls where they were from and when they both said the UK, he laughed and asked them 'but where are you *really* from?' God, I hated that. As if to suggest you don't belong in the UK because your black skin color tells a different story. All I'm trying to do is to help you embrace your Ghanaian heritage because you're always going to be asked about it."

"Yes, that was annoying," said Kakra.

"I don't care," said Panyin, looking away.

"How you feel inside is more important than what anyone else thinks," said Ben, repeating his favorite mantra.

Abena felt her entire family was ganging up on her. Why could none of them see how much this meant to her? She at least expected Ben to understand. To be fair, he had been nothing but supportive, picking up her slack on both the home and work fronts. But he didn't get the level of stress Abena was under. There was the external stress of coordinating and executing International Day, but then there was her guilt for failing the girls, for being a hypocrite, for lying to her closest friends over here, and the stress of feeling adrift from an identity that had once provided comfort and solace.

How would people react if she told the truth? Would it

be such a disaster to confide in her close friends? Would they judge her and ostracize her? Call her a hypocrite? Turn her in? And what about the girls—didn't she owe them the truth? Not the half-truths she'd been telling them their whole lives, but the full, unadulterated truth.

For all these years, Abena had forced herself never to look back at what she had done. She kept pushing ahead determinedly. She focused on building the future instead of dwelling on the past—because what was done could never be undone. But running away from it all, first to the UK and now to Portugal, had only made her more anxious, not less. It had only increased her anxiety, doubled her paranoia, multiplied the size of her guilty conscience, and resulted in a world of sleepless nights.

Now, confronted with her own identity crisis and that of her girls, Abena realized what her mistake was. It didn't matter where she lived or where she moved to. This thing would always follow her. Like a dark scourge, it would color all of her experiences. She had to stop running away and come clean about what she'd done. She could start by telling her friends. Then the girls. She realized that nothing else would bring her the peace she craved. Perhaps this was the real freedom her life abroad had given her: the courage to examine the source of her conflicted identity and the chance to come clean and bury those old skeletons once and for all.

## *Cascais, Portugal*
## April 2023

Abena looked at Fatima and Kate sitting across from her on her sofa. This was going to be harder than she thought. She had messaged them both and asked if they could meet for a casual coffee at her place—away from Portuguese lessons and preparations for International Day. A chance to talk. They had both accepted right away and now here they were. Abena had told Ben what she intended to do. She'd told him about her inner turmoil, that she wanted to confide in her friends. Ben had been skeptical but had eventually agreed that Abena would benefit from talking about it with people she trusted and who had no stake in the matter.

"Can I get you guys some biscuits with your coffee?" asked Abena.

"Sure," said Fatima, taking a long hard look at her. "You seem nervous."

"Yeah, you do seem a bit on edge," said Kate. "Forget about the biscuits and tell us what's going on."

"I probably seem nervous because I am. The thing is, I called you both because you're my closest friends over here. And what surprises me is that even though we are all so different, and you come from such different backgrounds than me, I feel like you get me, y'know? I don't know how I would have managed this first year in Portugal without you guys to keep me sane—through the new school year, settling in the kids, the Portuguese lessons and the moral support with learning a new foreign language, and just in general, with finding my feet in a new country. But I guess I've found more than my feet. I've also found the courage to share who I really am. It's scary sharing something I haven't shared publicly with practically anyone, except Ben, but I think … I *know* it's the right thing to do. Lately I've felt like such a hypocrite, extolling the virtues of International Day and encouraging our kids and parent community to be proud of who they are and where they come from, but all the time I haven't been honest with myself or with Kakra and Panyin about who we are, or where they come from. And it's been killing me from the inside."

Fatima looked confused. "What do you mean exactly?"

"Abena, are Kakra and Panyin adopted?" said Kate, coming straight out with it and voicing what she had suspected for some time.

The three women looked at each other as the word "adopted" lingered in the air like an overpowering smell that refused to go away.

Abena clasped her hands together and said slowly, "Yes, Kakra and Panyin are adopted," as if it was the first time she had said it out loud. "How did you guess, Kate?"

"I saw the panic on your face when the school asked you for their medical records that first day—that's when the thought first kinda crossed my mind. But I didn't want to pry or say anything in case it wasn't true. But I mean … it's not so bad if they're adopted. I understand it's a *huge* thing. But why do you feel bad about giving them both a loving home? You're an excellent mother, and I hope you know that." She reached out to touch Abena's knee, but Abena jerked away.

"I'm an awful person," Abena whispered.

"Sweetie, you can tell us, and we won't judge," said Fatima gently.

"Wait, do the twins know they're adopted?" asked Kate.

"Yes, the twins know they're adopted, but they don't know the full story. I think I had better tell you the full story. I'm not sure where to start …"

Then she took a breath and told them everything.

# 25

# ABENA

*Accra, Ghana*

September 2012

*F*rom the moment the airplane landed at Kotoka Airport *and the immigration officer welcomed her with an upbeat "Akwaaba," Abena knew she was home. She looked at Ben as if to say there was no time to waste, and while she quickly exchanged their British pounds into Ghanaian Cedis, he went to hail a cab. It took them directly from the airport to the hospital in East Legon in record time, bypassing Accra's notorious gridlocked traffic.*

*Then Abena was pushing open the dusty doors of her sister's hospital room, her heart thumping loudly in her chest and her mind racing, fatigued with jet lag from the journey and the stress of reaching a decision with Ben. When she got inside, her sister was nowhere to be seen. But there he was— looking over two incubators with two tiny babies—her brother-in-law, Daniel. It had been a while since Abena had seen him, and although he had aged, he was still dressed youthfully, with baggy black jeans and an oversized blue shirt.*

He turned around to look at them. "Abena. Ben. What are you doing here? Did you hear the news already?"

"Where is Akosua?" Abena realized she was panting. "Wait a minute … there are two babies?"

"Yes, Akosua has just delivered. Twin girls—didn't she tell you? They're both doing fine, as you can see. But Akosua …"

Abena walked over to the incubators in a daze and looked at her tiny new nieces, who were sleeping peacefully. Her heart surged with love. "Wow. They're beautiful. Congrats, Daniel. God bless. What about Akosua? You're scaring me."

"She's in the intensive care unit. After the C-section, her blood pressure began to drop, and they had to revive her. She's undergoing a full blood transfusion right now."

"No! My poor Akosua. I need to see her."

"You can't. We must wait. The doctor will let me know. In the meantime, I don't know what to do with … them. I didn't want them to begin with."

Abena looked at Ben.

"Hey, brother," Ben said. "The reason Abena and I flew over right away was because … we have been trying to have a baby for a long time, but it hasn't happened." He seemed to be grappling with what to say next. "When we heard that you and Akosua were fighting over having more children, we thought … we wondered …" He couldn't bring himself to say it.

Daniel stared at Ben. "You want to take them?"

"We were going to offer to adopt and raise your baby," said Abena.

Daniel looked utterly shocked. He paced around the hospital room, bringing his hand to his mouth, then thinking better of it, looking out of the window, turning around to look at Ben and Abena, then glancing at the incubators. Perhaps ten minutes passed by, perhaps fifteen. To Abena it felt like forever.

"Akosua will kill me," he said, "but my gut feeling is yes, take them, take them both, they are your girls to raise. I don't want to separate them. The truth is, you might be saving our marriage, not just solving your infertility problem. It's the best thing for everyone."

Abena was stunned. "How can you even say that? This is madness!"

"Actually, I don't think I have ever been more certain about anything before. Once Akosua is better, she'll see that too. I'll make her understand that it's best. I mean, we already have Afia, Yaa, Kofi, and Kwame. Having two more is going to bankrupt us. I … I lost my job recently, and the stress of providing for everyone is turning my hair gray. I can barely pay for schooling as it is. The shop in Makola is not bringing in much business these days either. You let me handle Akosua, okay?"

"Daniel, I can't just take my sister's babies! I need to talk to her. To explain our situation. She doesn't even know how long we've been trying to have a baby of our own. She has no clue about all our failed IVF attempts. All I know is that she's been struggling. And that the two of you have been fighting. And I know that Ben and I can provide a safe and loving home for these precious babies. But I have to talk to Akosua first."

"Then be prepared for her to say no. You don't know her the way I do. She's as stubborn as an ox. If it's a choice between me and the babies, she'll gladly give me up."

Abena took Ben's hand and they walked over to the twin incubators and peered inside. One of the baby girls was *stirring. She raised her tiny dark arm out of her swaddle and yawned.*

*Abena couldn't stop staring at her. "Can I hold her?" she asked Daniel.*

*"Yes, go ahead."*

*"Have you thought of any names?" she said.*

*"Not yet. Akosua wanted to see which one was born first and then give them traditional Ghanaian names."*

*A nurse peeked her head in to give an update about Akosua. Abena was breathing in the intoxicating newborn baby smell, and all she heard were the words "unconscious," "iron transfusion," "low hemoglobin," and "dangerously low white blood cells." Her heart started pounding. Who knew if Akosua would even make it out of the ICU to look after her two babies?*

*She looked at Ben and could see he was thinking the same thing. "Daniel," she said, "how about I offer to stay here and look after them till Akosua is better and has hopefully recovered?"*

*"If you do that, you can forget about adopting the twins. Akosua will never agree to it. Your only chance is now, while she's in the ICU. I will look after Akosua. But I can't look after her, the twins, and the four of them back home. Your mother is too senile to handle any more child-rearing responsibilities and won't be any help."*

*By now, Ben was panic-stricken. He was on board with the adoption of one child, but the thought of kidnapping twins was sounding more preposterous by the minute. "But how can we adopt them so quickly and without the mother's consent? That would amount to kidnapping!"*

*"First of all, you forget, brother, anything is possible if you*

*know the right people or pay the right kind of money on the black market. Secondly, it won't be kidnapping if you have the father's consent. And I am ready to give you mine and forge Akosua's signature. I'll even help you get around the hospital procedures. But only if you're sure you want to do this."*

*Abena felt like her whole world was collapsing. Her mind had become a blank canvas accosted by confused, jumbled thoughts. And yet all she could think was that this catastrophe, this heinous act, this ultimate betrayal, could give her exactly what she had dreamed of having for so long: her own complete little family. She wished it didn't have to come at such a price, but she was tired of waiting for her luck to change. She looked at Ben and recognized the look on his face. It was a look of determination. They both held hands, united in their plans, and turned to Daniel and said, "Let's do it."*

## Cascais, Portugal
### April 2023

When she finished talking, the room went completely quiet. Nothing was said. Not a word. It was only the howling of the wind outside that broke the silence.

Kate was the first to say something. "Wow, Abena, I have no words. I mean, how did you even manage to smuggle Kakra and Panyin to the UK? Weren't you stopped by border control or immigration control? Isn't all of this covered under the Hague Convention?"

"Ghana only became a signatory of the Hague Convention

in 2017; a lot has changed in recent years. But ten to fifteen years ago, it was a different story. It took a while for us to arrange everything. Application forms for an adoption by a close blood relative, forged signatures on all the adoption paperwork, hurried applications for temporary passports for infants. Daniel provided the contacts and we provided the funds."

"So, you … so you basically stole your sister's kids to raise them as your own?" said Fatima, finally finding her voice and barely able to comprehend the story she had just heard.

Abena nodded. "Stole them. Kidnapped them. Fake adopted them. Raised them."

"Wow. But what happened to your sister … Akosua? Did she survive?"

"Yes, Akosua survived. She was hospitalized for about five months. She suffered major nerve damage and short-term memory loss. The trauma of the birth, the medical emergency, and the subsequent complications all took a toll on her health."

"But what did you tell your friends and family back in the UK when you suddenly showed up from Ghana with two babies?" asked Kate.

"We said we had gone to Ghana particularly to adopt a baby, after having been in correspondence with an adoption agency there and initiating the paperwork process. We talked about seeing photos of the newborns and how it was love at first sight. So our friends and family in the UK knew the girls were adopted, but they had no idea they were actually my nieces and that I'd taken them without my sister's knowledge or consent."

"But what did your sister say when she found out her babies were gone? And that her husband had not only known about it, but had encouraged it?" asked Fatima. "Didn't she ever contact you or try to get her girls back?"

Abena was shaking. "It wrecked her. She divorced Daniel. She didn't really have the means to do anything to get them back, even more so after leaving Daniel; she was struggling enough as a single mother … Sometimes I feel like she decided to accept the awful reality because she knew deep down that Daniel was right, that it was for the better … in the best interests of the girls. At least that's what I like to believe." She swallowed hard. "Either way, she blamed me and has refused to speak to me since … and I can't say I blame her. What I did to her was absolutely unforgivable."

She broke down, and Kate and Fatima huddled in close.

"I know you must think I'm a horrible person. I blame myself too. For the longest time, I've been hiding the truth and living in fear. Battling my guilt, hating myself for what I've done, and knowing I can never take Kakra and Panyin back to Ghana. I've been terrified that the adoption papers would be questioned or that my sister would press kidnapping charges against me and try to take the girls back. I can't … I don't know how I would live without them, so I've never taken them back to Accra. Now they're getting older and wonder why I keep bringing up their Ghanaian heritage and roots when I've never taken them back a single time. There's been so much tension in our household since I started the preparations for International Day. The more I push the girls, the harder they resist." She unclasped her charm bracelet and held it up. "This is all I have left of my sister; it was a present from her when I left Ghana originally."

"First, Abena, you've been through a lot," said Kate, "and second, thank you for confiding in us; I can only imagine how nerve-wracking it must've been. But how can we help you? I mean, aside from providing moral and emotional support. Are you even ready to tell the twins the truth about who they are and where they come from?"

"I think that will be my next step. But I need Ben to be on board first. He agreed to me telling you ladies, but I don't know if he'll be so ready to accept that it's time we tell the twins."

"I think it's good to take baby steps," said Fatima. "I'm so glad you told us. Now we can be there for you." She got up to embrace Abena, and a second later, Kate joined them.

When her friends pulled away, it didn't escape Abena's notice how quiet they both were. Fatima looked like she was ready to cry. Kate looked as determined and steely as ever. But Abena could never have guessed how her admission of guilt would touch the lives of her friends and affect the decisions they would make in the coming weeks.

# 26

## FATIMA
*Copenhagen, Denmark*
September 2009

*F*atima had a date tonight and she'd been fretting about
what to wear. He had already seen her in her formal
office attire, so she planned to dress in a more casual yet
feminine style for their first date. All she knew was that Stefan
was taking her to his favorite restaurant to eat smørrebrød.
In the end she opted for the classic Copenhagen combination
for fall—all black, with a hint of lace.

She stepped out to make her way to the restaurant. She
loved Copenhagen at this time of year, with the deciduous
trees producing dazzling displays of earthy ochres, burnt
oranges, and rusty reds. Fall in Copenhagen was crisp like a
ripe Danish apple that's tart and ready to pluck. She watched
in admiration as a few cyclists rode past while she made her
way along Magstræde. They made it look easy, but she knew
from bitter experience that riding a bike on the old
cobblestone streets was not for the fainthearted.

She was pleased to see Stefan waiting for her outside the
restaurant instead of at a table inside. She wanted them to go
in together. He looked much younger out of his work suit, and

*his boyish blue shirt and gray khaki pants gave him a more relaxed vibe.*

*"Hej!" she said, waving from the other side of the road, and when she got to him, she looked into his blue eyes, and they hugged.*

*"Fatima, you look amazing."*

*They went in hand in hand. They said hello to the waiting staff and were led to a little table by the window. Fatima noticed his Danish pronunciation wasn't particularly good, even though he was a native German speaker and many of the words were similar. Obviously he hadn't been taking his Danish lessons seriously. Fatima, on the other hand, had learned to mimic her colleagues at work—she could make all the glottal sounds and speak like she had a hot potato in her mouth.*

*Stefan looked at the menu. "Okay, how about we try a few different types of smørrebrød?"*

*"Sure," said Fatima. "I'll be adventurous tonight." She winked at him.*

*"Okay, I recommend we start with the* Marinerede Sild. *It's a classic combo of marinated herring on rye bread, topped with red onions, brined capers, and fresh herbs."*

*Fatima made a face. "You know I'm not a fan of herring. But tonight I'll keep an open mind."*

*"Just wait, you'll love it. It's usually washed down with a small glass of aquavit. Would you like some?"*

*"Sorry, Stefan, I don't drink alcohol." She waited for his reaction. Western men were invariably put off by the fact she didn't drink. She had already fielded some questions from Danish colleagues at last year's Christmas party. Alcohol was such a big part of life in Denmark that it seemed incom-*

*prehensible to them that she had never touched a drop and wasn't curious to try it. If you told someone in Denmark you didn't drink because you were Muslim or for religious reasons, they would feel uncomfortable, like you'd told them you came from Mars. But the irony was, if you told them you didn't drink because you were a recovering alcoholic, or trying to be healthy, or doing dry October, you'd get a load of winks, endearing looks of support, and encouragement—even applause—for being sober. It would be interesting to see how Stefan reacted.*

*"Oh good," he said, "neither do I."*

*"You don't drink any alcohol?" she asked, checking if he was just being polite.*

*"No, I never really liked the taste. My parents are huge wine connoisseurs, but I was never into it. I used to drink beer occasionally as a teenager, but it was more of a social thing. As an adult, I prefer not to drink any alcohol. I know, I know, not what you'd expect from a German guy, but hey, life is full of surprises." He smiled at her.*

*That was the moment Fatima fell in love with him. It was refreshing to meet a man who was honest and who respected her choices, and who had the courage to make his own choices and not blindly follow social norms for the sake of fitting in. Perhaps they were the perfect match, even though they might stand out as a cross-cultural couple. The world would expect them to be so different based on their different backgrounds, not realizing how alike they were and how much they had in common. It was the perfect plot twist, and she had a sudden rush of unbridled happiness. Not even pickled herring could ruin her mood.*

## *Cascais, Portugal*
## April 2023

Fatima didn't usually take this long to get ready. Stefan was taking her out on a dinner date so they could try one of the neighborhood restaurants they'd had their eye on for some time. It was a little hole-in-the-wall Italian place down the road from them, famous for its handmade pasta. She put on a red lace sweater, then took it off. Too fancy. She was usually such a decisive person, but today she couldn't make up her mind, maybe because her mind was so preoccupied and her thoughts were so jumbled up.

Whether she chose to admit it or not, Abena's confession had really shaken her up. She had admiration for Abena for being so brave and vulnerable to share the story of the twins' adoption, or rather how she took them away from her sister. But it had awoken something inside Fatima, feelings of immense guilt for not having been honest with Stefan from the moment they met in Copenhagen. She'd had more than ten years to tell him the truth, but she never had. And now she regretted it because she had failed to be honest with her partner for life, even though she expected complete honesty from him. At least Ben had known the truth alongside Abena. At least Abena had been able to count on her husband for support. Not so for Fatima.

Also, she was becoming increasingly paranoid. The spooky phone call before the winter holidays, the unsettling feeling of being followed on the streets of Alfama last month, not to mention the sheer torture of Ammi staying with them for months, had all taken their toll, and she had withdrawn into her own little shell. Perhaps Stefan had noticed this. Perhaps that's why earlier that week he had suggested they go out on a Friday date night while Ammi looked after Maya. Ammi never said no to her favorite son-in-law, so here they were.

"Hey, *mein Schatz*, are you ready?" Stefan had his jacket on and looked eager to go.

"Yes, I'm ready," she said, finding it rather endearing he had called her 'my treasure' in German. "We're walking, right? I've put my sensible shoes on."

They said their goodbyes to Maya and Ammi in the lounge and set off along the cobblestone road hand in hand. The sun was setting in São João do Estoril, painting the sky a magnificent purple. Sometimes the pavement narrowed so much they had to walk in single file, and Fatima felt a burst of déja vu.

"Hey, do you remember our first date," she said, "when we walked on the cobblestones in Copenhagen and you forced me to eat weird Danish food?" She laughed, suddenly nostalgic for those simpler, carefree days.

"Yes! And I seem to remember you *did* enjoy it after all." Stefan smiled at the memory of that night.

"I still married you, didn't I?" Fatima linked her arm through his, feeling the warmth of his body.

"It's good to see you smiling. And it's good to go out— just us for a change. I feel like since your mom arrived, you've been so distant."

So, he had noticed. "I want to say *I told you so* but I'll bite my tongue because I don't want to spoil my mood."

"Look, I know it's not been easy having her here," said Stefan, "and I know coming home to find your entire kitchen has been rearranged and receiving endless unsolicited advice has driven you up the wall. But the other day I even overheard you arguing with her. And what did you mean when you said to her 'I was just a child'? What were you talking about?"

Fatima picked up her pace. She didn't want to lie to Stefan again but she wasn't sure she was ready to tell him the truth either. "Can we please not talk about Ammi on our date? I thought you were taking me out to get my mind off of her, which is hard to do if we keep talking about her. I really need a break!"

"Sure," he said. "I get it."

Their dinner at the little Italian place was pleasant. It was a tiny restaurant with space for ten tables; just as well they had made a reservation. The ate their way through bruschetta with anchovies, pappardelle pasta with mushrooms and truffles, and ended on a sweet note with pistachio cheesecake.

Afterwards, full to the max, Stefan suggested a little digestive walk on the *paredão*. The evenings were starting to get balmy and it was more than pleasant enough for a stroll.

"Hey, Fatima, promise me you'll tell me if there's something upsetting you, okay?"

Damn it, she said to herself. Stefan wasn't going to let this go. "Why do you say that?"

"I can't help but notice how different you've been these past few months," he said. "Quiet, broody, lost in your own thoughts half the time."

"Have I? I'm sorry. I guess it's been a massive transition

year for us, with everything going wrong from the moment I had that car accident at school with Kate."

"Fatima, were you ever involved in a car accident before the one at the school?"

"No, I wasn't. Well, actually, yes, I was, a long time ago, but that's not the point."

"For God's sake, can you just be honest with me. I'm getting really frustrated; you're obviously not telling me the full truth. I'm your husband, Fatima, but lately I feel like I barely know you. We never make love; you're never in the mood. You're constantly on edge. And then I overhear you fighting with Ammi. And I wonder what happened in your childhood. Please don't keep secrets from me, no matter how bad it was or how long ago it was."

"Look, I've been trying to leave it all behind, and unearthing everything would not only bring back my darkest demons, it would change everything between us."

Stefan went quiet, and Fatima's panic gave in to his brooding silence. She knew she couldn't risk alienating him, not now, especially not now. She needed him on her side more than ever. But would he still be on her side when he found out the truth? She shrugged and walked on, but the memory of Abena's confession came back to her. How brave she had been to share the ghastly truth about what she had done. Could Fatima be that brave and finally confide in Stefan? What if he hated her or resented her? But what if it brought them closer and he felt even more protective of her? What if she finally had an ally to stand up to Ammi with her? What if she finally felt some relief at unburdening herself to her husband?

"You'll hate me," she said.

"No, I won't."

"It'll change *everything* between us."

"Only if we let it."

"You'll be hurt I didn't tell you earlier."

"I'll be hurt if you don't tell me today."

Fatima realized it was now or never. She turned to Stefan, looked him in the eye, and finally confessed.

# 27

# FATIMA
*Karachi, Pakistan*
August 1996

*A* wedding would often announce itself in subtle ways.
*Many* months before the festivities began, the closets
would start to fill with shopping bags full of embroidered
clothes fetched from the tailor, the kitchen would brim with
trays of dates packed in little silk pouches ready to be
distributed after the nuptials, and the coffee table would be
stacked high with a pile of invitations waiting to be hand
delivered to friends and family. And now, the many layers of
delicate and ruffled petals of the fiery orange-yellow
marigolds bathed the garden of Fatima's grandmother in a
warm glow. The garden was filled with family members
sipping cardamom chai from old teacups, twinkling fairy
lights were draped on the outdoor façade of the house, half the
lounge was taken over by ladies getting henna drawn on their
hands in intricate designs, and there was a steady stream of
relatives walking in and out of every room.

It was still one week before the wedding, but tonight the

*bride's family was hosting the* dholki, *and the sound of the* dhol *was drowning out most of the conversations. The women of the family were dressed in predominantly yellow or green and sat on crisp white sheets with yellow* gao-tukiye *as floor cushions for back support as they sang their favorite wedding tunes. Outside, the tandoor was on, and the smoky flavors of chicken tikka and seekh kebabs drifted through the air as they were turned back and forth on the grill. A mint yogurt dip was whisked up while the fresh naan was baked in another tandoor. The men sat outside in the garden in starched white shalwar kameezes and smoked while they chatted about politics and cricket.*

*Fatima's cousin Abiha was the first to get married on her mother's side of the family, and her grandparents and aunt and uncle were throwing the most lavish wedding, as if to set the tone for the rest of the marriages in the family to come. But as she sat cross-legged on the floor, waiting for her turn to get her henna applied, a familiar feeling of dread took over Fatima's tiny body.*

*Fatima used to believe in fairy tales: Prince Charming, good conquering evil, the happy ever afters. But now, at eleven years old, she knew better. Evil came to her in the middle of the night. Slowly at first, creeping, like the literal thief in the night, then more forceful, more demanding.*

*She looked up nervously at Ammi sitting across from her in the lounge, who was still not talking to her. Fatima had struggled with immense guilt, then shame, then more guilt, until she had finally decided to confide in her mother a few months ago. Telling Ammi had been Fatima's last course of action, but it had backfired on her completely. Her courage had been met with a stinging slap across her face.*

*"How dare you accuse your uncle of something like that! Your Ali Mamoo has brought you up, he moved in with us and has been like a father to you ever since your own father passed away so suddenly. We owe so much to him. Where did you hear such horrible stories? What are you thinking, making things like this up? We are a respectable family. What will people say if they hear you make such baseless accusations?"*

*So now Fatima knew she was on her own. Her own mother didn't believe her—or protect her.*

*Her cousin Sarah came bouncing towards her, eager to show off her henna design, and Fatima pretended to be interested in the paisley on her palm. And then someone else took her hand, and Fatima, too startled to say anything, refused to look up.*

*It was him. She could smell him before she saw him—that distinct smell of cigarettes and aftershave.*

*Ali Mamoo, her mother's younger brother, exclaimed, "Oh, but your hands are still bare—no henna on them yet? Perhaps you can come and help me with something upstairs." He straightened his green kurta and smiled, except underneath that smile, Fatima knew this was not a request but an order.*

*She got up without a word and followed him out of the lounge and into an upstairs guest bedroom full of wedding paraphernalia spread out on the double bed. He had never dared to touch her outside of their house, but he had been getting bolder and bolder because he had been able to get away with it for so long, and tonight he had decided no one would notice their absence amidst the full house and the dholki festivities. He didn't even bother locking the door anymore. She used to fight back in the beginning, but now she looked away with a defeated sense of indifference. He unbuttoned the back of her blouse and was about to undress her completely when the door flung open and Ammi marched in.*

*There was a moment of deafening silence. Ammi fiddled with her dupatta, trying to understand what she had just walked in on.*

*"What the hell is going on in here?"*

*"Nothing, Baji." Ali Mamoo had turned around to face his older sister and used the respectful form of address.*

*"Fatima?"*

*Fatima turned to Ammi, tears streaming down her face. But she refused to say a word. This time, she would let her mother reach her own conclusions.*

*Ammi found her voice. "Khuda key liye! Ali, in the name of God, what are you doing with Fatima? I can hardly believe my eyes! I saw you come into the lounge to look at her henna and then watched her go upstairs with you. Fatima told me, but I refused to believe it. Until now that I see it with my own eyes!"*

*"Baji, it is not what you think." Ali Mamoo stepped forward with his hands clasped together in front of him, pleading to his big sister for understanding.*

*"Then what is it, Ali? Answer me right now. What are you doing here alone with Fatima? Why were you unbuttoning her blouse? Do you think I'm an idiot?"*

*"She enjoys it," he said, and he smirked.*

*Ammi raised her hand and slapped her brother across his right cheek with full force. Before he could recover, she yelled at him. "I cannot believe it! You are my brother. Her uncle!"*

*She grabbed Fatima, quickly helped her to put on her sparkly silver sandals, and with her face red and full of rage and fury, she turned back to him and shouted, "I am leaving. I am taking Fatima and I am going home. Do not dare to follow us. You do not live with us anymore. I will throw your things outside. I do not care where you live from now on. But you will not step one foot into my house again!"*

*Fatima hurried to keep up with her mother. Tears were streaming down her face, but she remained silent. Ammi rushed out of the dholki without a word to anyone, and she and Fatima got into their car. Their driver, Muhammad, surprised to see them leaving so early, asked if everything was okay, and she responded curtly that everything was fine, putting the blame on Fatima not feeling well, and asked him to drive them home.*

*Ammi squeezed Fatima's hand and gave her a look. Ammi knew they couldn't speak openly in the car, or they could only speak in English as Muhammad didn't understand English, but as soon as they were home, Ammi would unleash her full scorn and fury—in Urdu and English.*

*The white gate was opened and Muhammad prepared to pull into the driveway, but before he could, there was an almighty crash as another car hit them from behind.*

*Everything went still.*

*When Fatima opened her eyes, she wasn't sure if ten minutes had passed or ten hours. She sat there in the back seat, shocked and numb, wondering if it was all a bad dream that she would wake up from any second, that maybe her mind was now playing tricks on her. But then she saw the smashed window, and right at that moment, she knew that evil most definitely existed; it had a face, and she was looking straight at it.*

*There he was.*

*Ali Mamoo.*

*He had hit their car in a fit of rage, and now he stood there with a look of utter hatred.*

*To Fatima it was the face of the devil. But before she could do or say anything, Ammi grabbed her. They got out of the car and ran into the house, and Ali Mamoo followed them inside.*

*"Have you totally lost your mind?" Ammi screamed at him, "jamming your car into ours? Are you trying to kill us, Ali?" She took off her jewelry and flung her dupatta across the lounge.*

*"It was the only way to get your attention. I had to follow you here before you shut me out."*

*"How could you do this to us? I have cared for you like a mother instead of an older sister."*

*"Oh please. You are so selfish, only out for your own gain. All you've ever cared about is maintaining appearances in front of others. You've never really cared about Fatima or me."*

*"How dare you. How dare you!"*

*"How dare I what?"*

*"How dare you touch my Fatima. You … you make me sick."*

*"Oh, I make you sick? Well, how about I tell you how much Fatima enjoyed my attention. Because God knows, you don't give her any. You don't give her any love, any attention, any praise—nothing."*

*"So you decided to give all this to her? How noble of you—wah, wah!" She mocked him with applause.*

*"She enjoyed it!"*

*"She's eleven years old!"*

*"I know. But I love her, and I'll fight for her if I have to."*

*He lunged at Ammi with a knife. Reacting quicker than*

*the adults, Fatima grabbed the knife and stabbed it into his foot. He screamed out in pain, blood already beginning to ooze from the force of the knife, and before he could react, Ammi grabbed a vase and smashed it over his head. He fell, hitting his head on the coffee table, and lay still. They waited, but there was no movement, no sound other than their own breathing, and they stared down at the crumpled body, the pieces of shattered glass, and the pool of crimson blood.*

*When she was sure it was safe, Ammi looked over at Fatima, her eyes ablaze with terror, and said firmly, "Do exactly as I say."*

*Fatima nodded, too scared to speak. There were no words left in her mind anyway. She felt pain and looked down at her left arm and saw blood and a deep red gash. From a piece of broken vase? She didn't know, she wasn't sure.*

*FATIMA WAS TOO groggy to remember what time it was. Or how long she'd been sitting there on the floor nursing her left arm. She'd looked up to see Ammi bringing in Muhammad. His shocked reaction. The exchange of rupee notes. She'd watched him wrap up Ali Mamoo's body in Ammi's red Persian carpet. Transport it into the trunk of the car. And now Ammi's directions are clear: "Drive out to the Indus Delta. Leave the body there in the mangroves. Don't come back for a few days."*

*Muhammad would not look at Ammi or at Fatima but instead looked up to the heavens and prayed. "Yaa Allah, please forgive me." Then he unclasped his hands, and he was gone.*

*Fatima imagined him driving into the interior of Sindh, far into the Indus River and delta. When you drove two hours out of Karachi, you found the remoteness and desolation of the mangroves, and she pictured him dumping the body in a remote creek and covering it with leaves.*

*When she saw Muhammad one week later, he said nothing. But as his hands reached for the steering wheel of the car on their way to school, she noticed the giant blisters.*

*Their scars would forever bind them in silence.*

## Cascais, Portugal
## April 2023

Stefan slumped onto a bench in the *paredão* in shock and disbelief. He looked down, he looked up, he looked out to the ocean, but what he couldn't do was bring himself to look Fatima in the eye.

"I'm sorry, Stefan," she was telling him. "I'm sorry I didn't tell you earlier. I was too ashamed. Too guilty. Too weak. Too insecure. Too confused. Too angry. Too vulnerable. Too unworthy. I know this changes everything between us, but I hated you not knowing. Now I hate myself for dragging you into this mess."

He finally met her gaze. "This is a *lot* to digest, Fatima. Sexual abuse, murder in self-defense … I hardly know where to start. One thing is for sure—you didn't deserve what happened to you. For God's sake, you were an innocent victim of a power-play between two power-hungry adults whose primary job was to protect you. I wish you had trusted me and told me earlier. I would've made sure Ammi was never invited here if that's what would bring you peace after all these years. But I still don't get it. Why would she blame you?"

"It's more complicated than that. Ammi is a product of her own conservative upbringing in a predominantly patriarchal society, where the woman is automatically to blame for drawing attention to herself. Ammi has never stopped blaming me for what happened when I was eleven, even though I was a child. She has been holding this against me, and it was she who told me I should never tell you because you would leave me right away if you knew I was 'damaged goods.' She has been determined to tell lie after lie to keep our sordid family history buried away and hidden from prying eyes. That's all she cares about ultimately: keeping up appearances and protecting the reputation of our family. And there's something else I should probably tell you ..."

"What's that?"

"The way Ali Mamoo initially gained my trust was by telling me the truth about my father's death. He died when I was only six years old, and I barely remember him. He was always working late evenings and traveled a lot for work to promote his textile and garments business. He started having business troubles, and fears of bankruptcy eventually drove him to commit suicide. Ammi couldn't bear the thought of anyone finding out, especially as suicide is a big taboo in Islam, so she covered it up by saying he had died of a heart attack. Only Ali Mamoo knew the truth because she had confided in him and asked him for help in taking over the family business."

"Oh. My. God. How come you never told me?"

"I learned how to suppress the truth from such a young age. I too was shocked when I found out. I was only ten. He only told me to gain my trust, and sadly it worked. It also drove this huge wedge between me and Ammi because then I stopped trusting her."

"Did you ever confront Ammi with the truth about your dad?"

"Of course I did, and what do you think happened? She blasted me and refused to apologize or acknowledge that she'd hidden the truth from me and from everyone else. She was even upset with Ali Mamoo for telling me."

Not for the first time, Stefan shook his head in disbelief. "Talk about dysfunctional family dynamics."

"Tell me about it. One thing is clear: Ali was our savior. He turned the family business around thanks to his business acumen, and we owed everything to him. Ammi couldn't stop singing his praises. For far too long, I remained silent because I didn't want the 'fairytale' to come crashing down. When I finally did break down and muster up the courage to confess to Ammi about the abuse, she refused to believe me—because she didn't want to believe that our family savior was also my abuser. She doubted me for months, said I'd made it all up to seek attention. You can't imagine how desperate, how alone I felt. I knew I should be grateful to him for saving our family but God how I despised him."

Stefan squeezed Fatima's hand. "I can't even begin to imagine what you've been through. I'm so proud of you for speaking up. Trauma like that doesn't go away if you hide it."

"But the self-hate and self-loathing still haven't gone away. Sometimes the thirty-seven-year-old me still weeps for the eleven-year-old me. I wish I could go back and give her a hug and tell her it would all be okay."

Stefan put his arm around his wife. "I love you and I'm here for you." He thought of another question. "There's one thing I still don't get: how did you both explain his sudden disappearance? Surely your extended family and friends asked where Ali was?"

"Ammi took care of all that. She concocted a convincing story of how Ali took off under mysterious circumstances and, of course, painted herself as the victim. The disappearance of her brother still left a stain on that perfect family picture, which was difficult for Ammi to accept, but still, it was a small price to pay for the ridicule, shame, and dishonor the real story would have produced. She was always more ashamed of the sexual abuse than she was of the murder! Of course, in the end she always blamed me and has been holding it as leverage over me ever since."

Fatima nuzzled deep into Stefan's shoulder. She felt a strange sense of calm now that her husband knew the ugly truth about her. She wanted him not to see her as a victim of child sexual abuse but as a survivor.

"The thing is," she said, "abuse is never contained in that present moment; it lingers on. Sometimes the flashbacks are so real in my head I can literally feel him on top of me and smell his breath and wake up and be trying to push him off. And this is years after. And now Ammi staying with us for so long has brought all the long-buried trauma back for me, the nightmares, the paranoia—it's all back. I even thought I was being followed in Alfama one day after my Portuguese lesson."

Stefan had tears in his eyes. "*Mein Schatz*, your healing journey begins today. You took a big step in telling me. This is our breakthrough moment. In hindsight, a few things are starting to make sense."

"What do you mean?"

"At the beginning of our marriage, you were nervous to be intimate with me. I thought it was because of your strict upbringing, the conservative culture, where discussions around sex are not discussed or encouraged, only expected after marriage. But it was more than that, wasn't it? The sexual abuse, the molestation you experienced as a young kid. I wish I'd known. I'm so sorry. I'm beginning to finally understand you better now. Things will get better from now on, I promise. But have you never confronted Ammi with how you feel?"

"No, never. I don't know, I suppose … I feel like she has this power over me. The truth is, I've never had the courage to stand up to Ammi directly. So I've tried to rebel in other ways: moving abroad, marrying you, marrying outside of my culture …"

"Wait a minute, what do you mean? You only married me to spite your mother?"

"No, of course not. I love you and want to be with you. But what happened is also a part of me, and I honestly don't know where I'd be or who I'd be with if it hadn't happened. I guess everyone reacts to abuse differently. In a way, my awful experiences made me stronger, made me grow up more quickly than others. Ironically, the abuse has made me the person I am today. It made me determined to leave Karachi as soon as I could and move abroad and live my own independent life. It led to me meeting you, which has been the best thing that has ever happened to me. I think that's why it's taken me so long to tell you. I didn't want to mess up the one great relationship I've had in my life. But not telling you was slowly eating me up from the inside. The guilt has been crippling."

"So what made you confide in me finally?"

"Actually, it was Abena."

"Abena?"

"She recently opened up to me and Kate about her twins being adopted. Her strength and courage inspired me to do the same. I'm so sick of hiding the truth. Running away from my own sordid past by constantly moving to a new country has never brought me the closure I was so desperately searching for. Facing my fears and acknowledging my story and confiding in you was the right thing to do all along. I'm just sorry it took me so long to realize it."

"Don't be sorry. I wish I had known earlier, but I'm glad you've told me now. I have your back now, okay?"

The words she had long wanted to hear from her mother had finally been uttered by her husband instead. Things would only get better from this moment on. She was sure of it.

# 28

# KATE
*Lisbon, Portugal*
April 2023

K ate sat twiddling her thumbs in her office. She was still in a state of shock. Ambassador Hill accepting her invitation to be a chief guest at the school's International Day was the last thing she'd expected. She had assumed he'd be way too busy to attend or that the event wouldn't be prestigious enough or big enough to warrant his presence in an official capacity. But no. The ambassador had said his team had recommended an "image makeover," and that included more visibility and less pomp and ceremony. Officiating a day celebrating diversity at an international school was exactly the type of event that would encourage him to meet parents and educators and pose with children. It was the perfect opportunity.

Kate knew Abena would be thrilled. She'd been thinking about how their friendship had propelled Abena to confess to her and Fatima. But Kate wasn't so easily convinced. Yes, her friendship with the girls was precious, but unlike Abena, Kate couldn't afford to confide in her friends. If anything, Abena's confession reminded Kate of how much she had to lose if the truth ever came out, and it made her even more determined to keep her guard up and protect her past.

She checked her watch. It was time for the next therapy session with Dr. Teixeira, and Michael was picking her up so they could drive there together. She started packing up her bag. Her phone pinged. It was an email from Ambassador Hill. It was blank apart from the subject line: "The internal investigation is continuing. Let's discuss a plan of action tomorrow."

*Shit. This is really happening.*

So the State Department wasn't giving up easily. Not until they'd fully investigated the matter, talked to Maryanne, and drawn their own conclusions. She'd also had a message from Michael that he was only ten minutes away, and there was a WhatsApp message from her new BFF Patricia. Ugh. That woman would not leave her alone. It read:

> **Patricia**
> Hey Kate. Guess what? Remember the Martin family from Singapore? They're interested in moving to Portugal too. They're coming on a scouting trip next month. I've invited them to International Day. They're keen to check out the school. Maybe we can all catch up for coffee there?

Kate closed the message with an exaggerated tap of her phone. It was like the walls were closing in on her, like everyone wanted a piece of her: Ambassador Hill, the State Department, Michael, Dr. Teixeira, Patricia ....

She liked to keep her worlds separate. It was one of the things she loved most about expat life: the anonymity that came with moving to a new country where no one knew who you were. The blank canvas. The chance to start from scratch again. To not repeat the same mistakes—to have the chance to make new ones instead. But now it seemed all her worlds were colliding: Singapore, the US, Portugal, work, family, school, friends. It was like being pushed into a cage she didn't want to be in.

When Michael picked her up a few minutes later, she got in and slammed the car door. "Why on earth did you suggest I apply for this damn role in Portugal?"

"What's going on? Are you blaming something else on me now?" said Michael, not best pleased at being greeted with an accusation.

"We should have known how bloody popular Portugal has become with Americans. It seems like half of the US is moving here overnight. We should never have moved here!"

"So, this is my fault too? Geez, Kate, you give me way too much credit. It was merely a suggestion from my end. You're the one who lobbied so hard to get here."

"And now it's all coming back to haunt me. The State Department is launching a full investigation into Maryanne's allegations." Her bottom lip was quivering. She bit it to prevent the tears from streaming down her face.

"You're not going to lose your job," he said gently.

"It could get even uglier. They could disbar me from ever serving again. I could go to jail! Do you get that?" She was getting hysterical.

"Look, we're almost there. You really need to calm down."

"What, so I can lie some more in our therapy session?"

"Kate. Please. Don't let your anger and frustration affect our marriage counseling. We discussed this. We have to be a team, remember? For Eric's sake?"

She didn't answer, but the mention of Eric brought back the guilt, the immense guilt about letting her son down.

"YOU SEEM QUITE preoccupied, Kate," remarked Dr. Teixeira half an hour into their session.

"I have a lot on my mind, that's all."

"Would you care to share what's on your mind?"

"Let me," said Michael. "Basically she would love to blame me for all her problems."

"Well, it IS your fault we're living in Portugal." Kate was tired of beating around the bush.

"This marriage is never going to work if you blame *everything* on me, Kate. You've made some mistakes too. How about you own up to that? Oh no, no, we can't have that. Kate is perfect, Kate is innocent." Michael was spitting out his words like he had a nasty taste in his mouth. "Only I'm to blame, and I'm the one who needs to change. As usual, the onus is on me to change!"

"I need both of you to calm down," said Melissa calmly. "Blaming each other and hurling accusations is never productive. In fact, it's counterproductive. Now, Kate, is there something you're not telling me? Did anything else happen in Singapore I need to know about?"

For one brief second, Kate imagined telling her the truth. Not about Singapore, but about Houston. To see how Melissa's face would contort with confusion and shock. What would she say? But the moment passed.

"Look, there's nothing more to say or do or to tell you. I think you know enough. But I also think these sessions are turning out to be a waste of time and money because instead of moving forward, all we do is keep re-hashing the past. And it's exhausting. I'm exhausted. And it's affecting our son. Eric is *not* okay. And I feel guilty as hell, and the worst mother in the world, and I don't know how to stop this train-wreck!"

"I feel like you're giving up because things are hard," said Melissa. "No one said this would be easy, but you and Michael both committed to working together. And now I can sense your commitment wavering. What I want is for both of you to take some time out—to reflect—to decide if you would like to continue working on your marriage with me or not. But this has to be a properly thought-out decision. Personally, I feel we have made some important headway, but I need full commitment from you both. Take a couple of weeks to think about it. Think about Eric. You know where to reach me." She closed her notebook, got up, and showed them the door.

It was another awkward walk to the car for Kate and Michael. He went to put his arm in hers but she gave him a look that said don't.

Once they were in the car, Kate turned to him. "I'm sorry. This is too hard. I don't know where to go from here." Her eyes filled with tears.

"Honey, this is a setback. We need to stick together and we'll be fine." He sounded as tired as she did.

"I wish … I wish I'd never kept that newspaper clipping to begin with. Look at what damage it's caused us."

"Kate, we know why you kept it. It was a commemorative tribute to Carla Mosely, your favorite history teacher and mentor."

"She was the only one who believed in me all throughout high school. Ms. Mosely was the first teacher who encouraged me to think about applying for the foreign service and helped me write my college admission essay for Mount Holyoke. She was so thrilled when I got my acceptance letter. More thrilled than my parents were. She even brought a cake to school to celebrate."

"I'm glad you had someone like her in your corner."

"Mom and Dad always looked at her suspiciously because they knew how close we were, and they saw how traumatized I was by her death. Then at a family barbecue months after her death, they saw the *Houston Chronicle* article highlighting the 'Carla Mosely Grant for International Relations' set up by my high school in her honor. They thought it would give me some kind of comfort and closure. But they never knew the full story. They never knew it wasn't the grief that was eating me up from the inside, it was the guilt." Tears engulfed her.

"I know. Come here." Michael hugged her, and she allowed herself to feel his familiar warmth before pulling away.

"I know I haven't been the easiest person to be with lately," she said, "but I want to thank you for not shunning me when I told you the truth. We weren't even married then. You could have broken up with me when you learned the awful reality, but you didn't. You could've turned me in, but you didn't. I can't tell you how much that meant to me, and has meant to me over the years. You are the only person in my life that I have ever been completely honest with. Listen, you go ahead and drive back to Lisbon. I really need to clear my head. I'll take the boat back."

Michael looked at her like she might need protecting from herself. "Are you sure?"

She was already walking away. "Yes, I'm sure."

A few minutes later she boarded the boat that would ferry her from Almada to Lisbon. It cost less than two euros and took just ten minutes, making it the fastest and cheapest way to cross the Tagus River. She looked out at the water, and the gentle rhythm of the waves and the salty sea air transported her to a different time and place.

## Galveston, Texas
## July 1999

*Kate looked out to the island city of Galveston on the Gulf coast of Texas as the boat rocked back and forth in the calm waters of the Gulf of Mexico. Galveston was a popular escape for Houstonians in the summer, and her senior class at high school had decided it would be the perfect spot to celebrate the end of term and high school graduation. Someone had handed Kate a red plastic cup, but she couldn't bring herself to take a sip of the beer. She'd sworn the night before that she would never touch alcohol again, and she meant it.*

*It was the morning after the accident, and her memory was still blurry. She'd been driving home from her friend Melissa's house after an evening of partying. She'd had a bit too much to drink, and at eighteen years of age, that wasn't legal. Neither was driving while under the influence. Either could have landed her in jail. But it had gotten late. Eager to get home, she sped over Highway 6 before turning right on Lexington Boulevard.*

*That's where it happened. Instead of stopping at the stop sign, she sped through. A blue Ford was coming through the intersection, and when Kate didn't stop as expected, the driver turned the steering wheel sharply to avoid a collision and hit a large oak tree by the side of the road.*

*Fragmented pieces of her memory came back to her: the screech of the tires, the giant thud as the Ford crashed into the tree, the complete silence that followed. Here, her memory stopped, as if someone had erased what had happened next.*

*Did she step out and check on the driver of the blue Ford? Did she call 911? Did she scream for help? The reason Kate couldn't remember was because she had done none of these things. At eighteen, with her head clouded by alcohol, she had feared a drunk driving charge and panicked. She'd committed multiple felonies, any of which could land her in jail. She simply fled the scene without bothering to check if the driver or passengers in the blue Ford pickup were alright. Her car had no physical damage and was unblemished.*

*And now here she was on a boat in Galveston with her senior graduating class, pretending all was fine.*

*When she finally returned to Sugar Land that evening, she caught sight of the Houston Chronicle on the kitchen counter, left by her dad in its usual pristine state. She dropped her backpack on the floor and casually flipped it around only to see the headline:*

*"ACCIDENT ON LEXINGTON AVENUE CLAIMS ONE"*

*The color drained from her face and the house keys crashed to the floor. She looked back at the article, her brain struggling to make sense of the words.*

*"Driver Carla Mosely, aged 49, a teacher at Clements High School, was transported by an ambulance to the Houston Methodist Sugar Land Hospital, where she passed away within the hour."*

*She felt sick to her stomach and threw up on the kitchen floor.*

*"Kate, honey, is that you?" her mother called from upstairs. "How was the boat party?"*

*"Umm, not so well, Mom. I got a bit seasick. In fact, I just threw up." She grabbed a kitchen towel to clean up the mess.*

*"Oh, you poor darling! I'm coming down ..."*

*Kate put the newspaper back on the kitchen counter and finished clearing up.*

*LATER THAT DAY, Kate cut out the news clipping and hid it in her little red box. She imagined sitting in a court room and pleading guilty. She imagined her offer of admission being revoked from Mount Holyoke College. She imagined never being able to study journalism or International Relations. Never being able to travel. Never choosing her dream career in the foreign service. She imagined sitting behind bars. She imagined prison life.*

*The guilt was crippling. She was responsible for the death of her favorite teacher, her mentor. The only one who had believed in her. It was too awful to share with anyone, and she would never confide in her parents. How could she? This was one secret she would have to keep buried forever. And so it became her motivation to join the Foreign Service, to give back to her country as Carla had encouraged her to do. Her need to serve was born primarily through her overwhelming guilt and her penitence—to make amends for her unspeakable crime. She had failed in her civic duty on the day of the accident, but from now on she would make her civic duty the focal point of her education and career. This was one promise she would keep.*

*The next week, she made an appointment at a tattoo parlor in town, and when she left Texas that summer, there was a tattoo on the inner wrist of her left hand: the Chinese symbol for truth etched onto her skin in two syllables, a powerful reminder of her promise to herself.*

# 29

## FATIMA
*Cascais, Portugal*
May 2023

The sun was shining brightly when Fatima woke up that morning. It was May, and the Jacarandas were starting to bloom all over town. All things seemed possible. She had always loved May, her birthday month, but this year it held a particular promise of peace for her. And the best part was, she hadn't had the nightmare last night; her mind was clear and free. She sat up in bed, thinking about all those late-night conversations she'd had with Stefan as they worked through everything to come to a place of renewed trust. And there he was, still in his pajamas, coming up the stairs with her coffee.

"Here you go, *mein Schatz*." He was carrying her favorite white mug with the letter 'F' in Urdu printed on it in black.

She loved it when he made German-style filter coffee for her in the morning. She'd choose it over a fancy latte any day. She looked up and smiled at him. "Thanks, honey, you're the best."

"Enjoy. Gotta go down and help Maya with her homework." He gave her a quick kiss on her forehead and dashed downstairs.

Normally she loved sipping coffee in bed over a lazy weekend, each sip awakening her senses till she felt ready to start her day, and Stefan and Maya both knew to leave her well alone until she'd had her morning coffee. But today Fatima climbed out of bed and made her way to the balcony and sat on one of the white wicker chairs. Past the neighbors' aquamarine pool and the skyline of pine trees, she could see the glistening sea. She never tired of the view but today she felt liberated by it, emboldened by it. This was it, a chance to finally live her life on her own terms.

Since her 'confession,' she and Stefan had been working hard on their marriage, through constant and careful communication. They'd created a safe space for each of them to express their emotions and feelings without blame, and it had brought them closer than ever before. Stefan finally understood Fatima, and she was grateful that this 'thing' that happened to her no longer defined her. She *was* capable of having a loving relationship with a man who made her feel loved and safe.

She thought about Abena and Kate. In the past few weeks, she and Abena had met regularly, and through talking and sharing openly, they'd grown closer. They had leaned on each other for moral support and comfort, and they felt supported by each other. Of course, she hadn't told Abena the full story about the sexual abuse, and at times she felt a pang of guilt for not baring her soul the way Abena had done. But she'd talked about her difficult relationship with her mother, and how the extended visit had been testing her.

Kate, on the other hand, had grown distant, broody, and quiet. She seemed to be avoiding them, with one excuse after another for not being able to meet up, and she had skipped the last two Portuguese lessons. Fatima was concerned, but at that moment she had her hands full with preparation for International Day, which was now just one day away.

*Cascais, Portugal*

May 2023

One day later

Fatima came down to the kitchen as her mother was layering the *biryani*. First, Ammi covered the pot with a layer of fluffy white basmati rice and then came a layer of the aromatic chicken korma with cinnamon sticks, star anise, and cardamom. *Layering a biryani, burying her family secrets under a veneer of respectability.* She mixed some saffron with milk in a separate glass to dilute it before pouring it onto the layered biryani. *Diluting the saffron, diluting the truth. Ammi had enough experience of both.* Finally, she topped the biryani with onions that had been fried golden brown, sprinkled on some freshly cut coriander, and adding a few lemon wedges on top before putting it in the oven for the finishing touch. *The last step, the camouflage—in the kitchen and in life.* It was then she finally looked up and saw Fatima.

"All done, *beta*," she said with a look of satisfaction. "Now it needs to be in the oven for fifteen to twenty minutes." She took off her apron.

"Thank you for your help, Ammi." Fatima was careful to express her gratitude so she wouldn't be blamed for not being thankful enough for everything Ammi had done. In truth, Ammi had made herself indispensable over the last few weeks. She had meticulously planned the food menu for the Pakistani stall, done most of the grocery shopping, and taken care of the lion's share of cooking. Fatima knew that Ammi enjoyed showing off her culinary skills, and this had been an opportunity too good to let go.

"Help? I don't think you could have done it without me, Fatima," said Ammi, washing her hands at the sink. "Isn't it a good thing that my visit coincides with your International Day?"

She had crossed the line, as usual, and this time Fatima wouldn't let it go. Emboldened by Stefan and his trust in her, she knew it was time to finally speak up.

"Actually, Ammi, I've been wondering when I should tell you." She faced her mother head-on, hands on hips.

"Tell me what?" said Ammi, drying her hands with a kitchen towel.

"Stefan knows."

"Stefan knows what?"

"He knows *everything*. I told him *everything*."

Ammi stared at her for a moment, her face frozen in horror, then put down the towel. "You foolish girl!"

"Actually, it's the smartest decision I've ever made. And I wish I'd done it earlier. But better late than never, right? Because Stefan loves me and supports me, even after finding out about what I suffered and what we did. And for the first time in my life, I feel free. I've not had a single nightmare since I told him. Every night, we talk and share our feelings and really listen to each other. We're a stronger team now. More than ever before."

Ammi stared at her, momentarily lost for words, as if she didn't quite know how to react to a confident Fatima. But Fatima wasn't done and moved closer until she was standing barely an inch away from her mother.

"You know what this means, Ammi? You don't 'own' me anymore. It has taken me twenty-six years to finally confide in someone other than you. Someone who believed me—instantly. Someone who didn't doubt me, or blame me, or guilt me, or shame me."

"Fatima, I never blamed you—"

"*Yes you did!* You acted like it was *all* my fault."

"He was my brother. I trusted him with my life. I didn't want to believe the worst about him."

"No," she hollered, "you'd rather believe the worst about me—your own flesh and blood. Do you have *any* idea what this did to me?"

Ammi opened her mouth to say something, but Fatima wasn't having any of it.

"I was in pain. *Pain.* I'm still in pain. You didn't hear me. You didn't see me. I felt invisible. You know … I felt like I had no father or mother. You didn't protect me. You never explained anything to me. I had no clue about men or their advances. I thought his advances were all my fault. I actually felt guilty … *guilty* … because your brother, my uncle, decided I was a convenient distraction for him. How dare you! How dare you just leave me to deal with his sick advances on my own. I tried to tell you … I told you and begged you to believe me. Can you imagine how abandoned I felt? You are my mother. You are supposed to protect *me.*

Do you have any idea … do you have any idea about the trauma I've been carrying with me ever since? So much childhood trauma that a minor car accident on Maya's first day of school derailed me. Did you ever stop to think what this had done to your innocent little eleven-year-old? Did you ever offer to seek therapy or counseling for me to help process the trauma? Did you ever assure me that none of this was my fault? That I wasn't broken. Or damaged." Fatima knew she was shouting and ranting and rambling, but it felt good to let all her bottled-up rage spill out. "Shame on you, Ammi! For twenty-six years I have carried this burden around with me, no matter where I went. I never had the strength to tell you what you did to me. Yes, I hated Ali Mamoo, but I think I hate you even more!"

Fatima was done. And as Ammi stood there, lost for words, Fatima started to pack all the prepared food into containers for International Day. Once done, she took the biryani out of the oven, packed it into a takeaway container, and placed everything into a large grocery bag.

"Now, we'll be late getting to the school," she said calmly. "We have a show to put on today. And God knows you excel at that. But once we're back, we need to have a serious word about your departure from Portugal. You have overstayed your welcome. I want you gone."

Ammi was breathless with rage. She wasn't used to being spoken to so directly by her own daughter. But when Maya and Stefan came down ready to go, and the whole family marched out of the door, Ammi followed them without saying a word.

Fatima smiled at Stefan. "Give me the keys," she said. "I'm driving."

And she set off for International Day, determined and focused. So focused, in fact, that she didn't notice the small black car pulling out behind her.

# 30

# FATIMA
*Cascais, Portugal*
May 2023

Fatima barely recognized the football field at Maya's school. The goalposts had been removed and dozens of stalls had been set up under white tents that flapped in the breeze, each featuring a country and its flag. Flamenco dancers were rehearsing to loud Spanish music on a stage in the middle of the field, and somewhere at the other end, the sound of *fado* poured out of a loud speaker. The air was thick with the smell of a South African *braai* where chargrilled *boerewors* sausages were being turned back and forth, and the Belgians were preparing fresh waffles, which accounted for the sweet aroma of batter, vanilla, and toasted pecans.

"This is amazing," Fatima shouted. "C'mon, let's go find the Pakistani stall and set up." She and Maya were dressed in matching gold *gharara* skirts for their performance later on. Fatima couldn't walk as fast as she'd like to in her long gharara, but even so, Stefan and Maya couldn't keep up with her and exchanged looks of amusement as they followed on behind carrying bags bursting with food and decorations.

Ammi hung back. She hadn't said a word on the way over, choosing silent defiance as her weapon of choice. But Fatima had more important things to worry about right now, and once they'd found the Pakistani stall, she took out the elaborate handmade fabrics and cloths with mirror-work, and Stefan and Maya helped her create the display: a Sindhi *ajrak* outfit in red and black handmade embroidery to represent the rich heritage of the Sindhi people in Pakistan, colorful truck art, green and white flags, poster-sized images of famous Pakistani personalities such as Malala, and landmarks such as K2.

Ammi was put in charge of the food. To her credit, she had prepared a fantastic menu: hot potato fritter *pakoras*, okra fries, *keema* samosas filled with minced meat and peas, *tandoori* kebabs, chicken *biryani*, garlic butter *naan*, and individual *sheer* portions of rice and milk puddings set in traditional clay pots with crushed pistachios and a gold leaf on top. They were the only Pakistani family on campus, and Fatima felt a surge of pride as she surveyed the completed stall. It felt good to represent her country on an international stage, and she hoped she was setting a good example for Maya so she would be proud of her heritage. They'd also prepared a contribution for the German stall—a Black Forest cake she and Stefan had baked. She was about to head off to find the German contingent before the cake melted in the May heat when a breathless Abena turned up.

Abena had ear pods in and was holding a clipboard and talking a mile a minute. She'd been dashing from one stall to the next to check on progress, looking stunning in an exquisite turquoise and blue Ghanaian skirt and matching peplum blouse that cinched in her waist. "Fatima, there you are. Oh good, you're practically set up. You look beautiful! Anything you need?"

"Thanks. I love your outfit too. Think we're all set up. Just need to grab some extra plates and napkins from the kitchen and then we're ready. Oh, and I need to take this cake to the German stall."

"Okay, great. The German table's about ten stalls to the right. Now, in twenty minutes, the event will formally start in the auditorium. That's where we'll kick off with a welcome ceremony and the flag parade. See you in there, okay?"

"Sure. Wait, before you rush off, have you seen Kate?"

"Yeah, she's over there. Better warn you, though, she's acting really strange."

Fatima had no idea what had been going on with Kate lately. She spotted her across the field standing in front of the American stall. Michael was with her but he looked like he'd rather be somewhere else, and judging by their body language—both had crossed their arms—they were in the middle of an argument. They were interrupted by Patricia, who came over to them with some people Fatima didn't recognize, and although Kate hugged them, there were no smiles. It was as if Kate was seeing straight through the people around her.

She tried to catch Kate's attention by waving at her and shouting across to her. "Kate! Kaaaaate!"

Eventually Kate looked up and came over. "Hi, Fatima. Didn't see you there."

She didn't seem to notice Fatima's Pakistani clothes either. Or if she did, she didn't say anything. And she looked like she'd been crying.

"What's going on, Kate? Is everything okay?" said

Fatima, touching her arm. "I've barely seen you. You seem so stressed out."

"Oh, it's nothing. I haven't been feeling too well lately, that's all."

"Are you sure? It's not like you to miss so many Portuguese classes."

Kate snapped back. "Yeah, well, I don't see the point in continuing with the lessons anymore."

"Since when did you give up on learning a language? I thought you needed it for work?"

"Let's not talk about work. Work is such a shit show right now."

"Kate, what's going on?"

"It's too complicated to explain."

Fatima was getting tired of beating around the bush. "Too complicated to explain, or you don't want to explain?"

"Listen, I wish I could tell you more, but it's boring work stuff. It's confidential, okay?"

"Okay, but if you are *personally* in trouble, I hope you'll reach out to your friends. Abena and I are here for you, you know."

Kate looked touched. "I appreciate that, I really do." She started to say something else but then caught herself. "I better get back to the Martins—they're over from Singapore— before I seem rude."

Fatima sighed in exasperation. It was time for the ceremony and there was already a long queue forming in front of the auditorium. Once inside, Stefan and Ammi went with Fatima to find some seats, and Maya joined the other flag bearers on the auditorium stage. The crowd buzzed as the chief guest of the ceremony, the American ambassador to Portugal, made his way in. He was all smiles and was clearly enjoying himself but he seemed to have an issue with Kate, who was walking beside him. There was a brief exchange between them and then Kate stepped away—and kept her distance. Fatima wasn't within earshot but she could see the tension between them and noticed the lack of eye contact. What in the world was going on and what was the "shit show" at work all about?

A booming announcement came from the stage. "Ladies and Gentlemen, please take your seats. We will begin soon." It was none other than Abena, the master of ceremonies. Kate went to sit between Michael and Ambassador Hill, looking like a cornered animal resigned to its fate, and Fatima went to sit next to Stefan and Ammi.

The program began. Abena welcomed the parents, students, teachers, principal, and the chief guest, highlighting the importance of the event in promoting and celebrating diversity in their community. The elementary students filed onto the stage and sang *We Are the World*, cheered on by the parents. When it was time for the flag parade, a representative from each country was handed a flagpole by Ambassador Hill, and applause and cheers rang out as one by one they accepted their flag and marched out to the football field with a number of kids gathering behind them.

Abena announced each country in turn alphabetically, her voice blaring clearly and confidently through the loud speakers.

"Ladies and Gentlemen, please put your hands together for ... GHANA! AKWAABA GHANA!" The Ghanaian flag was being carried by Kakra and Panyin to the sound of West

African drumming. Fatima glanced up and saw Abena beaming with pride.

"And now, Ladies and Gentlemen, please help me welcome ... GERMANY! GUTEN TAG GERMANY!"

Fatima squeezed Stefan's hand, both of them welling up at the sight of Maya waving the German flag. Finally, an International Day that allowed their Third Culture Kid to express all parts of her identity.

After each of the fifty-two countries was introduced, Abena declared the International Day festivities open. Fatima hurried back to the Pakistan stall and was taken aback by the long queue in front of it. They were lining up to sample the feast Ammi had prepared, and she quickly took her place next to her mother and helped serve up the biryani and kebabs. Ammi had prepared twenty cups of rice, but at this rate, it wouldn't be enough. She stole a furtive glance at Ammi, who was relishing the attention and nodding excitedly. "Yes, yes, I cooked all this food. But you must try some of this too ..."

Ammi was less friendly to Fatima, continuing with the icy stares, and conversation between them was at a bare minimum, though to any outsider they would just have appeared busy. Fatima could feel the tension as she stood next to her mother, but for once, she didn't care. She was done pretending.

Half an hour or so later, the performances started, with each country showcasing its culture through dance. Fatima and Maya had been practicing their bhangra dance for weeks now, but as Fatima watched the Korean kids perform with their turquoise and pink fans, and the Japanese kids dance in their beautiful kimono robes, she was getting nervous.

"Ammi, here, take the spoon," she said. "Stefan will help you. It's time for Maya and me to go on."

"*Acha*, okay, *beta*," said Ammi, feigning disinterest.

Fatima grabbed Maya's hand, and together they made their way to the red stage in the middle of the football field. They climbed the few steps up to the stage, smiled at each other, took their positions, and waited for their music to start. Fatima took a minute to look at the crowd gathered around the stage. Stefan was at the front, smiling and waving, and Abena was clapping excitedly next to him. She could see Kate looking blankly ahead and Ammi's frosty, cold stare. And then she looked over to the entrance of the field, and all of a sudden her world froze in shock.

Voices shouting.

Music blaring.

Ears ringing.

Breath stopping.

Heart racing.

Eyes dilating.

*Impossible.*

# 31

## FATIMA
*Cascais, Portugal*
May 2023

She was running. She mumbled a half-hearted apology after colliding with a fellow parent on the football field. She ran, past the colorful stalls, past countless people, all of them looking surprised. She ran as fast as she could. Panic boiled up inside her and made her forget all about her surroundings. She ran, and she didn't stop to think. All she wanted was to get out, to get as far away as possible. She ran blindly. She couldn't believe that after all these years the past had finally caught up with her. She was afraid. She ran, and nobody tried to stop her. She was running from the little voice in her head, the one telling her to stay where she was, that everything would turn out alright.

It was him.

How could she ever forget his face?

The face of the devil.

The face that had been haunting her in her nightmares.

The one face she could never forget.

While she ran, the whole world stood still around her. Voices were muffled, like she was swimming underwater. She saw the concerned faces of Maya, Stefan, Abena, and Kate as she ran past them. But it was Ammi's face that made her run even harder. Ammi stood there motionless and expressionless until suddenly she handed the spatula to Stefan and then did the most unexpected thing.

Ammi started to run too. She ran behind Fatima as fast as she could in her *shalwar kameez* and silver strappy sandals.

Fatima ran into the school parking lot towards her car, quickly got inside, and turned on the engine. There was a thud of a hand on the window and she froze. It was Ammi. She let her mother in and Ammi fumbled with her seatbelt, but her hands were shaking too much. Fatima leaned over to help her, then locked the car doors and sped off.

They didn't speak. They were worn out from the running. There was just the sound of them catching their breath before Fatima let out a bloodcurdling scream, like a wounded animal that had been trapped. "What the hell, Ammi! *How*?"

Ammi was still trembling. "I don't know, Fatima ... I am as shocked as you are ... I don't know how this could be happening."

"But how can he still be alive? I thought you took care of it!"

"I did! I asked Muhammad to take care of it. You know I did, decades ago ..."

"Well then, how in the world is he still *alive*?"

"*I don't know!*"

"How did he know I was living in Portugal? How did he find out what school Maya was going to?" Fatima's eyes were darting back and forth to the rear-view mirror to see if he was following. Nothing. She simply couldn't take it in. What else did he know about her, this ... monster?

"He must have tried to track us down, but ..." Ammi was at a loss to explain, to understand. How could she come to terms with the fact that her dead brother was suddenly alive?

"The phone call!" Fatima shouted. "I should have known."

"What phone call?"

"I didn't tell you. Before you arrived, last December. I had a strange phone call ... no one spoke when I picked up, just heavy breathing."

"And why didn't you mention it to me?"

"What was there to mention? Just a prank call—but it must have been him. How did he get my number, Ammi?" Fatima was hysterical. "Why here? And why NOW?"

Ammi had no answers and Fatima had no plan.

They drove along Cascais's Guincho Beach road. The beach was rugged and windswept. The May winds had blown the sand inland, and now the dunes stretched as far as the eye could see towards the Serra de Sintra mountains. Cabo da Roca towered in the distance.

Ammi was still shaking. She'd started to recite verses from the Quran, and her hurried murmuring of Surah Fateha was unnerving Fatima, who had been forced to memorize it as a child. *'In the Name of Allah—the Most Compassionate, Most Merciful. Master of the Day of Judgment. You alone we worship and You alone we ask for help.'* A prayer for troubled times. And they could do with some help right now.

"Where are we going?" said Ammi all of a sudden.

"I don't know ... as far away as possible!"

"What about Maya? You just left her on the stage—she must be distraught."

Fatima pulled out her phone and saw eleven missed calls from Stefan. "Here, take my phone and call Stefan. Tell him to take Maya home."

"How can he when you have the car?"

"For God's sake, tell him to take an Uber," Fatima shouted, "and to stay far away from HIM. Just tell him to keep Maya safe, take her home—immediately."

They headed up the winding mountain road towards the red and white lighthouse, and Ammi called Stefan and put him on speaker phone.

"Stefan, *listen to me*," yelled Fatima. "Take Maya home. Immediately. I'm driving to Cabo da Roca. Ammi's with me. I can't risk coming home. Just take Maya home, and do *not* let that man into our home—he may follow you."

Stefan started to say something but Ammi cut him off so Fatima could focus on the winding road. When they reached Cabo da Roca, she parked next to some tour buses in the parking lot and slumped onto the steering wheel.

"Why are we here?" said Ammi, touching her daughter's shoulder.

"I don't know … I need to clear my head … I need some fresh air. It's the first place I thought of, far away from everything; it's literally the edge of the continent. I come here sometimes." She got out of the car and walked along the gravel path towards the headland. She turned around. Ammi was following her, her hair caught by a gust of wind, and behind Ammi, in the parking lot, a little black car pulled up next to hers. In an instant, Fatima froze.

Someone stepped out of the car. It was *him*.

She needed to think, but gripped by panic she just ran towards the top of the headland. Then she remembered: the monument. There would be tourists—the most westerly point in mainland Europe—there were always tourists. *Safety in numbers.* "Run," she screamed to Ammi. "Run!"

And soon she saw them, just ahead of her, day-trippers and hikers admiring the view and taking selfies, and she ran towards them, almost laughing with relief, dashing into the path of one of the tour guides and mumbling an apology before looking back for Ammi.

"Fatima, is that you?" said the tour guide, a woman with short hair and glasses. "Is everything okay?"

Fatima was startled. *Oh my God.* The matching active-wear set and baseball cap. It was Inês. Of course, her private weekend tours.

"Fatima, are you okay?" Inês asked again. "What's wrong?"

"Inês, please … you've gotta help me." She looked back down the path. Ammi was about to join them.

"God, Fatima, what's going on?"

"I don't have time to explain. My mother and I are being followed. We need to escape. Can you help us get up that restricted path?"

"It's restricted for a reason—the cliffs are steep and unstable. Hold on …"

Inês asked a fellow tour guide to take over her group, quickly handing her a sheet of paper, then turned back to Fatima and Ammi. "Okay, both of you, follow me."

They ran behind Inês, their Pakistani clothes and shoes slowing them down as they passed the hordes of tourists with their Nikon cameras and iPhones, until they reached the end of the gravel path. Inês had climbed up the hill without a break, but Fatima was gasping for breath and went back to help Ammi. Inês lifted one of the "Entrada Proibida" barriers and led them onto a steep, stony path that climbed through a remote part of the headland and then onto a narrow track high above the cliffs, Fatima looking over her shoulder whenever she could. There was no sign of him.

Even Inês was breathless now, and all three of them crouched behind a giant boulder near the edge of the cliff.

"Okay, we're safe here," said Inês after a minute or two. "Will one of you please tell me what in the world is going on?"

Fatima tried to speak but nothing came out. She looked over at Ammi.

And then he was there—from nowhere—staring down at them.

Fatima gasped, then leaped up to stand her ground. She'd had enough of this. But Ammi was faster and stood in front of Fatima, holding her back with one arm.

"Noooooo!" Ammi screamed at him. "Stay where you are. Don't you dare come even one step further. I let you hurt my child once, but I will not let you come near her again!"

Fatima let out a muffled scream, overcome with emotion at what Ammi had said.

"My dear sister. We meet at last. After twenty-six years. Is that correct? My memory is still a little fuzzy, but that's all thanks to you." Ali stepped forward to greet his sister as if running into family members on the edge of a cliff on the other side of the world was just a chance encounter, as if nothing was out of the ordinary.

"Why are you here?" said Fatima, her voice steady. "What do you want? Why are you even alive?" If she felt fear, it didn't show. She took in his appearance: same crooked smile, same nicotine-stained teeth, same sinister mustache twirled upwards at both ends, same arrogant strut. But he looked so much older. No longer the debonair twenty-seven-year-old, as the receding hairline and expanding waistline attested to. But she would have recognized him anywhere.

"Well," he said, "it looks like my perfect sister here didn't clean up after herself the way she should have."

"But how did you survive?" whispered Fatima.

"I was practically dead, but not quite. I would have died had it not been for the fishermen who found me near the Indus River. They took me to their village, to a pathetic little hospital where I lay for months until I recovered from my fractures."

Ammi screamed at him. "You deserved it!"

Fatima pulled at her arm. "Let him talk, Ammi."

"You always did enjoy listening to my stories when you were a child, Fatima, didn't you?"

She felt bile in her throat but gulped it down.

He continued: "The trauma to my head was severe—retrograde amnesia, they said. I lost all memory of what had triggered it, and much of what came before … then bits and pieces gradually came back to me."

Fatima had a rush of adrenaline. She couldn't believe what she was hearing. "How did you survive?" she said again.

"I was a beggar on the streets of Hyderabad. It's a miracle I survived, but I was always in such excellent health in my youth. I migrated inland to the farming lands and worked on the mango plantations there. I was lucky my business savvy stayed with me, so over the years I worked my way up and started a business exporting mangoes and chutney to the rest of Pakistan and even abroad. But as for the past, my head was still blurry. I remembered some details, our house, my sister, but these were just pieces. I couldn't put them together."

"Letting you stay in *my* house was the worst decision of my life!" yelled Ammi.

"So, how did you figure out what had happened to you?" said Fatima, forcing herself to appear calm. She stole a look at Inês, who nodded in encouragement.

"I might never have figured it out, except, one day, seemingly randomly, I ran into your old driver Muhammad in Hyderabad. I couldn't place him at first, but then I couldn't stop thinking about where I had seen him before. It triggered something in me and then I remembered the accident—when I hit your car. It was Muhammad behind the wheel. I confronted him and put two and two together. Of course, there was no way my perfect sister would do her dirty work herself. I told him I remembered everything. I threatened to expose him. And he confessed it *all*. How my own sister erased me from her life."

"*Buss.* Enough. This is enough!" Ammi screamed, her voice catching in her throat.

"*Kutiya!* Worthless bitch! All you ever cared about was keeping up with appearances, willing to kill your own flesh and blood for the sake of a perfect facade."

"How dare you blame me when you're the one who brought this shame upon our family with your sick urges, you sick, sick bastard!"

"Oh, as if you could ever understand. What Fatima and I had was special. And you were jealous and tried to destroy it. You should have seen how she wanted it, how she asked for it, how she enjoyed it."

Ammi covered her ears. "*Chup kar*, shut up! You make me *sick*!"

The wind was howling. Fatima broke free from behind Ammi and took a step forward. "You still haven't explained how you found me in Portugal. Or why you have come here."

"All these years, Fatima, all these years. I have been biding my time. I knew I couldn't simply march back and reclaim my life. Too many awkward questions would be asked. It would be too risky. I focused on building my business and honing my new identity until one day I came to Karachi for work, and I passed by the house, my house, the house I supported and kept afloat after my brother-in-law passed away, and it was then that I decided I would not only claim my identity back, I would make you two pay for what you did to me. I discovered you had lived in Dubai, Fatima. If I had only known back then ... so close. But no, I had to have you together. Instead of blackmail, I chose money. I gave Muhammad what he badly needed. You know, Gulzar, you really should pay your staff better. Or at least not entrust them with the phone number and address of your precious daughter in Portugal. It seems you never learn from your mistakes. And so, Fatima, I had your address, and I booked my plane tickets—I can write it off as a business expense, you know—and I found you and followed you. Then I learned of Maya and where you send her to school. Now *she's* a looker. Much better than you were at that age, Fatima, if I may say so."

Fatima wanted to lunge at him—to tear his skin, gouge out his eyes, hear him beg for mercy. But she wouldn't give him the pleasure or the satisfaction of knowing he was getting to her. Her eleven-year-old self had succumbed to him, but her thirty-seven-year-old self would not capitulate.

"Well, this has been a lovely family reunion," she said, edging closer to him. "Did you imagine we would all kiss and make up? All these years, I thought death had been too light a punishment for you, so I'm happy to hear of your suffering. You needed to pay for what you did to me, for the innocence of my childhood you stole from me. But I think it's time for you to go now. Unless you want me to report you for sexual harassment and stalking. They take these charges quite seriously in Portugal, you know. And don't forget, I have witnesses." She looked over at Ammi and Inês.

Ali looked her up and down lasciviously. "It's so fulfilling to see how you've matured. That in itself has made my trip worthwhile. But no, I won't be going anywhere, at least not yet. Thanks to the tracking device I put on your car, it was easy to follow you here, and the more I see of your new hometown, the more I like it. First I plan to have a lovely little holiday in this beautiful country of yours. Perhaps your friend here can help me?" He looked over to Inês and rocked back on his feet in excitement, inches from the cliff edge.

"Careful!" screamed Inês to warn him.

But he just laughed and held out his hand. "Come here, Fatima."

"Stay away from me or I'll break your balls, or whatever's left of them."

Something in him snapped and he hurled himself at Fatima, but in that split second Ammi moved back between them.

"Don't even think about touching my daughter!" she yelled, and she held out her outstretched arms in a dare.

"Get out of my way, Gulzar."

"NO!"

He lunged at her and she fell to the ground and screamed. "Fatimaaa, watch out!"

But it was too late. He'd already grabbed Fatima by the wrists. She tried to wriggle free, but his grasp was rock solid, and he held her tight, laughing at her like it was some kind of game. "You can never get away from me, Fatima."

He moved closer and ran his hand over her face. She smelt his putrid breath, and her eyes burned into his, seeing nothing but pure hatred. She spat in his face. Momentarily startled, he stumbled, then fell to the ground, trying to break his fall and ripping the palms of his hands on the jagged stones.

Before she had a chance to realize what was happening, Fatima felt a pull at her arm, and with all her force, Inês dragged her away from the cliff edge, away from him.

He was on his hands and knees like an animal, mad with rage. They watched as he pulled himself up, the wind howling over the headland, and he roared and plunged towards them.

There was a rumble, then a deep thud. A crack opened up and cut across the ground in front of him, causing him to lose his balance, and when he tried to scramble up and stand on the unstable earth, a gust of wind knocked him back down, and he lay there on his belly, squirming on the edge of the crumbling cliff, the wind swirling around him. His eyes pleaded for mercy and his outstretched arm begged for help. But they just watched, and after another powerful gust, he was gone, falling deep into no-man's land, where the land ended and the sea began.

# 32

# FATIMA
*Cascais, Portugal*
June 2023

"Hey, Stefan," said Fatima. "I could do with a hand taking the suitcases to the car."

"And you thought this day would never come," he said.

Ammi was leaving for the airport and Fatima was having mixed feelings about it. In some ways she wished they had more time together to sort out their complex relationship, but deep down she knew her mother would never change, not really. And looking after herself and focusing on her own healing journey was Fatima's priority now.

Her mother was a nervous traveler and Fatima had been helping her pack. Ammi insisted on stuffing everything—suitcases, carry-on, handbag—with handwritten verses from the Quran to protect her against any misfortune during her journey home. Maya had asked if they would prevent Nani Ammi's luggage from being lost and Fatima had laughed. But she knew Ammi believed in it and that old habits die hard. Besides, when it came to Ammi, she had learned to pick and choose her battles wisely.

As she waited for Ammi to get ready, she reflected on the tumultuous events of the past few weeks. Inês had promised to keep their secret. She'd also given Fatima some incredibly helpful advice about what to do after the 'accident.' Fatima hadn't known whether or not to report the fall as a witness and whether or not to call an ambulance. Both would have drawn attention, and in the absence of CCTV at Cabo da Roca, uncomfortable questions would have been asked. Besides, what was Fatima doing in a restricted area in the first place? The irony wasn't lost on Fatima. What had seemed like irrational madness at first, driving to the ends of the earth from where there was seemingly no escape, had turned out to be their saving grace; the remoteness of the cliffs had ensured there were no witnesses, bar Inês. And that's why they decided to do nothing. His rental car would have been found at some point and the security deposit withheld. People vanished all the time. And if Ali's body was ever found, there was nothing to indicate foul play, and nothing to tie it to Fatima. In the meantime, Fatima had helped Ammi see that Muhammad was not to be blamed— or fired—once she was back home in Karachi. He had simply been caught up in the crossfire and was a victim of circumstance, she'd said, and Ammi had agreed.

"Ammiiiii, are you ready?" Fatima called out, trying not to sound annoyed but looking at the time.

"*Beta*, I am coming. I am just checking I have not forgotten anything."

"Don't worry, if you have, I can always send it to you. You don't want to miss your flight."

"There's plenty of time. Let me say goodbye to Maya and Stefan."

"Sure, Ammi, but can we talk for a second first?"

"*Haan*, Fatima." She nodded and then put her handbag down.

"Ammi, I know I said many hurtful things to you that day in my kitchen. I want to say … that I saw how you stood up for me—finally—in Cabo da Roca."

"Who knows what I would have done if you had not said all of those things to me," said Ammi, staring into her daughter's eyes, "even though it was painful to listen to you. I wonder if you ever understood my side of the story. In your eyes I am the guilty one."

"Ammi, in my eyes, I was the child and you were the adult. I expected you to know better, to notice what was happening inside your own home, but most of all to believe me and protect me when I confided in you."

"Things are not always that easy, Fatima. You of all people should know that. I thought I *did* protect you. I took on the biggest burden and responsibility to shield you."

"Look," said Fatima, "we're not going to solve all our grievances in one conversation. I know that. But for the longest time, I didn't even want you to be a part of my life. I used to dread your visits. But for what it's worth, I realize I do want you in our lives from now on. No more pretending, no more keeping up appearances, no more dreading our time together. Perhaps this can be the first step towards our reconciliation, even though I know we still have such a long way to go. But I'd like to believe it's never too late to start." Fatima gave Ammi a gentle hug and her mother reciprocated and then went to the living room to say goodbye to Maya.

Fatima wanted Ammi to have a close relationship with Maya, and the extended time they'd spent together in

Portugal had done them both good. For one thing, Maya's Urdu had improved dramatically with her grandmother around.

On the drive to the airport they chatted about how quickly the months had gone. Ammi was full of advice for Fatima on how to keep her kitchen running smoothly, and Fatima rolled her eyes as she always did, knowing her mother would always be her mother: annoying, interfering, and believing she could always do things better. But Fatima had finally seen Ammi put her daughter first, and she would never forget how Ammi had twice defended her, physically and emotionally, in front of that man. As long and as unwelcome as the visit had been, it had given them a second chance. Nothing about their relationship was perfect or resolved, but at least they could finally be honest with each other.

"I guess it's time to say goodbye, Ammi." Fatima had helped Ammi check in at the Emirates counter and walked her to security control. She pointed out the gate number on the boarding pass; Ammi always doubted its existence unless she'd seen it with her own eyes.

"Goodbye, Fatima. I want to thank you for everything." Ammi choked back some tears.

It wasn't like Ammi to get so emotional. "I hope this can be a fresh start for both of us," said Fatima, and she enveloped her mother in a long, warm hug.

After waving goodbye to Ammi at the airport and promising to visit her soon, Fatima checked her phone for messages. Abena was waiting for her at Hygge Kaffe in Lisbon, and Fatima was eager to dig into their apple cinnamon cake, which always reminded her of her time in Copenhagen.

As usual, finding a parking spot in central Lisbon was impossible, so when she was close to the café, she did what any Portuguese person would—she parked on the nearby roundabout. Was it legal? She didn't know, but it was common practice, and anyway, the fact she didn't think twice about doing it was a sign she was slowly becoming Portuguese.

It was good to feel the breeze on her arms as she walked to the café. For the first time in her adult life, she was wearing a sleeveless dress. At last, she didn't care about that scar on her arm. It was a symbol of her survival, like a talisman, a source of power after what she had overcome, and she was proud of it.

Abena was sitting by the window and got up for a hug. "Love the dress, Fatima."

"Thanks. I've been looking forward to this all day. Just dropped my mom at the airport. Feels like I'm officially on summer holiday, even though technically we still have a few more days to go till school lets out."

"How did it go?"

"I wouldn't say we parted on good terms, but we parted on better terms. There's a long way to go, but it's a start."

"I'm so happy you and your mother are willing to work together to patch things up." She smiled. "Speaking of patching things up," she whispered, "what did you think of the email from Kate?"

"It was such a shock," said Fatima. "First she wasn't responding to any of my messages on WhatsApp, then all of a sudden I get this email from her. Hold on, let me pull it up. I read it in such a rush earlier … here it is …" and she read it out, lowering her voice to a whisper.

*"Dear Fatima and Abena, I'm sorry to do this over email, but I wanted to let you both know that Michael, Eric, and I have left Portugal. It was a rushed decision and I'm sorry I didn't get to say goodbye to you both in person. The truth is, there had been a toxic environment at work for me lately and I just wasn't happy. Baseless allegations were made against me and after an internal investigation, the Foreign Service has revoked my security clearance. I've been back in the States for a few weeks now. I'm awaiting a formal hearing in DC. Through a mutual decision, Michael and I have also agreed to go our separate ways. Our focus is on sharing custody of Eric and concentrating on his well-being above all else. I hope our paths may cross again. Until then, lots of love, Kate."*

"Wow," said Abena. "I can't believe she's under investigation. Sounds like she may get fired. And she broke up with Michael. I didn't even know they were having problems. It felt like I barely knew her sometimes. I hardly know how to reply."

Fatima nodded. "Isn't that exactly what that other woman—Patricia—said? About how she left Singapore in a rush, without saying goodbye. Sounds like it's a bit of a pattern with her. Maybe she felt guilty because she had something to hide and decided not to confront it, to keep running?"

"It's possible. Sounds like there were pressures at work. I think she decided to take her chances on her home turf. I really wish she had confided in us."

"Me too," said Fatima, "but it takes guts to face your deepest, darkest demons. And if there's one thing I've learned it's that your problems don't go away when you move countries. There they always are, till you tackle them head-on. But sometimes moving abroad can give you the strength you need to turn your life around. And it's only by sharing your stories that you can live your best life."

"So true," said Abena, looking emotional. "What you seek to leave behind is something inside you. Which reminds me, there's something I wanted to share with you. I've made the difficult decision to go back to Ghana this summer and face my sister."

Fatima reached across the table and squeezed Abena's hand. "Oh my God, Abena. That's huge. Are you taking the twins?"

"Yes, all of us will go."

"How do you feel about it?"

"I'm scared. Terrified actually. But I'm also determined to face what I did all those years ago. Now that Kakra and Panyin know the truth about their adoption, it's the next logical step."

"Right. And how have they reacted to the news?"

"Well, it's a lot for them to take in of course. But they've said they want to get to know their birth mom. And I have to respect that."

"I'm so proud of you, Abena. What you're doing takes strength. If there's one thing I've learned from Ammi's visit it's that people you think you know well can still surprise you."

After the International Day fiasco, Fatima had divulged the details of her sexual abuse at the hands of her uncle to Abena, who had listened in shocked silence. It was the second time she had confessed and shared what had happened to her, and just as Stefan had instantaneously supported her, so had Abena. It still felt weird to say the words out loud, but each time she did, she felt herself reclaiming her story, bit by bit. While she'd told Abena about the abuse and her toxic relationship with Ammi, she'd left out the part about Ali Mamoo's return. The less people knew, the better, and she couldn't drag Abena into that as well. Yes, Abena had seen her rushing off on International Day—the whole school had—but nobody had seen *him*. Nobody knew who he was except for her and Ammi, and Fatima was determined to keep it that way. The public embarrassment and raised eyebrows were a small price to pay for her newly found freedom. Besides, it had been so loud and busy that many people hadn't actually noticed what was going on. When she'd confided in Abena, Fatima had blamed her public meltdown on an earlier confrontation with Ammi and her intent to finally take back control of her life. Telling a half-truth was better than concocting another lie. She wanted no more of that.

"I know you've been through a lot recently," said Abena. "If anybody has been strong, it's you, Fatima."

"It wasn't easy. I've started seeing a therapist to help me process everything. Stefan got the ball rolling and insisted on making that first appointment for me, and I'm so glad he did. It was time. And I'm finally starting to feel free. You will too. Let me know if I can do anything, how I can support you. Okay?"

"Thanks, I appreciate the offer. I'll keep you posted. There's already a lot of emotions to process, especially for the girls. I'm doing it for them. Finding peace will heal them and help them move forward. It'll help all of us."

"I'm in awe of you," said Fatima. "And I'm always here to help."

"I know, thank you. What about you? What are your plans?"

"Nothing too exciting. We'll stay in Portugal and explore it to our heart's content, I imagine. And first up is a long overdue visit to the town of Fátima." She laughed.

"Sounds like a plan. In fact, it sounds like the perfect place to rediscover yourself."

Stefan and Maya were waiting for her when she got home, and with the sky turning a bright, burning orange, the three of them took a sunset walk along the *paredão*. With her past firmly behind her and her future beckoning, Fatima Khan finally felt free to move forward—without looking over her shoulder.

# RECIPES

Several characters in the book are featured cooking and serving their traditional food. Even though they all come from different backgrounds and cuisines, their recipes feature a common ingredient: rice.
This highlights how different cultures cook rice and how their expectations of it, in terms of taste and texture, can vary a great deal. It also reinforces the commonalities we share with others; food really can help us cross cultures.

Here are three of the multicultural recipes shared by the characters that may have made your mouth water as you were reading: Michael's Italian Butternut Squash Risotto, Abena's Ghanaian Jollof Rice, and Ammi's Pakistani Biryani.

# Butternut Squash Risotto

Serves four to six
Cooking time: 1 hour

Michael makes this in *Chapter 2* for their first dinner in their new home in Portugal. Ironically, at the mention of Maryanne, Kate storms out without eating a bite.

*Ingredients*

- 3 cloves of garlic, finely chopped
- 2–3 small shallots, chopped
- 1.5 liters or 6 cups of vegetable broth
- ¼ slab of butter
- 1 butternut squash peeled and cut into cubes
- 500 grams or 2¾ cups of Arborio risotto rice
- 1 tablespoon olive oil
- 250 grams or 1 cup of freshly grated Grana Padano (or Parmesan)
- 1 bunch fresh parsley or sage for garnish, chopped
- Salt and pepper to taste

*Method*

1. Finely chop the shallots and sauté them in a bit of olive oil and most of the butter.
2. Peel and cube the butternut squash and add it to the pot with the shallots.

3. Keep stirring and let it cook until the squash becomes soft.
4. Add in the minced garlic and stir well.
5. Heat up the stock in a separate pan.
6. After 5–10 minutes, mash the butternut squash so it becomes a coarse puree.
7. Add the risotto rice with the remaining butter and stir well until all the rice is coated.
8. Add salt and pepper to taste.
9. Add 1 cup of stock and reduce the heat. Let it simmer and keep stirring. Gradually keep adding more stock as the liquid is absorbed.
10. When all the liquid has been absorbed, stir in the Grana Padano and the chopped parsley.
11. Sauté the sage leaves in butter for garnish and serve.

# Jollof Rice

Serves six to eight
Cooking time: 1½ hours

Abena makes this in *Chapter 8* to welcome her friends over for brunch at their new apartment in Cascais. The Jollof rice draws a comparison to a biryani and helps Abena bond with Michael over their joint love of multicultural food and cooking. It's also her friends' first introduction to Ghanaian food and Abena's bold attempt at expressing her Ghanaian identity on a plate. She serves it with some shito sauce on the side (see recipe below) and a side of cabbage salad.

*Ingredients*

- 150 ml or ⅔ cup of groundnut oil or vegetable cooking oil
- 1 kg or 2.2 lbs. of fresh meat (beef, chicken with bones, or turkey)
- 600 grams/3 cups of long-grain rice like Thai jasmine or basmati
- 2 big onions, chopped
- 4 cloves of garlic, minced
- 2 medium-sized ginger roots, chopped
- 7 medium-sized fresh tomatoes, blended
- 200 grams or 1 cup of tomato paste
- Salt and pepper to taste

- 1 scotch bonnet pepper or habanero pepper, chopped. For spice-sensitive palates, you can substitute with ½ a teaspoon of paprika instead
- 500 ml or 2 cups of concentrated meat stock/broth

*Method*

1. Season the meat by using 1 chopped onion, garlic, ginger, the scotch bonnet pepper or the paprika, mix thoroughly, and add to a saucepan.
2. Add the concentrated hot meat stock.
3. Cover the saucepan and leave it to simmer for about 20 minutes to let the spices add flavor and intensify the taste of the stock.
4. Take the meat out and set aside the concentrated stock.
5. Blend pepper (to taste), 1 onion, and garlic together. Then blend the fresh tomatoes separately.
6. Get your tomato paste and 1 chopped onion ready.
7. Pour the cooking oil into a saucepan and allow it to heat. Then add the chopped onion to fry for about two minutes. Then add the tomato paste and stir well. Let it simmer for about 15 minutes.
8. Add in the blended tomatoes, scotch pepper, garlic, and onion. Stir to mix thoroughly.
9. Let it simmer for 30 minutes, stirring in between.
10. Add some more concentrated stock to the tomato sauce and stir to mix.
11. Add the rinsed rice and stir for 10 minutes. Add water to 1 cm above the rice and cover the pan with a lid.

12. Allow it to steam under medium heat for 15 minutes. Put foil over the pan and put the lid on. Keep stirring and checking for about 20 minutes until the Jollof is ready.

## How to Make the Ghanaian Shito Sauce (to serve on the side)

Shito is a Ghanaian condiment that can be used as a dipping sauce, marinade, dressing, or spread. It has a deep, earthy, fishy flavor, with a spicy kick from the chilies.

*Ingredients*

- 350 ml or 1½ cups of vegetable oil
- 3 medium-sized onions, peeled and sliced
- 4 cloves of garlic, peeled and cut into small pieces
- 5 cm ginger root
- 2 scotch bonnets with the stalk removed
- 2 tablespoons of tomato puree
- 60 grams or ½ cup of dried fish pieces (or blended anchovies)
- 1 tablespoon of chili flakes/powder
- 60 grams or ½ cup of ground shrimp (or fresh shrimp)
- 1 teaspoon ground cloves
- Salt to taste

## *Method*

1. Cut the dried fish into smaller pieces and remove the bones. Wash and soak in some water before you start cooking. This will make it easy to blend later.
2. Heat oil in a pan (use a nonstick pan if you have one) under medium heat.
3. Add the onions to the oil. Stir until the onion slices are translucent and beginning to brown. This will take about 10-15 mins.
4. Remove from the heat and allow to cool. In that time, drain the fish and pour into a blender. Prepare the scotch bonnet and garlic. Add into the blender with the tomato puree and ginger root.
5. Add the onion and the oil into the blender and puree. Pour the blended mixture back into the pot and place on a low heat.
6. Add the dried shrimp, pepper flakes, cloves, and a dash of salt.
7. Allow it to simmer gently, stirring frequently to prevent burning. If the sauce appears dry, you can add more oil.
8. The color will change gradually, and by the time the sauce is done, it will be quite dark. This will take around 20 minutes.
9. Allow it to cool, and keep in a closed container. Refrigerate and use as needed.

# Chicken Biryani

Serves six to eight
Cooking time: 2½ to 3 hours

In *Chapter 29*, Fatima observes Ammi cooking her chicken biryani to serve at their Pakistani stall for International Day. We've already heard about Ammi's famous recipe in *Chapter 8*, but this is the first time we see her cooking it through Fatima's eyes. Each step of making the biryani reminds Fatima of what her mother is good at—camouflage, layering, deception, and diluting the truth. It is a dish that not only captures Ammi's culinary expertise but also her personality.

*Ingredients*

- 2 large onions
- Sunflower oil or vegetable oil
- 800 grams or 4 cups of basmati rice
- 1.5 to 2 kg or 3 to 4.5 lbs. of chicken leg and thigh pieces, skinned
- 1 inch of ginger, peeled
- 4 cloves garlic, peeled
- 2 teaspoons red chili powder
- 1 teaspoon ground cumin
- 1 teaspoon dried coriander
- 5 medium-sized tomatoes
- 500 grams or 2 cups of fresh full fat yogurt
- 1 bunch of fresh coriander

- Biryani spice mix: 5–10 black peppercorns, 5 small green cardamoms (crushed with shell), 2 large black cardamoms (crushed with shell), 4–5 cloves, 1 teaspoon whole cumin, 2 bay leaves, 3 cinnamon sticks, 3 star anise and 1 teaspoon of garam masala
- 2 lemons
- 2–3 teaspoons of turmeric powder
- 5 green chilies, chopped
- 1 glass of full fat milk
- Salt and pepper to taste

*Method*

1. Start by soaking the 4 cups of basmati rice in water for at least an hour.
2. Prepare a ginger garlic paste. You can use a store-bought paste, but it's very quick to prepare a fresh one at home. Simply blend the ginger and garlic with a bit of vegetable oil in a blender and put it aside.
3. Slice the 2 large onions and fry in vegetable oil in a big pot until golden brown.
4. Take out half the onion and put it onto absorbent paper to use for garnishing afterwards.
5. Add in the biryani spice mix and stir together for 2 to 3 minutes.
6. Add in the chicken pieces and coat the chicken with the spices and oil, frying it for a few minutes.
7. Add in 2 tablespoons of the ginger garlic paste, 2 generous teaspoons of salt, and stir well to make sure the chicken is coated well.

8. Sprinkle in the red chili powder, the ground cumin, and the dried coriander, and stir well.
9. Let the chicken simmer for 5–7 minutes and then add in 5 chopped medium-sized tomatoes and cook until the tomatoes turn liquid.
10. Once the tomatoes have dissolved and you have a tomato base, it is time to add in the yogurt and stir well. Let the yogurt mix with the tomato base on low heat for at least 15–20 minutes.
11. Once the curry starts to thicken, add in the chopped green chilies, a generous bunch of the chopped fresh coriander, and the juice of one lemon.
12. Stir well and cook on high heat, stirring regularly to prevent the chicken from burning. Cook until the sauce has completely reduced and is as dry as possible (this can take up to 45 minutes, so be patient).
13. Transfer the chicken curry from the pot into a large frying pan.
14. Start cooking the rice separately in a big pot. Add 8–10 cups of water and bring it to a boil. Then add in the soaked 4 cups of rice.
15. Do not cook the rice completely yet. When it is only half cooked in about 5–6 minutes and the grain can still clearly split into two, turn off the heat and drain the rice.
16. Now take the large pot in which you have previously cooked the chicken. Cover the base of the pot with a layer of white rice.
17. Then add a layer of chicken curry on top.
18. Followed by another layer of rice, another layer of chicken curry, and finally another layer of rice.

19. Dissolve the turmeric powder in a glass of fresh milk and mix well. This is your food coloring. Once the turmeric has been diluted well, sprinkle this mixture over the rice. It is important *not* to cover all the rice, just some of it, to create the multiple hues of your biryani rice: orange, yellow, and white.

20. Garnish with the remaining fried onions, sprinkle on some fresh coriander, cut the remaining lemon into lemon wedges, add a bed of lemon on top of the rice, and put the lid on.

21. Preheat your oven for 20 minutes at 150 Celsius and leave the pot in for another 45-60 minutes.

22. Serve alongside a cucumber raita (mix ½ a cup yogurt with grated cucumbers and dried mint, topped with coriander and pomegranate seeds).

# BOOK CLUB
# DISCUSSION QUESTIONS

1. The novel is set in present-day Portugal. To what extent do you think the setting affects the story? Do you feel Portugal is a passive backdrop for the story, or is it an actual character in itself because you see the main characters actively interacting with it?

2. As a South Asian, North American, and West African who move to Europe, Fatima, Kate, and Abena experience living in Portugal through a very different lens. How much do our countries of origin, race, ethnicity, gender, language, and previous places we have lived in shape our experience of moving to the same country?

3. This book has three points of view: Fatima's, Kate's, and Abena's. How would it affect the story if the whole book was only told through Fatima's point of view?

4. Guilt is one of the major themes running through the book. Different characters feel guilty for different reasons, and this leads them to make some guilty moves. Is guilt just an inherent part of moving and creating a life abroad?

5.  Several nationalities are featured in the book: Portu-
    guese, Pakistani, British, German, Ghanaian, American,
    etc. To what extent is each nationality stereotyped, and
    how is this either achieved or avoided?

6.  How important is food to the story? Do the characters
    present themselves through the food we see them cook-
    ing?

7.  The novel plays out in present-day Portugal, but there
    are also flashbacks to Singapore, Dubai, Accra, Karachi,
    Houston, Copenhagen, Berlin, and Brighton. Did these
    places add any character and depth to the story or help
    you to understand the main characters better?

8.  In your opinion, does the novel represent the diversity
    of experiences and backgrounds of the modern expat
    family, as well as their reasons for moving?

9.  Language plays another key role in the novel, and there
    are references to many words in different languages,
    such as Portuguese, Urdu, Twi, German, Danish, and
    Arabic. Did you notice a clear hierarchy in how these
    languages are perceived and used? How can language
    enhance or limit our experiences when moving abroad?

10. What point is the author making about moving to a new country with children? What kind of awareness, preparation, and support do Third Culture Kids (TCKs) need to help their transition?

11. Why does it matter that the guilty can't say goodbye to their secrets, to their old selves, to their old homes, and to their family and friends? How important is closure, acceptance, and reconciliation with their pasts for those who move to a new country?

12. Which character was your favorite and why?

# ACKNOWLEDGMENTS

I would like to thank many people for their help in writing this book. First and foremost, my incredible husband, Martino, who was my main sparring partner and never said no when I asked to read passages of dialogue to him out loud to test if they sounded real—even at eleven p.m. He miraculously continued to sleep next to me in the dark, even after reading the insidious way in which my mind works. My three amazing kids, Mina (twelve), Mikail (nine), and Miro (three), who watched the hours I spent sitting with my laptop and who remain my biggest cheerleaders, but also kept asking me impatiently, "Mama, why are you never finished?" My loving family—my parents, Nighat and Navaid, my mother-in-law, Marlies, and my late father-in-law, Salvatore—for your emotional, mental, and practical support, including all the unsolicited advice that helped bring my writing to life. And, no, none of the characters are based on our family; I just wanted to reiterate this point before it comes up at the next family gathering in Pakistan or Germany.

I'd like to thank my UK book publishing team; even Brexit couldn't keep us apart. Thank you to my incredible editor, writing mentor, and trusted friend, Jo Parfitt, who has borne witness to the gradual development of this book from one draft to the next. Without your help, guidance, support, two developmental edits, chapter-by-chapter feedback, and extra-long voice notes on WhatsApp, I would still be figuring out how to write this book and what to call it. Special thanks to Paddy Hartnett for doing an incredible job on the line editing and proofreading on a tight deadline. I hope you still enjoyed working with me even though I have a hard time staying consistent in either UK or US spelling as a result of going back and forth between British and American education systems my whole life. And a big thank you to Jack Scott, author and book design specialist extraordinaire at Springtime Books, who has helped to guide my vision at every step of the way and provided fantastic (and realistic) advice, and coordinated all aspects of book production, editing and design, including a new author website. After months of working together, when I invited Jack to come to Portugal for the book launch, he said, "I'd love to, but I really need a relaxing holiday!" Okay, point taken.

When I was writing this multi-POV expat fiction novel with a diverse cast of characters from all around the world, I knew I would need an equally diverse group of sensitivity readers who would tell me if I had misrepresented a culture, a person, or their voice. In this regard, I owe a huge thank you to my six wonderful sensitivity readers—Enyo Bruku, Lisa Lyn Ericson, Karla Camp, Becky Grappo, Amanda Graham, and Sarah Khan—whose feedback as Ghanaian, American, Portuguese, British, and Pakistani readers helped tremendously in shaping this book. In fact, this book would not have been possible without all of your generous help, cultural know-how, and professional backgrounds. Any errors are mine. I resorted to some extreme measures when it came to research. These included stalking the current American Ambassador to Portugal on Instagram to get a sense of a typical working day.

Getting feedback from fellow writers was an important (but nerve-wracking) part of the process that shaped this book. I am grateful to my wonderful Lisbon Writers Group for welcoming me into the fold with open arms, for reading the early drafts of my chapters, and for giving me both positive feedback and constructive criticism. Thank you to Mary Fowke, Katie Gray Craven, José Marques, Jean Page, and Daniel Sellen for helping me to become a better writer. I am also grateful to the many writers groups I turned to for questions, advice, and support, in particular the Expat Writers Group run by Andrea Barton and the Women's Fiction Writers Association in the US, which helped me to learn the writing craft and other areas of the book publishing process while also allowing me the chance to connect with other fantastic authors.

I was definitely hungry while writing this book, craving daal chawal one day, risotto another, and I may have put on an extra five kg between drafts one and two. I would like to give special thanks to two Ghanaians for sharing their precious jollof rice recipe and their shito recipe with me for inclusion in this book. A massive thank you to the Ghanaian woman who became part of our family when we lived in Ghana: our housekeeper Mavis Nyator, who cooked her way into our hearts. And thank you to the lovely Agyan (Alice) Owusu Asare, a Ghanaian friend in Lisbon who brought me some homemade jollof rice one day, which resulted in me begging for her recipe.

As a struggling writer I needed a great group of friends to keep me sane, especially when imposter syndrome struck and I felt like quitting or packing up my bags and skipping town anonymously. A big thank you to my wonderful support squad in Portugal: Cassie Bodily, Ilaria Penzo, Victora Welton da Cunha, April White, Angie Hickson, Kimberly Mitchell, Nicole Robertson, and Emma Nascimento. Several book clubs helped me to read Portuguese writers and literature, such as the PLIE (Portuguese Literature in English) book club in Cascais, from where I drew inspiration and creativity. My introduction to Portuguese authors such as Dulce Maria Cardoso, who wrote *The Return*, helped me to understand my host country of Portugal through a historical lens. I'd also like to thank the international parent community and school administrations at TASIS Portugal and Amazing Kids Estoril, who have been big champions of my work and true partners in raising the next generation of global citizens. And a special mention to Lincoln Community School in Accra, Ghana, for hosting one of the best International Day celebrations I have seen around the world. To the wonderfully loyal readers of my blog 'And Then We Moved To' who volunteered to be advance readers, shared in my joy at the publication of this book, and were the first to subscribe to my email newsletter, thank you so much for your continued support. None of this would have been possible without my online and offline international tribe.

Last but not least, to my current beautiful home, Portugal, and its wonderful people—thank you for welcoming me and my family with open arms, even though life for many Portuguese people has not been easy of late. Soaring prices, a housing crisis, and a very low minimum wage are the unfortunate reality for many. As someone who moved here in 2020, I think it is important to be mindful of this, to not exacerbate the problems that already exist, and to acknowledge my own economic privilege while living here. Moving as an economic migrant, immigrant, or expat is a beautiful thing; the exchange of ideas and the mix of different cultures and different perspectives brings positive things. But there may also be an impact on the local population—so the land, the people, the culture, the language, and the history deserve our respect. I hope my respect is evident in this book, which I consider to be my unofficial love letter to Portugal for the many ways in which it has inspired me and shaped my writing.

Mariam Navaid Ottimofiore
Cascais, Portugal, February 2024

# ABOUT THE AUTHOR

MARIAM NAVAID OTTIMOFIORE is Pakistani by birth and Italian through marriage, but her identity is not confined to the passports she holds. She is an author, writer, speaker, researcher, and economist. She was born into expat life, joining her parents on their first global expatriate assignment in 1982 in the Kingdom of Bahrain. Her early childhood was spent growing up in Manama, New York City, and Karachi. To date, Mariam has lived in ten countries as both a Third Culture Kid (TCK) and an expat adult: Bahrain, the United States (NY, MA, TX), Pakistan, the United Kingdom, Germany, Denmark, Singapore, the United Arab Emirates, Ghana, and Portugal.

Her life on the move is messy. A 40-foot container, an expat husband from another corner of the world, and three children born in three different countries 3,000 miles apart have added complexity, challenges, and many joys to living a multicultural, multilingual, and multi-mobile life. Passionate about languages and cultures, Mariam speaks fluent Urdu, English, Hindi, and German, with some Italian, Danish, Arabic, Twi, and Portuguese on the side. She is an expert at making embarrassing mistakes in every new language she picks up, is perpetually lost in every new city she calls home, and can never remember her new phone number or address, or where she packed those suede boots!

Mariam has a BA in Economics and Political Science from Mount Holyoke College in the US and a specialization in Economic Development from the University of Sussex in the UK. Her debut non-fiction book, *This Messy Mobile Life: How a MOLA can help globally mobile families create a life by design*, comprises personal reflection, expert advice, and survey research to help global expatriates embrace their transitions and thrive in their international journey. *The Guilty Can't Say Goodbye* is her second book, but her debut novel. She currently lives in Cascais, Portugal with her German/Italian husband and her German-Pakistani-Italian kids, born in Singapore, Dubai, and Lisbon. You can follow her writing by visiting her author website or by connecting with her on social media.

| | |
|---|---|
| *Website* | mariamnavaidottimofiore.com |
| *Instagram* | mariam.navaid.ottimofiore |
| *Facebook* | authorpagemariamnavaidottimofiore |
| *Twitter* | @MariamNavaidO |
| *Goodreads* | 104772670-mariam-ottimofiore |

Printed in Great Britain
by Amazon